Sex
A Love Story

Jerome Gold

Books by Jerome Gold

FICTION
Sex, A Love Story
In Georgia: A Yankee Family in the Segregated South
The Moral Life of Soldiers
Sergeant Dickinson (originally titled *The Negligence of Death*)
The Prisoner's Son
The Inquisitor
Of Great Spaces (with Les Galloway)

POETRY
Stillness
Prisoners

NONFICTION
Children in Prison
In the Spider's Web: A Nonfiction Novel
The Burg and Other Seattle Scenes (Mostly True Stories)
The Divers and Other Mysteries of Seattle (and California, but Just a Little): More Mostly True Stories
Paranoia & Heartbreak: Fifteen Years in a Juvenile Facility
How I Learned That I Could Push the Button
Publishing Lives, Volume I: Interviews with Independent Book Publishers
Obscure in the Shade of the Giants: Publishing Lives, Volume II
Hurricanes (editor)

Sex
A Love Story

Jerome Gold

Black Heron Press
Post Office Box 614
Anacortes, WA 98221
www.blackheronpress.com

ISBN (print): 978-1-936364-36-7
ISBN (ebook): 978-1-936364-37-4

Cover art and design by Bryan Sears

Black Heron Press
Post Office Box 614
Anacortes, Washington 98221
www. blackheronpress.com

For Jeanne

"Oh, who really knows why? I mean, what motivates any of us to do anything?"

—Jean-Louis Brindamour

"How clear is the border between the world in bed and out of bed?"

—Simone Zelitch, *Judenstaat*

Part One
(1960)

Elliot and Earl

That summer, shortly before school ended, Bob met two guys in a coffee shop he liked to go to who were planning a cross-country drive to New York. It would be a kind of Kerouackian, *On the Road* adventure. They had both read *On the Road* and a lot more of Kerouac besides, and even some Ginsberg and Corso, and when Bob told them that he also had read *On the Road* as well as *Howl*, they invited him to go along.

His parents did not agree, of course—"You're only sixteen. When you're older…"—and this made it all the more alluring. But he hadn't yet made up his mind to go when Elliot and Earl disappeared. He could not find them in the cafes where he was used to seeing them and he was too young to get into bars to look for them.

Then one night he saw Elliot in a line waiting to go into a movie theater. He and Earl had had a falling-out, Elliot said. The trip was off. He had last seen Earl puking his guts out on the curb in front of a bar he had been thrown out of. He had been drinking sloe gin and tossing pills of a kind Elliot didn't know. Elliot had been disgusted. He had been disgusted then and he was disgusted now as he told Bob how Earl was the last time he saw him. Elliot was straighter than Earl, not long out of the Army, and he had no tolerance for men who relinquished control over themselves, not to the extent Earl had. It had not been the first time he had seen Earl helpless and he didn't want to see him that way again.

So he was sorry, but the trip was off. The car they would have been driving was Earl's, if he still had it, but Elliot wouldn't trust

Earl to drive across town now, or even to be in the same car with him and Bob. Bob could go with Earl if he wanted, and if Earl still wanted to go, but Elliot wouldn't advise him to. Also, Elliot said, he had a girlfriend now, so he had no reason to go to New York. He introduced Bob to the young woman standing beside him. She was attractive and her face was round and open and she seemed guileless. Bob would have thought Elliot would go for a harder-looking woman.

Bob never saw Earl again; he wouldn't have gone with him alone anyway. Elliot was the one he trusted, and if Elliot wasn't going, then Bob wasn't going either. But it bothered him that his parents thought he hadn't gone because they had objected.

Doreen is wearing red panties today. Yesterday she wore blue. The day before they were white. Is Doreen a patriot? But didn't she wear green panties one day last week? Oh, I get it: this is the week of July fourth. Yes, Doreen is a patriot.

She was sitting cross-legged on the floor and Bob sat across from her in the circle, and when she uncrossed her legs to stand up she raised her knees and her skirt slid up her thighs. Her panties were the color of a red licorice stick, say, or a Lifesaver, and they were in bright contrast to the ivory white of her legs. She seemed not to know that she had revealed her underpants, even though she had stood up in the same way many times, each time showing what she was wearing under her skirt.

Today they had a visitor, the director of the program, a round, balding man who appeared jovial but who Bob suspected wasn't jovial. At the break he and Mr. Amos stayed inside while the students went out in the corridor to talk or get something to eat from a vending machine. The director was leaving as they returned to class and he smiled while holding the door open for them and they filed through the doorway.

The class was in one of the faculty lounges that weren't otherwise being used this summer. The floor was thickly carpeted and they began to take their places again on the carpet. But this time Mr. Amos told them that the director had objected to their sitting on the floor and they would have to sit in the chairs. However, aside from this objection, the director had only good things to say about the program and believed he could get it funded again for next summer.

When Mr. Amos said the director had objected to their sitting on the floor, a blush spread over Doreen's face and her eyelids seemed to swell until Bob thought she was going to cry, but she didn't. Maybe one of the other girls, or maybe more than one, had already spoken to her, or maybe she knew without anyone telling her.

Another girl said it was ridiculous, we were all mature people here, and if they would let girls wear shorts or Capris—it was summer, after all—then nobody would have to worry about what they might see. Mr. Amos agreed but said it was a small price to pay to keep the program in good standing. Even if he himself did not return next summer, he felt he owed it to his successor and those who would want to attend it, to do what he could to keep the program alive. He corrected himself. "We," he said. "We owe it to the students as well as the teacher who will want to come here next year."

Bob was between his junior and senior years in high school and he was taking a creative writing class at Fullerton Junior College for which he would receive both high school and college credit. The class was limited to ten students and was open to kids from high schools in Orange County who had been identified as "talented" by their English teachers. It was Mr. Amos' last teaching job, as he would be going to work as a writer for television in the fall. He was looking forward to earning some real money, he told Bob, but he knew that writing for TV meant the end of his creative life in literature. But, he said, his daughter had a medical condition and he needed to be able to pay for her treatment. He told Bob all of this during their breaks while he smoked a cigarette in the corridor outside the classroom and Bob sipped coffee he had bought from the machine around the corner.

The class was made up mostly of kids who wanted to pass the summer in a way that would allow their parents to believe they were not wasting their time, that they were somehow being productive. One girl, Jennifer, was very smart and very incisive and seemed to enjoy displaying her intelligence and critical ability in conversation, but she put off the other girls who were not as smart or as incisive as she was. Like Bob, she seemed to reside in a place somewhat apart from the others. She was very small, certainly not more than five feet, she had short, nearly black hair that cupped her head like a hand, and her figure appeared to be perfectly proportioned. She was a dancer—"modern dance," it was called. She walked so that, behind her, you could see her hips sway with the shift of her weight from one leg to the other. Later, when they started going out, Bob asked her why she walked like that and she said she couldn't help it, it was the way she walked, but he was sure she had put sex in her walk as an affectation. It was probably another reason most of the girls in the class did not like her.

The class was six weeks long and at the end of it, a few of the students, including Jennifer and Bob, had poems published in the *News Tribune*. The publication, the first for all of them, was arranged by Mr. Amos and he also made up a list of the names and phone numbers of those in the class and distributed it to everybody with the idea that they might want to talk to one another about writing or about books or about something else entirely sometime in the future. He thought they could establish a kind of support network for themselves if they wanted to, but Bob, at least, never called any of the others except Jennifer.

The Wind in His Face

The sky was the color of slate. The wind had picked up during the day and had become a Santa Ana. Walking into it on the way home from school, Bob felt it pressing against his chest and legs, the fine sand it carried biting at his face. At one point the wind suddenly ceased and he fell forward, barely catching his balance before it gusted again. He loved days like this one. He remembered Sara telling him how much she liked to walk on these days too, the wind blowing so that she felt its tug on her scalp, its grit in her eyes, and afterward when she was home, how her skin felt like it had been scrubbed nearly raw by the sand.

When he got home, he saw that the plum tree in the front yard was down. Nothing to be done about that yet. Also, the thin ropes his father used to keep the slender trunks of the other young trees straight against the urge to grow toward sunlight had loosened or had torn away entirely from their pegs. A couple of pegs had been pulled out of the ground, still attached to the rope.

Bob changed into old jeans and a sweatshirt, got a mallet from the garage and went back outside to refasten the ropes and hammer the freed pegs back into the ground. His father would be pleased. Bob loathed yard work and ordinarily looked for a way to get out of it, but today was different: he got to be out of doors during a Santa Ana.

When he returned to the house, his mother was on the phone in the kitchen. She was still in the housedress she was wearing when he left for school that morning.

"Your father is worried about the fruit trees he planted. He wants you to take a look at them."

"Tell him some of the ropes had pulled loose, but I already tightened them." Hah! "Oh, the plum tree by the wishing well is down. Better tell him that too."

His mother replaced the phone on its hook. "He says he's proud of you." A quizzical look was on his mother's face. "Why did you do it without being told to?"

"I wanted to save the trees. I thought they might be blown down."

"Well, your father is very happy with you."

"Tell him to increase my allowance."

She laughed.

Bob took a shower and, back in his room, put on a clean pair of Levi's and a fresh sweatshirt and lay down on his bed. He had begun *The Subterraneans* the night before and now he picked it up from the night table. Jazz. The mad poets, though not so much their poetry. Sex, little of which matched Bob's experience.

His cousin Paul had introduced him to jazz the year before. Miles Davis. The Adderly brothers. Thelonious Monk. Cal Tjader and Dave Brubeck out here on the West Coast. The Modern Jazz Quartet was Paul's favorite, but Miles Davis was Bob's, especially after he heard *Sketches of Spain*.

Chuck Cotilla deejayed a late-night show at the lower end of the FM dial and he played the entire album when it came out. It broke Bob's heart. He had never heard music that could do that. He bought the album and played it over and over on occasions when his parents weren't home. He never tired of it. Its sound, the sound of Miles Davis' trumpet, made it seem as though an entire world had been irretrievably lost and now could only be mourned, and the trumpet was the instrument of mourning and sorrow. Of all of *Sketches of Spain*, Bob was most enthralled by

"Concierto de Aranjuez." Even much later in his life, when he would hear its first notes, whether instrumental or vocal, whether Miles Davis or elevator music, Bob would want to stop whatever he was doing and just listen, anticipating the entire cut as though he were seventeen again and Miles Davis was playing it as he had the first time Bob heard it, as though he, Bob, were his only audience.

He saw his life after high school as jazz and travel and writing. He did not intend to go to college, although his parents assumed he would. He wanted to know the world and he believed college would distract him from the education he needed in order to write.

What he needed to write was a combination of reading and the experience of the extremes of life as Hemingway and Kerouac had lived it. After all, Hemingway hadn't gone to college, and while Steinbeck and Kerouac had, they hadn't stayed long enough to graduate. Dos Passos had graduated from Harvard, but Bob saw him as less daring, less insightful, more reliant on stereotype in drawing his characters than the other prominent writers of his time, although he, Bob, would not then have phrased his criticism of Dos (as Hemingway called him) that way, not, at least, when he was sixteen.

The wind continued to whip the house but nothing more could be done outside and, anyway, Bob had had his fill of outdoor adventure for now. His feeling of serving a sentence in a kind of soft prison returned and he thought of Sara and then he thought of Jennifer, and he put *The Subterraneans* down and found the list of phone numbers Mr. Amos had given out and he called her.

A man he assumed was Jennifer's father answered. Jennifer couldn't come to the phone, she was sick with the flu. "We've all been sick," he said. Bob said he would call back.

"Who is this?"

"Bob Givens. Jennifer and I had a class together last summer and I just thought I would call her."

Her father said he would tell her Bob called.

He called again a couple of days later. She was still sick and they talked for only a few minutes. She said she remembered him, but sounded as though she wasn't certain. Bob asked if, when she was feeling better, she would like to go out and she said yes. He had not expected her to answer so decisively; he had thought she would want him to call a few more times before she agreed to going out with him. He said he would call her next week.

He sent her flowers. Later, recalling his choice of red roses, he was certain he did not know the significance of red as opposed to white roses, but perhaps someone had told him. (Who? The florist? He would not have confided in his mother.) He sensed, when he bought the roses, that he was doing something that would induce Jennifer to allow him to make love to her. And later she told him that her ex-boyfriend had said when they broke up that she would give up her virginity to her next boyfriend, that she was "ripe as a peach." (He had read that somewhere, or had heard someone else use that expression, Jennifer said. He was not that original, but he knew her and he was probably right.) Later, too, she told Bob how much the flowers had meant to her, coming from someone she hardly knew when she was so sick.

Bob Was Taken Aback

On their first date they went to a drive-in. She didn't object when he put his arm around her and when he kissed her, her tongue slipped between his lips even before he thought to do the same to her.

After a while she said, "Won't you touch me?"

He didn't know what she meant. He had undone her bra and was caressing her breasts.

"Between my legs," she said.

He was taken aback. He had touched other girls there, but only after he had persuaded them to let him do it, or they had been so excited that they didn't resist his fingers. No one had ever invited him to do it. He said no.

"Why not?"

He didn't have an answer.

"Do you want me to touch you?" she asked.

Only two other girls had touched his penis. Neither had asked him first; they had done it because they knew he would like it, or maybe because they were curious to see what his reaction would be. Putting things into words seemed to make everything more naked. Again he didn't know what to say. He kissed her and while they were kissing, he placed his hand on her mound. Her hips immediately began to thrust and her face became damp. She seemed to be in a trance. He was sure she didn't know what her body was doing. After a while she stopped. "Thank you."

He asked her if she had had an orgasm. She said she didn't know.

She said that when she was younger she and a girlfriend went to a matinee with her friend's older sister. At the theater the sister met her boyfriend and they found seats where they could be by themselves and they began to make out. Jennifer and her friend took seats where they could spy on them. The boyfriend's hands were all over Jennifer's friend's sister, under her sweater and under her skirt. In a moment, Jennifer's friend gasped, "She's feeling *him* up!"

Jennifer laughed when she told Bob the story. "Next time I'll feel you up."

Bob touched her again and moved his hand over her pudendum. She closed her eyes, but said after a minute, "I'm not ready yet."

He fastened on the inevitability implied by that word: "yet."

They played miniature golf the next time they went out, but neither of them cared for the game and they spent most of the evening over hamburgers and coffee at a Denny's restaurant. They sat beside each other in a booth and held hands until the food arrived. After they had eaten Bob put his hand on her thigh, but she removed it, saying, "Not here."

They talked about the writing class they had taken last summer and about one of the boys—"He was so quiet, I didn't know he was even in the class until we had that little Kool-Aid-and-cake ritual when we graduated," Jennifer said—and one of the girls.

"She always wore colored panties, almost always red," Bob said.

"How do you know?"

"Because when we sat on the floor, she always raised her skirt when she got up."

"Do you think she knew she was showing you her panties?"

"She didn't seem to, but she was consistent about lifting her skirt that way. But I don't think she was particularly interested in me. I think she just wanted to show off her panties to whoever was looking."

"And you were looking."

"Sure. How could I keep from it? I sat right across from her."

"You didn't have to. It wasn't assigned seating."

"I didn't have to. You're right."

"I used to do that when I was little. When I was four or five."

"Really?"

"We used to visit my grandmother in Mississippi when I was small, and my cousin was always there too. He's a couple of years older than me. We used to go into the barn and play with each other. I used to like to show him my panties, but he was more curious about what was inside them."

"Smart little kid."

She kissed him.

"Michael got angry with me when I told him about my cousin." She hadn't mentioned Michael before. "He's this boy I used to go out with."

"Why would he be angry?"

"I don't know. I guess he was jealous."

"Oh, I heard that Mr. Amos left his wife."

"Really? Where did you hear that?"

"My English teacher from last year, Miss Berkey, told me. She was very disapproving."

"Don't you always leave your wife when you go to work in Hollywood? My father's cousin is a lawyer in Hollywood and the first thing he did when he moved there was divorce his wife and get a newer, prettier one. She's very nice though. You and he were close, weren't you? Mr. Amos, I mean. I always saw you talking with him during our breaks."

"I don't know if we were close. Maybe. I liked him. He called me a couple of months ago, just to talk."

"That sounds suspicious."

"To talk about writing."

"That still sounds suspicious."

"Are you teasing me or are you serious?"

"Can't you tell?"

"No."

"Well, you're going to have to learn, Buckwheat."

"Buckwheat?"

"My father calls my brother and me that sometimes. It's the name of one of the characters in the old Our Gang movies. You have a lot to learn about me."

He didn't immediately say anything and she said, "Don't you want to?"

He felt something like a gate begin to give way onto a world he knew nothing about, and he nodded and said, "Yes."

"That's good," she said. She leaned closer. "I don't let just anyone touch my pussy. Hey. Give me your hand."

She grasped his wrist with one hand and began to massage the pad of his thumb with the thumb of her other hand. She looked directly into his eyes without blinking. "You may think I'm human because I look like you," she said, as though she were a robot reciting emotionlessly from a script. "But actually I'm from Mars, the daughter of a great civilization whose people, unknown to most Earthlings, have been interbreeding with the inhabitants of your planet for centuries. Don't be afraid. In almost all ways, we are just like you, except that our sex organs are in our thumbs."

A laugh roared out of him. He tried to stifle the loud sound, but it came out again. It was such a strange story, and told by such an interesting girl, and it was funny. "That's great. Where'd you get that?"

"I heard my father tell it. He can be really witty."

They parked in the driveway after he took her home, and they made out for a while. When he walked her to her door, they embraced and kissed again. "Put your hands on my ass. Anyone who touches my ass can do whatever he wants with me."

He tried to slip his hand into her pants but she squirmed away. They were standing under the porch light. "Just put your hands on my ass. One more thing. Call me Jen, okay? I hate 'Jennifer.' And not 'Jenny.'"

They saw each other once a week, usually on Friday night, and they talked on the phone a couple of times a week at first and then almost every night. One afternoon, driving around with Harry, Bob asked him to stop at a phone booth so he could call Jen. He had told her he would call at five and he wanted to keep his promise. They were talking about something inconsequential when he noticed that someone had written obscene lyrics to a song on the aluminum frame beside the phone. He laughed.

"What's funny?" Jen asked.

"There's these porno lyrics on the wall here, next to the phone. I just noticed them."

"What do they say? Read them to me."

Bob read them.

"That's terrible," Jen said.

"Why? I think they're funny. Kind of this weird little poem. He even divided it up into stanzas."

"What if a little kid saw it? What if Peter saw it?" Peter was her brother. He was eleven.

"I don't think Peter is likely to come to this phone booth." It was five or six miles from her house.

"I'd like you to erase it. Wait! Does it say 'For a good time, call this number' or anything like that?"

"No, it's just song lyrics, or maybe a poem."

"Write 'For a good time, call' and then write my phone number."

"Are you crazy? I'm not going to write your phone number in a telephone booth. Who knows who will call you?"

"All right. Just erase it then."

"What the hell were you thinking, asking me to give out your number like that?"

"I was just curious about who would call. The kind of person who would. But you're probably right. What are you doing?"

"I had to borrow a pencil from Harry. I'm erasing the poem, or whatever it is. I got some of it, but you can still read it. It's scratched into the metal."

"All right. Thank you for trying."

"If I didn't want to get into your pants so bad, I wouldn't have done it."

"Pussy power." She laughed. Then she said, "You didn't lie about trying to erase it, did you?"

"No."

"Thank you."

When Bob came out of the phone booth, Harry said, "What were you doing in there? You used up my whole eraser."

"There's a joke or a dirty poem on the wall by the phone. Jen wanted me to erase it."

"Jesus. You must really have something for her."

"It's starting to look that way," Bob said.

His parents owned a station wagon and a Renault sedan. When Bob and Jen began talking about making love, Jen asked where they would do it. In the back of the station wagon, he said. They were parked in Hillcrest Park. They crawled into the back of the wagon to see if there was enough room; they didn't want to hit their heads or their butts against the roof. They thought the missionary position would be possible. Bob lay on top of her and made thrusting movements with his hips. They decided the only danger was to his head, and only when he got on or off her. He suggested that since they were already here.., but she said no before he got the rest of the sentence out of his mouth. She wasn't ready yet, she said. He asked her if she thought she would ever be ready.

She said she wanted there to be a rule. Once they started making love, he could have her whenever he wanted; she believed a woman should never withhold herself from her lover. But she didn't want to be fucked in the ass. Her cousin had done something to her once and she hadn't liked it. As it wasn't something that had entered Bob's imagination, at least until she brought it up, he was able to assure her that he wouldn't do it.

The Other Girls Had Been Shocked

She wanted to tell him something herself before he heard it from someone else.

Who would he hear it from?

Your ex-girlfriend, Sara. She's friends with one of the girls I was with. But listen.

A few weeks before they started going out she went to Disneyland with some girls she knew and they met some boys and went back to their car to make out. She allowed the boy she was with to take her clothes off. She didn't know why she did it. The other girls had been shocked, and it had cost her their friendship. This was back when she was still seeing Michael and they were fighting and she thought their relationship might be over. In fact, it was over, but they didn't know it yet.

Her tone was explanatory. She didn't seem upset to be telling this to Bob, although there appeared to be an aspect of her memory that made her uneasy—perhaps the loss of friendships, perhaps her allowing the boy to demonstrate his power over her to his friends. She didn't seem to think that Bob might be disturbed by her confession. He wasn't. He was fascinated by her, and he didn't think that what she had let this boy do had anything to do with him.

They were in his parents' Renault, parked in Hillcrest after having gone to a movie. She wasn't looking at him, but into the distance, as though memory resided there. He brushed the side of her face with his fingertips and she turned. He kissed her and began to unbutton her shirt. She didn't resist, but allowed him to do as he wished. When her shirt was open and her bra unfastened, he placed his hand on her thigh under her skirt. He put his middle finger between her labia over the smooth cloth of her panties and then moved it inside her panties. At first she wasn't excited, and then she was. "Take them off," he said. She shook her head. Soon his fingers were inside her and their tongues were first in her mouth, then in his. He took her shirt off and then her bra. He put his mouth on one nipple and then the other. She placed the palm of her hand on the back of his head as though to encourage him. When he straightened up, she was smiling. "That was nice. I liked that."

She laid her hand on the bulge his penis made inside his pants. "Can I see it?"

He unzipped his pants and worked them down below his hips.

"My god, how am I ever going to get that inside me?"

He laughed. The eyes of the beholder, he thought.

"I know the walls of my vagina are elastic, but…"

She was working his penis with her hand. He was close to ejaculating and he tried to kiss her, but she was more interested in looking at his penis.

She had semen all over her hand. She turned it so she could see the back of it and then she turned it so she could see the cream coating her palm and seeping between her fingers.

"I never brought a boy off before," she said.

"There's a box of Kleenex on the back seat."

She shook her head.

At last she turned and picked a tissue out of the box and wiped her hand.

They sat beside each other. She put her hand on his penis again and let it rest there. He placed his hand on the inside of her thigh. He could feel the heat coming from her vagina.

"I think I'm ready now," she said.

He laughed again. "I'm not."

"I don't mean *now*. When will we do it?"

"Next week? I'll get the station wagon."

"What will you tell them? You can't tell them you want the station wagon so you can make love to your girlfriend."

"Why not?"

"What do you mean, 'why not'? You don't tell them what we do, do you?"

"Sure I do."

"What?"

"I don't, but don't you think they know? Don't you think your parents know?"

"I don't know. I hadn't thought of it. God, I'm blushing."

"I think they know. They were our age once."

"I don't think my mother realizes. I can't imagine that she ever did what we do."

"Do you feel guilty?"

"About what we do? No. Do you?"

"No."

"What's this? Are you getting hard again?"

"Yes."

"Do you want me to do you again?"

"Okay."

"'Okay.' As though you can take it or leave it."

"I prefer to take it, please."

"At least I know what to do now if I can't get it inside me."

"I want to give you pleasure too."

She slid her panties off.

"Angela's mother told her to always keep one foot in her panties when she makes out with her boyfriend, so she doesn't forget them in his car."

"Who's Angela?"

"A friend at school. Touch me and I'll touch you."

Jen's father asked Bob to follow him into his den after telling Jen and her mother that he wanted to talk to Bob alone. Jen's father was a dark-haired man in his mid-forties, about Bob's father's height, though not as heavy as his father. Bob had met him a couple of times before but they had not talked of anything of substance.

"Young man," he said, "I'd like you to tell me what your intentions are toward my daughter." He was smiling good-naturedly. He had framed his question as the opening of a kind of comedic act, Bob thought, because he anticipated that Bob would respond with awkwardness, perhaps embarrassment, and he wanted to spare him discomfort. But at the same time, he wanted an answer.

"I want to make love to her," Bob said.

Jen's father was silent. He wasn't smiling. After several seconds had passed, he said, "At least you're honest."

Bob parked on the shoulder of a road made of dirt and sand that ran parallel to the freeway. They waited a few minutes to see if anyone would come by. The moon was almost full. No other cars appeared. They climbed into the bed of the station wagon.

They lay together, both of them undressed, exploring each other as though for the first time. A towel was under Jen's hips. Finally she said she was ready and Bob rolled on top of her and she parted her legs.

He was hardly able to penetrate her. Neither of them had expected there to be so much resistance. After several attempts in which he pushed inside her until he was blocked and then withdrew, she said she'd had enough, the pain was unbearable. There was no blood on the towel. They lay beside each other. He touched her but she said she was too sore. She wouldn't look at him. He had not seen her entirely without clothes before and he didn't want to give that up yet—her short, black hair like a soft hat, the light brown nipples of her small breasts angled away from her chest, her dancer's legs, the black triangle where they met disappearing into the shadow between them—but she wanted to go.

They got dressed and moved into the front seat and Bob started the car. The back tires spun in the loose dirt. He turned the steering wheel this way and that, but the soil wasn't firm enough for the tires to get traction. He cut the engine.

He remembered passing a house maybe a half-mile back. He suggested that Jen stay with the car while he walked back to try to find help. She was uneasy but didn't think she could walk that far, as sore as she was, and she didn't know if she was going to start to bleed. Bob left the key with her and told her to stay inside the car and lock the doors.

There were tall eucalyptuses in leaf on either side of the road. After a short time, the trees on the side away from the freeway gave way to a furrowed field at the far end of which was a lighted house. Bob thought to walk through the field, but then decided not to; he didn't know if it had been seeded and he didn't want to get somebody whose help he needed angry with him. After another hundred yards he came upon the drive that led to the house. A pickup was parked in front of the garage.

A man in his late thirties or early forties opened the door. Bob explained about his car being stuck in the sand on the side of the road and asked if the man had a chain or a rope to help him out.

"That's my land," the man said. "What were you doing out there?"

"My girlfriend and I were parked."

The man left the door open while he went inside the house. He hadn't asked Bob to come in, so he waited on the step outside. The man came back wearing a pair of Wellington boots. They got in his truck and started out to where Bob had left Jen. Bob asked the man if he had a daughter.

"Yes," he said.

"How old is she?

"Sixteen."

Bob was silent.

When they stepped out of the truck, Jen left the car and came up to them. She told a story about them losing their way and then getting stuck when they tried to turn around. To Bob, she was still lying naked in the back of the station wagon, and then he saw her as she was now, an hour later, nervously lying to this fatherly man who was beginning to allow himself a smile.

He had a chain in the bed of the pickup and he hooked it up to the station wagon and then the truck. He pulled the car out of the sand as easily as if the sand had never held it.

They thanked him and he warned Bob to stay on the hump of the road, on the packed dirt where the road was solid, and then he said he would take them back to the freeway. Bob followed him to the stop sign where the road met the asphalted on-ramp and then waited while he turned his truck around. Bob waved his thanks as he passed and he waved back and then he was gone and Bob moved out onto the freeway.

Jen said, "I was so embarrassed. I was sure he could see it."

"That you were embarrassed?"

"I know he saw it. I was just prattling away with that stupid story that anybody could see through."

"He liked you though. He was smiling. He has a daughter our age."

"How do you know?"

"I asked him."

"You asked him if he has a daughter?"

"Yes."

"That makes it even worse."

"We don't have to do it if you don't want to."

"I know. But I want to. Next time let's go to a motel. Maybe I won't be so nervous if we're indoors. I have some money I saved from my allowance. I can help out." They had not talked about going to a motel before.

It was the same thing in the motel except that they could lie comfortably beside each other between Bob's attempts to break her hymen. He was frustrated. He had not been able to ejaculate and Jen offered to masturbate him.

"Try sitting on it," he said. He visualized her slowly easing herself onto his penis. He felt he had been battering her and he didn't want to do it again.

She started to object—she was depressed about her hymen's obstinacy and her consequent failure to reach her destiny as an adult human female and she had begun to find fault with everything: the temperature of the room, the hardness of the bed, the flickering and sound of the TV that they had turned on to mask her screams, should there be any—but then she straddled his hips and, her palms on his chest, lowered herself onto his erection. She stopped once about halfway down, then continued until she was sitting on him, her buttocks against his hips. He was completely inside her.

Cautiously, he began to move. She raised herself a little and he stopped.

"Don't stop," she said.

She lowered herself onto him again. Her eyes were closed. He moved away from her and then slowly returned inside her. He did this again and then again and then again until he was overwhelmed with pleasure and a mingling of emotions that included gratitude, affection, wonder, and love. She was only the second girl he had had intercourse with, and he had done it with the other girl only once.

He pulled Jen down so that he could kiss her and he pressed his face against the side of hers. The smell of her hair excited him again but she wanted to wait. "Let me check the damage."

There was blood mixed with semen and her discharge on his penis and in his pubic hair. There was a smear of blood on the tissue she used to wipe herself. She lay down beside him. He took her hand and then she moved so that her head was resting below his shoulder.

"That wasn't so bad." She was smiling. "In fact, it was pretty good. I didn't think it would be so easy."

"You look pleased with yourself."

"I am. I accomplished something."

He started to slip into a doze.

"Hey! Don't go to sleep!" She punched him on the shoulder.

"Just for a few minutes," he said.

"That's insulting."

"What is?"

"I want to talk."

"Talk. I'll listen."

She began to talk and he fell asleep. She punched him again. She had small fists and it didn't hurt, but she succeeded in waking him up.

"You said you'd listen."

"I was."

"No you weren't. You were sleeping."

"Just for a minute."

"No."

He sat up. He was irritated.

"I thought it would mean as much to you as it does to me," she said. She was genuinely hurt.

"Go ahead. Talk. I won't fall asleep this time."

"It's too late."

"Why are you crying?" He didn't think he had done anything to warrant her crying. Falling asleep was not something he could have avoided.

She turned her face so he couldn't see the tears, but of course he could. She was lying on her back, the top sheet and the blanket covering her in the cool room. He drew the blanket and the sheet away from her and kissed her breasts, one and then the other. He felt her nipples harden against his lips.

"Don't cry," he said. Then he said, "I love your body."

She put her hand on the back of his head. She was smiling, her eyes closed. He kissed her navel, lingering over it, darting his tongue in and out of the small indentation. He kissed her labia. She had told him that Michael had used his mouth to pleasure her. She had said he had kissed her there, so Bob kissed her there too. Her fragrance surprised him. It excited him and, not knowing what else to do, he pressed his lips against hers at the top of her thighs and then pushed his tongue between them as though her vagina were her mouth. She gave a start.

Her eyes were open. "What was that?"

"I don't know."

"Do it again."

He pressed his tongue between her labia again, but it had no effect. He moved up to suck her nipples. He settled his body against her hips and her legs parted and he slipped inside her.

"Be careful. I'm a little sore."

He moved slowly and felt her begin to cream and she opened more and he moved faster and faster until he came.

He lay on top of her, aware of the child smell of her skin now that the perfume she had worn had evaporated. Remembering the feral smell of her between her legs, he was amazed at the difference in scents that came from the different parts of her body.

"I almost climaxed that time," she said. "I think maybe next time I'll be able to."

He didn't fall asleep this time, but she didn't feel like talking. They nestled, his arms around her, her butt cool against his pelvis, his hands cupping her breasts. Occasionally he kissed her head or the skin behind her ear and she smiled when he did this. After a while she said, as she had once before, "You can have me whenever you want me. I'll never refuse you." She raised his hand to her lips and kissed it.

More Mysterious in the Dark

Neither of them had a job but they each received an allowance from their respective fathers and they began putting money aside so they could go to a motel once or twice a month. They continued to date once a week, going to a drive-in or out for a hamburger. Afterward Bob would drive Jen home and they would make out in the car. He would park on the street instead of in her driveway because it was less convenient for her father to cross the street than to walk through his garage to see what they were doing, although after they had been seeing each other for a couple of months, Bob thought her father went out of his way to avoid embarrassing them, or himself.

In the car they would explore each other's body. Their bodies were more mysterious in the dark of the car than in a motel room, perhaps because in a motel room they felt relatively safe from getting caught. In the car they would remove the clothing they needed to remove in order to do what they wanted to do; in his memory later there would be the rustling of her skirt or blouse and the rasping feel of his jeans as he pulled them down past his thighs. He found that sometimes, as he kissed and caressed her, her hips would work as if he were inside her, as they had when he touched her on their first date, and her skin would become damp and emit that little-kid smell he noticed the first time they went to a motel. Once afterward, when he told her what her hips had done, she said she had not been aware of it.

Sometimes he would drive over to her house during the week after ten when, he knew, her parents went to bed. He would go to her bedroom window and she would raise it and he would reach inside and touch her breasts. After they did this three or four times, he stopped going to her window but would call so she would know when to expect him and then he would drive to her house and park across the street near a light that was out of service and soon she would come running out of the house, barefoot and wearing a muumuu, and get in the car beside him. The first couple of times they did this, she said as soon as he put his arms around her, "I'm not wearing panties." Later she didn't say anything but he assumed it and as soon as she was in the car he slid his hand up under the skirt of her muumuu.

She liked to masturbate him. She liked to watch the semen pulse out of his penis; she liked to look at it on her hand. "All those babies," she would say sometimes. Sometimes, when he was erect, she would try to insert her small finger into his urethra. It hurt and he told her to stop, but she would do it again, and finally he would slap her hand. She didn't seem to mind his slapping her and after a while he wondered if she kept hurting him because she wanted him to slap her, but from the intent expression on her face as she caressed his penis or tried to enter him through his urethra or slipped her hand below his penis to cradle his testicles, he decided that she was curious about the reaction she would get from him when she did one thing or another, and his hitting her hand was simply one of the reactions she learned to anticipate. But later, remembering her facial expression, he thought she experienced a kind of trance, perhaps even ecstacy, when she played with him and when he came. She may not even have perceived his discomfort and his hitting her hand. As for him, allowing her to play with him, knowing that eventually she would try to slip her finger into his penis, the pleasure she gave him by doing the other things was such that he didn't want her to stop, and the pain she sometimes induced was not severe enough for him to prevent her from opening his fly.

On weekends they began going for a drive during the day, finding a secluded place to park, and making out. Sometimes a car would slow as it passed. Once a car passed, stopped, then backed up and idled beside them as Jen removed her jeans and panties. Bob asked her later if she had seen the car. She hadn't.

Once, in mid-afternoon, parked on a street in a residential area near the beach, he undressed her completely. Some kids their age were walking back from the beach when one of them noticed and they stopped. They were silent as Bob touched her breast, as he kissed her and placed his hand between her legs. She was dry as he slipped his finger inside her, but moistened almost immediately. Other kids were collecting outside the car and, beginning to feel fear, Bob straightened up and turned the key and they drove away as she put her clothes back on. She hadn't enjoyed that, she said. It reminded her of the time Michael undressed her while the couple in the back seat watched. But I thought you liked it that time, Bob said. That was why I wanted to undress you.

She *had* liked it. They had all been friends and she had once seen the other couple making love. Well, not making love like intercourse, but everything else. And that was the time Michael put his tongue inside her (inside? Bob had only kissed her there) and she had liked that. But now, when she thought about it, she sometimes thought she had made a mistake. Not the tongue part, but the naked part. But maybe that was because it was Michael.

Once, perhaps wanting to see how far they could go before the envelope pushed back, they went to an indoor movie and, instead of sitting in the balcony, they sat on the aisle in the main section. It was a Friday night and the theater was filled.

During the previews, they began to kiss. He had asked her to wear a skirt so it would be easy for him to feel her up, but he had only begun to touch her when an usher appeared and shined his flashlight on them. He asked them to come with him and they did without objecting. In the lobby the manager said they would have to leave the theater. He was angry; other patrons had complained. No, he would not refund their admission. Bob wanted to argue, but Jen said, "Let's just go." She was embarrassed. Humiliated.

They had only two dollars left, not enough to go to a restaurant or a drive-in or a motel. In any event, Jen didn't want to make love now. Bob didn't remind her of her vow not to withhold herself from him. Perhaps he was being considerate. Perhaps he didn't want to make love either.

He had the idea of buying a can of something at a supermarket and eating it in the car. They bought a tin of sardines because they didn't have a can opener and the sardines came with a key that allowed you to peel back the top of the tin without having to use a separate opener. For less than a dollar they were able to buy a bag of plastic forks.

They ate the sardines in the car in the parking lot outside the supermarket. When they had finished, Jen said she didn't want to go through what she had just experienced in the theater again. She was still upset. They agreed to rent a motel room for their next date.

Out of money, they went back to her house and watched TV with her parents and her brother. She told her father that their date had consisted of sharing a can of sardines in the car after they discovered that they didn't have the money for a movie.

"It was a cheap date," she said. She seemed genuinely cheerful, the upset of a half-hour earlier having passed. In her parents' house again, she felt secure. The implication, which Bob understood even as he listened to her talking to her father, was that he was taking her to places where she felt unsure of herself, perhaps even afraid, and sometimes she needed to be able to retreat to her parents' house to regain herself.

"How much did it cost you in gas and oil to drive to the market and back here?" her father asked Bob.

Bob didn't know.

"Maybe it wasn't so cheap after all," her father said.

It wasn't that either of them thought what they were doing was wrong. After all, how can something that gives so much pleasure be wrong? The very fact that it was so pleasure-filled made it right. Otherwise God or Nature would not have made it so wonderful. It was, rather, that they knew what adults, and even some of their friends, would think if they found out how far they were going.

When he told Harry what he and Jen were doing, some of the risks they were taking, Harry was appalled. What if...? he said. What if this other thing? What would Bob do? What would Bob do if yet something else? How could he endanger Jen like he was doing?

Harry was right. How could Bob endanger Jen? What if some of the boys in that group of kids by the beach had decided that they wanted her too? How could he have protected her?

And what did she want? Once, in a ground-floor room in a motel, she opened the curtains and stood at the window, nude, for several minutes before closing the curtains again. When Bob asked why she had done that, she said, "I wanted to see what was going on outside," which, of course, wasn't an answer. Perhaps she was daring herself to push forward, but also wanted his protection should something go wrong. Perhaps she simply wanted somebody other than Bob to look at her.

On some occasions when they rented a motel room they kept count of the number of times they had intercourse. He was able to come only six or seven times in an evening, but he was erect almost constantly. Jen was certain she was achieving orgasm, but he couldn't tell if she was or wasn't—her body did not do anything different when she came, if she came, at least the parts of her body that he could see or feel. On two nights they coupled so often and with such energy that her labia bled after the fourth or fifth time, raw from the friction created by the thrusts of his penis, and the shaft of his penis was scraped bloody from rubbing against her pubic hair. Yet, though they were in pain until her excitement swept her away to a place she couldn't afterward describe and the lubrication of her vagina coated his penis, they didn't stop but continued to copulate without restraint.

She talked to him sometimes, though perhaps the words were not meant for him but to release something in herself. She would say, "Fuck me" or "Fuck my pussy" when he was already moving in and out of her. Once, riding him, she said, "Hurt me, hurt my titty." He had no idea what she wanted him to do, how she wanted him to hurt her, and he didn't want to cause her pain. When they had finished and were resting, he asked her what she had meant when she told him to hurt her. At first she didn't remember saying it, then she decided that she had wanted him to suck on her nipple, but she didn't know why she had asked him to hurt her.

Once, as he was thrusting into her from behind, an aroma came from her that was a mix of vaginal arousal, the dampness of her skin, and the sea. Her anus opened and he almost withdrew from her vagina and plunged into it, but reminded himself of her prohibition against that. When he told her later what he had seen, she said, "Don't fuck me in the butt. I'll do anything else, but not that."

She fantasized about other men. She had read a novel that described a scene in which two men held a young woman in a kind of seat made from their locked arms and slowly lowered her onto the erect penis of a third man. In her fantasy she was the woman with the three men. She had a dream in which Bob's friend Tom made love to her. His penis—its color, its length, the way it looked when tumescent and after—was so real that she asked Bob what it looked like in actual life. But he had never seen it and he didn't want to ask Tom to describe it or show it to him. When Bob told her this, she laughed and said, "All right. I'll let you off the hook this time."

She often did not remember the specifics of their lovemaking, so lost had she been in the sensations she had experienced. Bob seemed to be aware of everything—what her body was doing, how her skin felt, what he was thinking, what different parts of him were feeling—up to the moment of climax when all went white inside his head and he collapsed beside her. He likened the intense pleasure of his orgasm and the vision of nothingness that accompanied it to what he imagined was the experience of death. He usually fell immediately into sleep afterward and slept for several minutes. Jen had learned to accept that he could not keep himself awake after coming if it was his first orgasm of the evening, and waited for him to open his eyes before trying to converse with him. She would console herself during his absence by holding his penis. At first it would shrink to almost nothing, she said, but then it would lengthen and sometimes it would get hard again if he slept long enough. She liked that. She liked being able to manipulate it into an erection while he was entirely unaware. At those times she had more control over his body than he had.

When he woke up after sleeping for five or six, perhaps even ten minutes, he usually felt depressed. This happened only after the first intercourse of the night and only if they were in bed. He thought the sadness had to do with his returning from the place of pleasure and light and nonexistence. He came to look at orgasm as a mystical experience, and he visited it as the land where life and death converged.

They took to playing with each other as he drove. He got her to promise not to try to insert her finger in his penis, and for the most part she kept her promise. He would open his fly and she would go inside his underpants and stroke him until he ejaculated into her hand. Or she would loosen her jeans or Capris and he would place his hand inside her panties and caress her vagina. He preferred her to wear a loose skirt when they drove around so she could kick off her panties and open her legs and he could put one or two fingers inside her. This way, too, he could withdraw his hand quickly if necessary—say, if a patrol car pulled up beside them—and her skirt would conceal her nakedness.

But sometimes they liked to have people watch them. Once, driving back from Los Angeles during rush hour—they had gone to Pershing Square to listen to the soapbox orators, something Mr. Amos had told them about—traffic was only inching along and she began masturbating him. He came after a couple of minutes and hadn't closed his fly before she undid her jeans and slipped them off and then pulled her panties off and he inserted his fingers in her. She slid her hips forward and opened her legs to allow him to penetrate more deeply. After a while he looked past her and saw that a bus had crept up alongside them in the adjacent lane. People were looking out their windows at them. He saw no emotion on their faces. He caught the eyes of a woman of about forty and offered a smile. The corners of her mouth lifted slightly and then she returned her gaze to the area of Jen's pubis and his hand.

"I just came," Jen said. "It was great."

The bus was pulling forward.

"I think it was all those people watching us," she said.

"I didn't think you'd noticed."

"Put your hand there again. There. Just touch me."

Finally their lane began to pick up speed and he had to use both hands to drive.

"I feel like crying," Jen said.

Late one afternoon they were in his parents' Renault in a secluded area of Hillcrest Park. They were in the front passenger seat, she sitting on him. She was naked below her waist and his hands grasped her buttocks as she rode. The violence of their ride drew them on, each of them seeking climax, and they were oblivious to everything around them. His penis seemed to grow and grow inside her until he thought it would burst its skin. At one point he heard her gasp, and this sound, this reminder of her as his lover, his partner, drove him still farther, his penis engorged beyond anything he'd previously experienced. At last he exploded—there was the encompassing light, which he had anticipated, but also bits of darkness strewn through it, like small holes in a white fabric, which he had not seen before—and he pulled her to him as though to merge his skin with hers and he kissed her face, her neck, everywhere he could reach. He felt he could not stop. Then he heard her say his name and he opened his eyes and it was as though the most intense experience he had ever known were a fiction, so far away did it seem from this gray day that existed beyond the confines of the car. When they began their lovemaking, it had been sunny, the broad leaves of the trees they were parked under dappling the Renault with shadow.

"Children are watching us," Jen said.

He looked out the side window. There were three of them, the oldest nine or ten years old, a few feet away. Jen slipped off him onto the driver's seat and they hurriedly dressed. He had to get out of the car to walk around to the driver's side while she slid back into the passenger seat. When he opened the door, the children didn't move. "Hi," he said. He forced himself to smile, but they only stared at him and at Jen behind him.

Most of the way back—to her house? Later he couldn't recall where they had gone—they didn't speak. Finally she said, "If we're going to do it outdoors again, we should do it at night." Then she said, "It felt like I had a fire hose inside me. Your jizz is still leaking out."

"Did you come?"

"Couldn't you tell? Jesus!"

After a moment, he said, "Do you think it's possible to go any farther?"

"I don't know. I didn't think I would ever get this far. I had no idea this even existed. Wait. Are we talking about my orgasm, or yours? Or something else altogether?"

He laughed. "I don't know what we're talking about."

"Well, you asked the question."

"I know."

Are Love and Sex the Same Thing?

In late spring, he got a part-time job stacking wood in a wood yard owned by his friend Justin's father. The wood came from trees uprooted as part of land clearance for new housing or shopping centers. The land-clearance operation was also owned by Justin's father. Of all the varieties of wood they cut and sold, live oak was the most popular because it burned clean and longer than most other woods. Walnut was also popular, because it burned hot and dry, and, of course, citrus—orange and lemon and grapefruit; this was Orange County, after all—for its scent.

Bob and Justin, when they worked together, would sometimes make up new names that the county might adopt after the orange trees were gone. "Deadwood County," "Orangeless County," and "Firewood County" were three of the possibilities they came up with. Once, when they were drinking Chianti, Justin's brother, Fred, had bought for them, they talked about writing the county commissioners or county councilmen or whatever they called themselves and proposing their ideas for a name change, but they never did.

Remembering this later, Bob's sense was that they thought the names they made up were funny and sad at the same time, but he thought that what he now recalled as sadness could more accurately have been labeled bitterness. They didn't like the changes they saw almost every day, but understood that Justin's father's business and the jobs they had, as little as they paid, owed their existence to these changes.

Bob liked the work. He enjoyed being outdoors, and sweating

made him feel good afterward. And he liked Justin and Fred. Fred had gotten out of the Navy a year earlier, was finishing up his bachelor's degree in mathematics at Long Beach State and was engaged to Toni, a girl he had met there. He would expound sometimes on the irrationality of love, but Bob thought it was obvious that love was irrational and he didn't usually comment.

Once when all three of them were in the yard, eating their lunch, and Fred was going on again about love and unreason, Bob blurted out, "Thank God for sex!" Neither Fred nor Justin responded at first, but then Fred said, "Do you think love and sex are the same thing?"

"No, but they're close enough for government work," Bob said, at which they all three laughed. He had learned that expression from Fred who, Bob assumed, had picked it up in the Navy. Bob had not meant to disclose that he and Jen were sleeping together, but his expressing his gratitude to God for inventing sex certainly gave them away.

Justin told him this story. Justin had sold a full cord of wood to a guy who lived out near Palm Springs and he had to deliver it. He and a man his father had just hired loaded the wood onto a fenced flatbed and drove it out to the desert. The other man was interesting. "In-ter-est-ing," Justin said, pronouncing the word with a kind of faux German accent. He was studying German in college and sometimes applied this accent to English words. Bob hoped that this habit would pass after Justin fulfilled his language requirement.

The man was from Mexico and sent money from each paycheck to his family there. It had not occurred to Justin or to Bob that the Mexicans who worked in the United States had obligations at home that they were trying to meet. But the more interesting thing was something the man had said while they were driving. He asked Justin if he had ever had the experience of his mind separating from his body such that he could see his body from above while it continued to negotiate the world. Before Justin could respond, the man said he had had that experience one time when he was out in the desert alone, on foot. That was the first time he had it, but he had had it two or three times since, even while working. Driving through the desert now, he said, reminded him of it.

Justin told him he had never had that experience, had never even heard of it before. The man was surprised. He had thought it was very common.

The man had been working in the wood yard for several weeks when, one day, he didn't come in. Neither Justin nor his father ever saw him again. Justin's father still had a paycheck for him, waiting to be picked up.

A couple of months later the man's body was found out near Mojave. He had been castrated and had apparently bled to death, or maybe he had died of shock. When the police notified Justin's father, Justin remembered that on the trip to Palm Springs, the man had told him that he had once cut off one of his testicles during a time when his mind was away from his body.

It was odd, Justin said, that he had blocked that out of his thoughts. But he remembered it now and told the police. The police said they would ask the Highway Patrol how many testicles had been found beside the body. It seemed to be a kind of police humor, Justin said, their saying that.

Though Bob had known Justin for years, he did not think Justin would have told him about the strange Mexican if they, Bob and Justin, were not working together in the wood yard.

Harry Loves Sara

Sara had gone camping up by Porterville with her mother and stepfather and she had invited Bob to come up too. He had not hitchhiked any distance before and decided to thumb his way there.

His parents did not want him to go. They were afraid something bad would happen to him, but they voiced their concern in terms of authority: "As long as you live in this house," etc. Bob ignored them. He had just graduated from high school. He was almost eighteen and he wanted to show them that they had no more power over him than what he chose to allow them.

He took off late in the morning on a hot day in the middle of June. He was able to hitch rides down to the beach easily enough, but when he got to 101, he waited for half an hour before a car stopped and the passenger door opened. The car was filled with boys only a little older than he was. From their short-sleeve shirts with their buttoned collars, their pressed jeans, their carefully cut hair that gave the appearance of having been swept by the wind, their even teeth, Bob took them to be college kids, probably fraternity brothers.

He didn't see room for another person, but he started toward them anyway. Then the boy in the passenger seat pulled the door closed and the car lurched forward. Then it stopped again. The door opened but Bob didn't move. "Come on," the kid said. "Do you want a lift?"

Bob walked toward them again, the boy shouting, "Come on! Hurry up!" He was almost to the car when it took off again, even before the door shut. It went twenty feet and stopped again. The door opened again and the boy asked, "Don't you want a ride?"

Bob didn't move. The door shut and the car backed up. The boy said, "Get in. Come on, give me your pack."

Bob walked over to him. The boy had not opened the door and Bob stared at him through the open window. He could see the two sitting in back. They would not look at him. They seemed to have absented themselves from this.

Bob stepped back so the kid in the passenger seat would have room to open the door, but the kid didn't move. Bob thought if he could get him to open the door, he would push it back on him while the kid's arm was still extended, or maybe he could get him to start out of the car before he slammed the door into him. Maybe he could catch the kid's leg or his hand.

"Come on," Bob said.

The kid looked at him.

"Come on," Bob said again.

The car took off, spraying Bob's legs with dirt and gravel.

Traffic had become denser. Rush hour was starting. Finally a sedan stopped. The driver was pudgy and middle-aged. No one else was in the car. The driver was smiling. Bob got in.

The driver was easy to talk to but after a few miles he put his hand on Bob's thigh.

Bob didn't know what to do. Finally he said, "Is your hand bothering you?"

"No. Why?"

"It's bothering me."

The man withdrew it. "Sorry."

They did not talk any more. An hour later the driver pulled off the road at a truck stop at an intersection where a county road met the highway. "I turn here," he said. Bob got out and went inside the café.

He was hungry and he ordered a bowl of chili and a cup of coffee. After a couple of cups he went outside to the restroom. At adjoining urinals were the man who had given him a lift and a tall, younger man wearing a leather motorcycle jacket. No one else was in the restroom and Bob went into a stall and peed. When he came out, the two men hadn't moved.

Bob stood, thumb out, a few yards up from the intersection. It was dark now. Cars and semis ripped by doing seventy, eighty. The traffic light seemed never to show red. Finally it did, but only for a few seconds. It did not turn red again for twenty minutes. Bob returned to the café and ordered another coffee. The counterman had been watching him. "You're never going to get a ride that way."

"I know."

"Where are you going?"

"Porterville."

The counterman called out: "Anybody going to Porterville? This man needs a ride."

There were maybe ten people in the café. Everybody looked up. A stout man with three or four days of gray-blond stubble came over. "I'm going up near there. I'll be leaving in about ten minutes. I can use somebody to talk to, keep me from falling asleep."

"Great," Bob said.

The man drove a small hay truck. He had bought hay from a wholesaler and was taking it back to his ranch to feed his cattle. His ranch was small compared to a lot of them in the valley, and he pinched pennies where he could. Transporting his own feed was one of the ways he did it. He had only a few cows, so it was worth fetching the hay himself. He had been driving all day and hadn't had much sleep the night before.

He was still talking when Bob dropped off. It seemed as though he had been out for only a few minutes when he felt the rancher bump his arm. He needed Bob to stay awake; he was afraid of falling asleep.

"Sorry," Bob said. Then he dropped off again.

Around dawn the rancher pulled into a parking lot beside a small restaurant. "I'll let you out here. I'll park this thing and meet you inside. Take your pack."

Bob got out of the truck and went inside and sat down on a stool at the counter. After a minute or two he looked for the rancher, but he hadn't come in. Bob went to the door. The road was straight and he could see the hay truck making its way up the slight grade.

He had eggs and hash browns and coffee and then asked the man behind the counter if he could ask around for a ride.

"Wait outside and catch 'em on their way out," the man said.

The second man Bob approached was going to Porterville and he agreed to give Bob a ride. He was in his mid-twenties and he drove a nearly new Chevy. He was an Army reservist on his way to a boring weekend at the Reserve Center in Porterville, he said. He had gotten his commission as a second lieutenant after graduating from ROTC. Then he had gone on to the Army's basic officer's course. That was last summer. Engineer Officer's Basic Course, it was called, to be exact. It had almost nothing to do with engineering. He knew because he was an engineer in civilian life.

He was assigned to a boat company. It was supposed to exercise its boats on the Sacramento River, but it didn't because, although it had boats, it did not have the trailers to haul them to the river.

A couple of other reservists had offered to bring in their own boat trailers, but the company commander said no, he didn't want to get embroiled in an insurance mess, should something happen. Life as an engineer officer in a boat company in Porterville was pretty fucking boring, the lieutenant said. He was thinking about going to jump school and then Ranger school, just for something to do. "How about you?" he asked. "What do you do?"

"I just graduated from high school."

"Yeah? You look older. Do you live in Porterville?"

"I'm going up there to see some friends. They're at the campground outside of town."

"I know where it is. I can drop you off about a mile from there."

"That'd be great."

"No problem. You know, you ought to think about joining the Army Reserve."

Bob had understood almost nothing the lieutenant said when he talked about his experience in the Army Reserve. Bob didn't know what the Army Reserve was. He didn't know what an Army engineer did or was supposed to do, and he didn't know how you exercised a boat on the Sacramento River if you could. He had heard of jump school, but he didn't know what Ranger school taught you.

"It would mean an income," the lieutenant said. "A small one, but still, it's better than a poke in the eye with a sharp stick." He laughed.

It was still early when he stopped the car where a narrow feeder road made a T with the highway.

"Just go up that dirt road. It's about a mile, maybe less. You'll see it."

"Thanks. I appreciate it," Bob said.

"No problem. I'd drive you, but I'm running late."

Bob started walking. Alfalfa fields and a shallow ditch bordered the road on either side. Water had been in the drainages recently but the damp earth at the bottom was beginning to crack. Through his shirt he could feel the heat that would become oppressive as the day grew older. The sky was already changing from pale blue to white. As he walked, frogs announced his arrival and then his departure. Crows in the fields and along the edges of the road ignored him.

A dented pickup with a couple of small hay bales in the bed pulled up beside him.

"Need a lift?"

"I'm looking for the campground."

"You're almost there. Another two, three hundred yards."

The driver put the truck in gear and it pushed forward, groaning with the effort.

Bob walked around the vehicle gate and was about to go into the office to ask where he could find the Simmons' campsite when he saw Harry filling a jerry can at a faucet at the side of the building. Harry looked up and his face went from disbelief to glad-to-see-you to quizzical in less than a second.

"What are you doing here?"

"Sara told me she was coming here and invited me to come up. I didn't know you were going to be here," Bob said.

"She invited me, too."

It was awkward.

"Did you drive The Beast up?" The Beast was Harry's old Ford V8.

"Yeah. I'm going to have to borrow some money for gas to get home." He looked at Bob, but didn't ask. Finally he said, "Did you bring a tent? I don't see one on your pack."

"No. Just a sleeping bag. I thought I'd pray it doesn't rain. Maybe do a non-rain dance."

Harry laughed. "You can share my tent if you want. Actually, it did rain a little last night."

Harry took the jerry can and lugged it to the campsite fifty yards away and Bob followed him. Sara was in her parents' tent, but they had gone down to the lake, Harry said. In a moment Sara came out of the tent. She looked like she always did, small and athletic, but somehow—perhaps in the way she carried herself—not at ease. Bob realized now that she was only a couple of inches taller than Jen. She did not look happy to see him, but she didn't seem unhappy either. She and Harry looked at him now with forbearance and Bob thought he had made a mistake in coming up here.

"If you want to show me where your tent is, I'd like to take a nap. I got hardly any sleep last night."

"Oh, yeah. Follow me."

Where the Simmons and Sara shared a walk-in tent that allowed for cots and folding chairs, Harry slept in an Army-surplus pup tent.

"We usually use this tent in the afternoon when Bill and Peggy go to town. She doesn't like to make love in their tent. Sara, not Peggy. I assume Peggy does like to make love in their tent, but I don't really know. What the hell am I talking about?"

"Sorry to be in the way," Bob said. "I misunderstood something, I guess. I'll leave after I get some sleep."

"If you want to wait, I was planning on going back tomorrow."

"Sure. I'll help out with gas."

"Thanks. You can use my sleeping bag if you want to. Oh, you've got your own. Okay, I'll see you later."

Something was pushing against his shoulder. Harry. It was mid-afternoon. "Sara and I are going into town to get something to eat. We thought you might want to come with us. Or if you want to sleep some more, you can stay here. We'll only be a couple of hours."

"I'll come with you. Where can I brush my teeth?"

"Bring your toothbrush. You can use the restroom there."

Bob felt the strain as soon as he got in the car. Sara smiled but was silent and Harry gunned The Beast hard before peeling out of the parking area, throwing up bits of dirt and small rocks behind them. Bob thought of the frat boys when they took off back in Huntington Beach.

"That was considerate," Sara said. "I'll bet the people who own those other cars like having their paint chipped."

Harry ignored her.

At the restaurant they got a booth by a window. Bob sat across from them. When they had ordered, Sara said, "How's our littlest angel?"

"She's fine," Bob said.

"I heard something about her. I'll tell you later, if you want to hear it."

"If it's about what happened at Disneyland, she already told me."

Sara was silent, her expression noncommittal. Harry's eyebrows raised but he didn't say anything.

The waitress brought their food and the tension lifted. Sara and Harry talked about things that had happened here in town or at the campground over the past few days and laughed and shook their heads. Bob didn't know what they were talking about and concentrated on eating his cheeseburger.

They were staring at him.

"What?"

"I said how long are you planning on staying here. Not to be discourteous," Sara said.

Bob looked at Harry. He didn't know what Harry had told her and Harry was giving nothing away.

"I don't know. I thought I'd leave tomorrow, or maybe the day after."

"That isn't very long. Did you hitchhike?"

"Yes."

"How was that? Hitchhiking," Harry asked.

"I'll bet he has some stories to tell," Sara said.

Bob told them about the man who put his hand on his leg, and the hay truck driver who dumped him at a truck stop and then took off, and the Army reservist who hated the Army and wanted him to join up. He told them about the traffic light that turned red for thirty seconds every twenty minutes.

Harry was watching him with interest. "You seem different. Or maybe you're the same and I'm seeing you differently."

"You've graduated. You're going to change," Sara said. Bob couldn't tell if she was talking to him or to both him and Harry. She said, "Those are a lot of adventures to have just to come up here for a day or two."

"I'll be leaving tomorrow," Harry said. "He can ride with me so he can avoid any other adventures."

Sara looked at her plate. "Everybody's leaving. Murphy asked me to marry him again. Maybe I will."

Harry pretended not to have heard. Finally he said, "If you had arranged to be born a year earlier, you could have graduated with us."

Sara and Bob were quiet.

They dropped Bob at the campground and then they drove off—to the lake, they said.

They left at nine in the morning. Sara was not there to see them off. They'd driven an hour without speaking when Harry said, "Six other guys have touched her cunt."

Bob asked him how he knew.

"I asked her. She told me."

"You asked if six other guys had touched her cunt?"

"I asked her how many other guys she'd screwed. She said six."

Bob didn't say anything. He remembered her telling him something like that when they were going out. He wondered if six were a special number for her, or if she had not been with anybody new between the time she told him and her time with Harry.

When they got to the coast the air was cool and the blue of the sky was hidden by a layer of cloud. Inland, the temperature had been climbing toward ninety again.

They stopped at a gas station with a restaurant attached to it. Bob gave Harry ten dollars to fill the tank.

"Is this one of the places you stopped on your way up?"

"No. This will be a new adventure."

Harry laughed. It was becoming easier to be with him. They had been close friends, the closest maybe, when Bob and Sara were together and Harry was on the outside. But then something happened between Harry and Sara and, though Sara would have liked to keep them both, Bob eased himself away from her and eventually began to see Jen. It had been months since he and Harry had been able to confide in each other or to laugh without restraint in each other's company.

Bob ordered an omelet and Harry ordered chili and beans with onions and cheese.

"Jesus. I'm going to keep my window down. I don't care how cold it is. Remind me to get my jacket out of the trunk."

"I think I'm going to enlist," Harry said.

Bob sipped from his glass of water. Harry hated the military. His sister had spent ten years in the Air Force, leaving only because she had fallen in love with a woman and someone had informed on them. Harry hated the idea that his sister was a lesbian and he hated the Air Force for making her leave when she hadn't wanted to.

"Why?"

"What else can I do? I can't afford to go to college. I don't know if I even want to go. I don't see myself, or don't want to see myself, changing tires and pumping gas for the rest of my life."

"What branch are you going to go in?"

"The Air Force."

"What!"

"My sister liked it." He shrugged. "I'll try to save some money. I should be able to save something in four years."

"Four years? The Army is only three. Two, if you're drafted."

Harry shrugged again. "The Air Force is four. Maybe they'll teach me something I can earn a living from when I get out. Have you checked out the Army?"

"I just remember when the recruiters came to talk to us at assembly last year. The Army was three years, the Marines four and the Navy four. I didn't pay any attention to the Air Force after I saw how fat their recruiter was."

The food came and for most of the meal they didn't talk. Bob picked up the check. When they were walking out to the car, he asked, "When will you be going?"

"I don't know. I don't even know if I will be going. Thanks for the gas money. I owe you a couple of bucks. It didn't come to ten."

It was almost dark when Harry dropped Bob off. His father said, "Well, look who's here." He was very angry. His body seemed to vibrate with rage. Bob went to his room, alert to any sound that would indicate his father was coming up behind him. Half a year earlier, he had slapped Bob on the back of his head after an argument.

Bob dropped his pack on the bed and went into the kitchen for something to eat. His mother came in and, without speaking, opened the refrigerator door and pointed at a plate of fried chicken. Then she started to laugh at the silliness of wanting to feed him but refusing to talk to him. Bob laughed too.

His father appeared. "Are you going to work tomorrow?"

Bob nodded.

"Do you think you're going to use one of the cars?"

"I assumed I would."

"Assume again, buddy." He walked away.

Bob found the newspaper and sat down at the table in the nook beside the kitchen and started looking through the classifieds.

"What are you doing?" his mother asked.

"I'm going to need a car."

She disappeared. After a minute or two, his father came back.

"You can use the Renault. You'll have to put gas in it in the morning."

"Thank you."

"Uh huh." He left again.

He came back. "How much money are you taking home each week?"

"Fifty dollars. Maybe fifty-five."

"Uh huh. Your mother and I decided that since you're working now, you ought to be helping out with expenses. Food, laundry, gas and so on."

"I pay for the gas I use."

"Uh huh. And rent. We're going to charge you twenty dollars a week for rent. I think that's fair."

Bob waited. When his father didn't say anything more, but only glared at him, Bob said, "And the other stuff?"

"What stuff?"

"Food and laundry. Whatever. What are you going to charge me for that?"

"We haven't figured that out yet. I'll tell you when we do."

"Thanks."

"Don't be a wise ass with me, buddy." He took a step toward Bob. Bob stood up. He was taller than his father. His father turned and walked out of the kitchen and Bob went back to the newspaper. After a while, his father returned.

"We're going to charge you twenty dollars a week for food and your mother's labor in preparing it. Same with laundry. Twenty dollars. Most of that is your mother's labor."

"That's more than I make each week."

"Uh huh. We'll forgive most of it, maybe all of it, if you do one thing."

"What?"

"Go to college in the fall. It's not too late to sign up for junior college."

Bob let his breath out. "How much time do I have to make up my mind?"

"This week. I'll give you till Friday."

"All right."

"All right you'll apply to the junior college?"

"All right I'll let you know on Friday."

His father went back out into the living room where Bob assumed his mother was waiting.

He found a scratch pad by the telephone and tore off the topmost bit of paper and wrote down some phone numbers he got from the newspaper.

It Is All a Series of Accidents,
Though You May Believe It Is Fated

"I missed you," Jen said. "I was surprised how much it hurt, not seeing you."

They were parked on the street a block from her house. He kissed her and breathed in the scent of her hair. It was one of the things he liked most about her, the scent of her hair.

"It must mean I love you," she said.

"You didn't know?"

"I didn't know it would be this painful. I don't want you to go away again."

"I won't."

"Really? You didn't like it?"

"Mostly it was boring, standing out in the sun, waiting for a ride. And you don't know when a car will stop."

"What are you going to do then?"

"I don't know. Work or go to junior college, or both."

"I'll be at the junior college."

"I know. I keep thinking about that. But I don't know if I can stay at my parents' house now. I don't think I can."

"Where will you go?" He could hear the fear in her voice.

"I'll stay in Fullerton, or near here. I'm going to talk to Tom, see if I can move in with him."

"He already has a housemate, doesn't he?"

"Yeah, but maybe I can sleep on the couch. At least for a while."

"Don't leave me."

"I won't. Why do you say that? Will you do something for

me?"

"Yes."

"Take your clothes off. I want to smell your skin."

She hesitated. "My parents might come out. Sometimes they go for a walk. What if Peter comes out and sees us?"

"We can go to the park. No one will see us there."

"I didn't know you liked my smell so much. I'll have to see what soap I'm using."

"It isn't the soap. It's you. God, I'm going to come."

"Not yet. I want you to come in my hand."

He opened his fly and she put her hand inside.

"Like this?" she asked. "Is this good?"

"God, yes."

"You missed me too, didn't you?"

"Yes, yes."

"I love your penis. Your big, fat penis. Your big, thick, juicy penis cock prick shaft stiff—what else do you call it?"

"Just don't stop."

She leaned forward and kissed it. "Your just-don't-stop. Give me your jizz, my Bobby. Give me…there. There."

He bought a nine-year-old Dodge two-door. It may have been green when it was new, or yellow if they ever painted cars yellow, but now it was something like chartreuse. The owner, a guy about thirty with hair slicked back and held down with some kind of gel like they used to do five or six years ago, drove it to Bob's parents' house, followed by a guy in another car. Bob gave the owner fifty dollars and he handed over the title and the keys and then Bob was the owner.

His mother had been watching through the bay window. It was late afternoon. He had just gotten home from the wood yard and his father wasn't home yet. When he went inside, his mother asked if he had bought that car and he said yes. She asked why he needed a car; he could drive the Renault or the station wagon. Bob said he wanted his own car. He went into the bathroom and took a shower and dressed in clean clothes. When he came out his father was home. He asked if that clunker outside was Bob's and then he asked what Bob was going to do about insurance. "Right now you're on our insurance, but I'm not going to insure that heap."

"I don't know. I hadn't thought about insurance."

"Uh huh. There's room for only two cars in the garage. You can't park in the driveway because we won't be able to get out when we want to. And you can't park it out front because it's an eyesore and the neighbors will complain. So what are you going to do?"

"I'm open to suggestions," Bob said.

"Uh huh. My suggestion is that you get rid of it. Sell it. Take it to a junkyard. You can drive your mother's car."

"Only when you say I can."

"What is that supposed to mean? Oh, I see. Well, I'm saying you can drive your mother's car when she isn't using it."

"I want my own car."

"How are you going to pay for gas and maintenance when you're going to school? Or are you planning on working part time when you're in college?"

"I haven't agreed to go to school. You said I had till Friday to make up my mind."

"Ah. So that's what this is about. Okay."

He walked away. For the rest of the evening he acted as though he didn't know Bob was planning to leave.

Bob knew Tom because Bob knew Justin. Justin knew Phil Reisser from Anaheim High and Phil was a friend of Kevin Crowe with whom he had also gone to high school, although Justin hadn't known Kevin then. Kevin's brother was Gerry and Gerry had gone to high school in Garden Grove with Tom. So Bob knew Phil and Tom because he knew Justin, and he met Kevin and Gerry Crowe because he knew Phil and Tom. That is how it works: you meet one person because you know someone else. It is all a series of accidents, one upon another, though you may believe it is fated.

Bob probably never knew what happened to the Crowe brothers' parents. Nobody talked about them. All Bob remembered later was that their parents were out of the picture and Gerry and his wife had taken Kevin in to live with them some time before Bob met them all, and Gerry had gotten Kevin a job doing what he did, painting houses.

Gerry's wife's name was Janice. They were twenty-three or -four and had a couple of kids. Phil was away at UCLA, studying philosophy, which Justin was studying at Long Beach State. Phil painted when he had time, often when he was drunk. He painted abstracts. He liked to paint with Kevin who also liked to drink. One of Kevin's oils was a workingman's shoe; he was indebted to Van Gogh for the way he pressed paint onto the canvas with his palette knife, and sometimes the subjects he chose.

When Bob met Tom he had been out of the Air Force for a couple of years and was taking classes at the junior college in Fullerton. He was serious about his studies. He loved history and read philosophy to try to understand what there was in the way Europeans and Americans thought that had led to World War II. He was older than most junior college students because of the years he had spent in the Air Force, but he had an advantage few other students had: the GI Bill. He did not have to work while many, perhaps most, junior college students did, at least part time. Another advantage to having more time to read and study was that this time could also be used to drink.

For most of the time Bob knew him, Tom was in love with a woman who did not love him, or did not love him enough to keep her from marrying his brother. She was the love of his life, and when, twelve years later, she divorced his brother, Tom left his first wife to marry her. Bob didn't know her and he no longer knew Tom when Tom married her, so he did not know whether, during their marriage or after, Tom continued to regard her as the love of his life. In his mid-twenties, Tom talked about her, at least to Bob, only when he was drunk. When he drank, he became sad and she inhabited that sadness.

Tom lived in an apartment over a garage behind a house on a street zoned for single dwellings. The owner of the house had built the apartment for his wife's sister who, after three months, vacated it and moved back in with her husband. It was a two-bedroom flat and Tom rented out one of the bedrooms. He did not tell the owner, but it didn't matter. One day when Tom went over to pay the rent, the owner said something about the other guy living there. He was not objecting; he was just letting Tom know that he knew. He didn't want Tom to think he had to deceive anybody, or perhaps he didn't want Tom to think he had been successful in deceiving him.

The apartment was within walking distance of the college and Tom had no difficulty in finding someone to live there. He chose a man around his own age who had come out from Chicago to go to college. Harold was studying political science; he wanted to be a lawyer. Bob did not know much about the life Harold came from. He knew that Harold knew something about fighting because he once described an incident with a co-worker that led to his inviting Harold to go out in the alley with him. Outside, the other man raised his hands as though he were a boxer, but positioned himself so that his back was almost touching the wall of the building behind him. Harold told Tom and Bob that if he hit the guy it would have been like hitting him twice with each punch, as each shot to the head would have bounced it off the wall behind him. Harold was surprised the guy knew so little, because he had been so aggressive. Harold said he had no heart to fight when he saw how ignorant the other guy was, and told him he was right about whatever they had been arguing about and walked away.

He fell in love with a girl he met at the junior college. Bob thought he must not have come from money because he often talked about his girlfriend's father's wealth. His girlfriend's father owned orange groves in Santa Ana and Tustin and walnut groves in Ventura that he said he would be willing to sell when offered enough money.

Harold lived under pressure. He worked full time and went to school full time and saw his girlfriend on weekends. He got a D in one of his classes once. This was all the worse because the class was in his major. He seemed to brush the grade off, but then just before the new semester began, he disappeared. Tom and Bob thought he had gone to Ventura where his girlfriend's family had another home; he often spent the weekend there with her and her family. But after three or four days his girlfriend called. She had not heard from him in nearly a week.

When he showed up, neither Tom nor Bob asked where he had been and he did not tell them. He went to his girlfriend's house that night and came back two days later. He had gotten engaged. They had not set the date, but it would be within the next year or year and a half. A few days later he told them his future father-in-law was going to help pay for his education. He had offered to pay for all of it, but Harold was uncomfortable with accepting so much, and preferred to continue to work, even if only part time.

He had talked to his boss and he had agreed to keep Harold on. Harold was a good worker and if his boss could not have him for forty hours a week, at least he could keep him for twenty.

But all of this happened months after Bob moved in with Tom and Harold. On the Thursday before the Friday when he was supposed to tell his father what he had decided about going to college, Bob packed what he could of what he owned in a duffel bag and a rucksack and he put them in his car and drove over to Tom's apartment.

Although he had talked with Tom earlier in the week about the possibility of sleeping on his couch until he could find his own place, Tom was surprised that he had actually left home. Tom hadn't even mentioned to Harold that Bob might be moving in. But no matter. Harold was away, who knew where? and Bob could sleep in his room for now. Was he sure he wanted to do this? Tom asked. Bob wasn't, but he didn't see what else he could do.

He needed a full-time job now. He had played tennis in high school with Vern Dornier. Vern's father ran a tree-spraying outfit where Vern worked summers and he had told Bob that if he ever needed a job he would talk to his dad about him. Bob called him. Vern said he would call him back when they started hiring crews to spray for black spider, which wasn't really a spider but a fungus that afflicted citrus trees. That would be later in the summer. In small talk he said he would be starting a mortuary science course in September. "I'm going to work with dead people. At least they don't talk back," he laughed.

Bob didn't know what that was an allusion to, but it was kind of funny and he laughed too.

Show Me You're Grateful

Jen and he had stopped going to motels. She had no money and Bob needed to conserve what he could from what he had coming in from the wood yard.

One night they were parked near her house. They had made love and were sitting quietly, still half undressed. His middle finger glided between the lips of her vagina; her hand rested on his penis. Her eyes were closed. She made a sound like "unh." It was the sound she usually made when he entered her. Was she fantasizing or was she only concentrating on the sensations?

"I'm getting hot again," she said. She squeezed his penis. "You are, too."

"Ride me," he said.

Afterward, she asked, "What do you think about when you're inside me?"

"About you. Different parts of you. How you feel when I touch you. How you look. How your face looks." He didn't say that he sometimes thought about other girls, that he imagined sometimes that he was touching Sara again, or that he remembered how another girl smelled when she was excited. He was afraid of these thoughts, afraid they would conflict with what Jen and he had if he admitted to them.

"What do you think about?" he asked.

"Sometimes I don't think. I just feel what's happening to me. Inside me." She bent and kissed the tip of his penis. He made it bob in response and she said, "Oh, look at it." Then she said, "Sometimes I think of you, how much I love you. How much I love what you do to me. Sometimes I think of Michael." She went silent. She was waiting for his reaction.

He said, "What do you think about when you think about him? When we're making love."

"I think about what he used to do to me." She was looking at his lap. He was raging hard. "Again? Does it excite you when I talk about Michael?"

Bob had never met him, but thinking of him undressing Jen and putting his fingers inside her both frightened and aroused him. "Apparently," he said. Saying only that one word, he began to soften.

"Don't," Jen said. "I want it to be hard. Is this what it's like when you get jealous?"

"I don't know. This is new to me too."

"Would you like me to tell you what Michael and I used to do? God, are you sure you don't have enough money for a motel room?"

"It'll have to wait until next week."

"Why couldn't I have fallen in love with a rich guy?"

"Or you could have been rich."

He kissed her. He tried to position her on top of him, but she resisted.

"I want you on top of me," she said.

"We can go to the park. We can lie on my jacket."

"Let's go."

He stopped the car at the top of a hill near where other cars were parked. They left the pavement and walked down the hill to a stand of pines. He spread his jacket over a level place on the ground softened by pine needles that had gone brown and they lay down.

"Can anyone see us from up there?"

"I don't think they're interested in us."

He put his hand between her legs. The skin on the insides of her thighs was softer and warmer than the skin on the front of her legs but the muscles under it were as firm.

"I feel like we're being watched."

"Sometimes you like to be watched."

"Not tonight."

"Nobody can see us through the trees."

She sat up and turned, then lay back again. "Okay."

They began undressing and working each other up. Finally she said, "Now. You on top."

Eyes closed, he thought about her buttocks, how they tightened as he withdrew from her vagina. He pictured her breasts and her hard nipples and he imagined someone else's hand on one of her breasts and he kissed her, his tongue going deep inside her mouth, her tongue gliding all around his. He felt his penis swell as a large knot of something worked its way toward the tip, and then it burst out in a flame of sensation and he heard himself sob and he fell down beside her.

Both of them were sweating.

"Did you?" he asked.

"Don't talk."

After a while, she said, "Kiss my pussy."

He leaned over her on one elbow. He didn't say anything.

"Show me you're grateful," she said.

"I am grateful."

"Show me."

He slid down between her legs and placed his lips on her lips there. He didn't know what else to do. He pressed her vagina with the tip of his tongue but he couldn't get it inside. After a moment she said, "Thank you."

The next week, after he got paid, they got a motel room. As soon as they were inside she threw herself on the bed, already pulling at her clothes, her jeans and panties, her shirt and bra. Naked, she kicked everything to the floor.

"Fuck me. Hurt me."

"Hurt you?"

"Fuck me. No foreplay."

"Jesus," he said afterward. "I thought you liked foreplay."

"I do. But this time I wanted you to put it in me while I was still dry."

"Why?"

"I wanted it to hurt a little."

"But why?"

"I'm just trying to please my pussy. Isn't that what you want me to do? But I couldn't come. I'd like some foreplay now, please. Or afterplay, I guess it's called. Would you touch me up now?"

He slipped his index and middle finger inside her. She closed her eyes and lay still. He imagined her imagining someone else doing this to her. He grew erect again. She raised and spread her knees and he ran his fingers in and out of her as he kissed her breasts. Her aroma was very strong and he moved on top of her and then inside her and he didn't think about her at all, but concentrated on his own sensations. He felt her fingernails on his buttocks and heard her moans in his ear and felt everything moving into his penis, engorging it so that he thought it would explode before he could come. Her smell was different and he realized that what he was smelling now was her scent commingled with his own and this smell and his knowledge of what it was and the sounds that came from her throat and her clawing at his back and buttocks drove him into her again until, again, his penis erupted and his arms would no longer support his weight and he aimed for a spot next to her and fell into it.

He could not stop kissing her, her face, her hair, her neck, her shoulders and down, down, her breasts, her belly, and he parted her legs and pushed his tongue against her labia and she began to move her hips in quick jerks until she came again, the fluid flooding out of her into his mouth. At last he stopped and crawled up beside her and kissed her breasts once more and then lay still.

"That was wonderful." She was smiling but her cheeks were wet and he thought she had been crying. "Thank you, thank you. That was wonderful," she said again. "I can't imagine anything better."

His sweat was drying on her breasts and he began to lick it off. She shuddered. "My skin is so sensitive. What have you done to me?" She put her hand against the back of his head. "Do it again. But not yet."

Vern called. The spray season was starting. Bob was looking at fourteen-hour days, a half day on Saturday. It was hard work. Was Bob sure he wanted to do it?

He was sure; he needed the money. He had been laid off at the wood yard. It was summer. The wood had been cut and stacked for the fall. Nobody was buying now. The little that needed doing could be done by Justin and Fred.

Wear boots, Vern said. Bring a lunch. See you on Monday.

Dick Miles Showed Bob How to Hold the Spray Gun

Dick Miles showed Bob how to hold the spray gun so his hand wouldn't get tired and then he showed him how to spray each orange tree, beginning at the top and working down to the bottom. Every leaf needed to be wet, but not soaked. The spray gun had an adjustable nozzle.

Dick was ten or twelve years older than Bob, tall and sandy-haired and angular. An Okie, he said, meaning his family had come out to California to escape the Oklahoma dust storms of the '30s and the loss of arable land. They each had a spray gun and they walked together behind the tank truck, one spraying the trees on the right side of the irrigation ditch the truck followed, the other the trees on the left. Periodically Dick called to the driver to stop so he could go back over a tree where Bob had missed the inside leaves.

The driver was Carl Richman. He made a joke about not being a rich man. Carl was in his fifties. He had cracked hands and his face was scored by sun and weather. He and Dick alternated driving the truck. They did not know Bob yet and did not want him to drive until they did.

Alberto Perez drove the nurse truck that followed them from a distance. Whenever Bob looked at him, Alberto smiled and gave him a thumbs-up. He had a small transistor radio on the seat next to him that was able to pick up a Spanish-language station in Tijuana.

They took a fifteen-minute break about nine o'clock and Dick, Carl, and Bob sat down on the soft soil amid the trees while

Alberto drove up beside the tank truck, clambered to the top with the hose from the nurse and stuck the end of it in the tank's hatch. Then he climbed down and went back to the nurse and turned on the pump. He came over and sat with the others while the tank filled with water and chemical.

Dick and Carl had taken their thermoses out of the cab of the tank truck. Dick sipped coffee while Carl ate soup out of his thermos cup with a spoon he kept in his lunch bucket. Alberto had been nibbling something from a cardboard container as the others sprayed and he wasn't hungry now. It had not occurred to Bob to bring either a thermos or a snack. Dick refilled his cup and passed it to him.

"Thank you," Bob said.

When he was finished he returned the cup to Dick. Dick shook it out and screwed it back on the thermos bottle, and then he and Carl and Alberto stood up and, following them, Bob stood up too. He did not feel tired yet.

The pump engine had stopped and Alberto climbed onto the tank truck and retrieved the hose. He brought it back to the nurse and laid it across the six supports welded to the side. Carl got into the cab of the tank truck and started it up. It started to creep forward along the irrigation ditch. Dick and Bob turned on their hoses and began to spray the trees on either side of the ditch. Lunch was three hours away.

When they stopped again Bob could feel the strain in his calves and thighs. The web of skin between the thumb and index finger of his right hand was torn where the spray gun nestled. He licked it as though he were a dog tending a wound.

He had brought a sandwich and an apple in a brown paper bag. He had forgotten to buy potato chips. Dick and Carl had brought lunches twice the size of his. Alberto ate only a sandwich, but he had been snacking all morning.

Bob was still hungry after he finished the apple. Dick offered him part of the slice of cake his wife had packed him, but Bob declined it out of pride.

"I like pie," Carl said. "Nothing I would like better right now than some hair pie."

Dick and Alberto laughed, so Bob laughed too, but it took him a moment to understand what Carl was talking about.

"You married?" Alberto asked.

Bob shook his head. "No."

"You ought to be," Carl said. "You wouldn't have to go looking for pussy all the time."

"Looking for it is the fun part," Alberto said. "How many times you been married?"

"Three so far. I'll probably wrap it up with number four," Carl said.

"You getting married again?" Dick asked him.

"I swore to myself I would never, but like you said"—to Alberto, although Alberto had not said it—"I get tired of looking for it. Also, I tend to lose interest after I get a few drinks in me."

"That's the problem in looking for it in bars," Dick said.

"But you got somebody lined up?" Alberto said.

"Yeah."

"How old is she?" Alberto winked at Bob.

"Twenty. Twenty-four. Something like that."

Laughter broke from Dick and Alberto. "See?" Alberto said. "You always marry those young ones. No wonder you can't keep them happy. That's why they leave you." Alberto was enjoying himself but Dick, though smiling, was watching Carl closely.

"Fuck you, Perez." Carl began packing the trash from his lunch into his bucket. "The next one I marry is going to be your daughter, and I guarantee she'll be as happy as anybody has ever made her."

"Yeah? You guarantee?"

"I guarantee, friend. I know what she likes, because she told me."

"She told you?"

"That she did. She told me."

"Well, it's too bad she didn't do more than tell you, or I can make you pay for the baby in her belly. You sure you're not its papa?"

"Whoa!" Carl stood up. "I never even met your daughter. I didn't even know you had one. It was your wife I was talking about."

Alberto laughed. "You okay, Carl. For an old fuck, you okay."

"That's what they all said. All three of 'em," Carl said. They all laughed.

They sprayed until four o'clock when they ran out of grove. The next one was half an hour away. Carl weighed the advantage of going back to the truck barn while they still had daylight and calling it an early day against losing a couple of hours' pay and possibly displeasing Marion, Vern's father, and decided to drive out to Placentia and get a start on tomorrow's grove.

When they got there they had to wait for Alberto to fill the tank, so by the time they started spraying they had less than an hour before they had to start for home. It was questionable whether Carl had made the right decision, whether the expense in fuel and driving time was worth going out to the new grove instead of waiting till morning, but when they got back to the barn, Marion didn't say anything. He clapped Carl on the back and told him he had been out to look at their work and they had done all right. He probably asked how the new guy had done, but Bob didn't hear that or Carl's response. After talking with Carl, Marion came over to Bob and told him he'd be sore tomorrow and to be sure to take a long, hot shower tonight.

On the way home, Bob stopped at a market and bought two kinds of lunchmeat and some cheese and bread and lettuce and apples and potato chips and candy bars and a thermos.

They finished the grove in Placentia at noon and sat down and ate their lunch before driving to the next one. Carl and Dick and Alberto all congratulated Bob on his thick sandwiches and Dick said he ought to invest in a metal lunch bucket when he got paid—the paper bags he was using would soak up the oil mix they were spraying on the trees. "I don't know what it will do to you, but I'm pretty sure you'll be better off if you don't eat it on your sandwiches."

After finishing his lunch Bob passed some candy bars around. Dick and Alberto seemed surprised, but each took one and began to peel the paper off it.

"This will make me fall asleep," Alberto said.

"I'll wake you up," Dick said.

Carl declined the candy bar. "Diabetes." Then he said, "How old are you, Bob?"

"Eighteen."

"Old enough," Alberto said.

Carl nodded.

"You got a girlfriend?" Alberto asked.

"Yes."

"Yeah? You do it with her?"

Bob didn't know what to answer. The others were quiet. Finally Carl said, "Hell yes, he does it! Look at him. This man's a stud."

The others laughed. Bob felt his face get hot.

"Yeah? You do it with her?" Alberto persisted.

"Sometimes," Bob said.

They laughed again.

"Sometimes is better than no times," Alberto said. "She do it with anybody else?"

Again he didn't know what to answer. He shrugged, then heard himself say, "How would I know?"

They laughed.

"That's a good answer," Carl said.

"It's the best answer," Dick said.

"How can you know?" said Alberto. "She ever come home and her pussy's all wet from somebody else?"

Dick and Carl glared at him. "That's enough," Dick said.

"That's enough?" said Alberto.

Carl got to his feet. "Let's get moving. We've been sittin' for forty-five minutes. We only get a half-hour," he said for Bob's benefit.

Alberto returned to the nurse truck. Dick and Bob disconnected the spray hoses and stowed them behind the cabin of the tank truck, then climbed up inside the cab. Bob sat between Dick and Carl.

"I hope the next one has soft dirt," Carl said. "That one was like walking on broken concrete."

"You got any other boots?" Dick said.

"It ain't the boots. It's my feet."

"What do you think of Alberto?" Dick asked Bob.

Bob didn't say anything.

"He'll ease up," Dick said.

"Or he won't," Carl said.

"He will," Dick said. "Don't let him get to you."

It was thirty minutes to the next grove. When they pulled in,

Marion and another man were waiting for them. Marion made a
show of looking at his watch but didn't say anything. Carl got out
of the truck and went over to him and spoke. Marion nodded.
Dick and Bob got out of the cab. Alberto was already on top of
the tank, inserting the hose from the nurse truck.

"I told him it was Alberto's fault. He fell asleep and we couldn't
wake him up," Carl said. Marion laughed.

"What's that?" Alberto shouted from the roof of the tank.
"You talking about me?"

"He was just sayin' you're a lazy s.o.b. and you made everybody
late," Marion shouted back.

"What? That's a lie! We had to wait because Carl was pulling
his pud and it took him a long time to get his nut."

"That true, Carl? You made these guys wait while you were
jackin' off?"

"Shit. Now we know what the motherfucker dreams about,"
Carl said.

"Okay," Marion said. "This man is James Little. I brought him
out to work the tower. But don't let him be the only one to do it.
Rotate it, you hear me?" He turned as if to say something to Bob,
but then changed his mind. "All right. I'll let you get to it. I'll see
you back at the barn this evening."

He walked out to the road where he had left his car.

Carl and Dick turned to James Little. He was a man about
thirty, a little shorter than most, with dark hair and sharply cut
facial features. Under Carl's interrogation, James said he had
worked for another outfit doing the same thing, but he had left
after an argument with his foreman. The argument had been about
something personal; James said he didn't want to talk about it.

"Well, you won't have that problem here. Marion's a good
man. He's fair," Dick said.

Carl nodded. "We better get at it. You been in the tower

before?"

James said yes.

"All right. You take the first turn." Carl looked down the lane separating two rows of trees. "These are pretty long trails. We'll change over after two or three and Alberto can fill up then."

Dick got in the cab and started the engine but did not put it in gear. James climbed to the top of the rig and hoisted himself into the tower's cage. He turned the knob and the tower began to rise. He took it all the way up and looked around. These were big trees and James could spray down on the leaves they couldn't reach from the ground.

Carl and Bob turned their hoses on and Dick put the truck in gear and it began to inch forward.

While Alberto was filling the tank, Carl told Bob, "You want to watch out for high tension lines when you're up there. If you see any coming up, yell down to me to stop the rig, and then lower the tower until you're low enough to get under the lines. There've been men electrocuted because they weren't paying attention, so pay attention. Be sure to turn off your spray gun. The electricity will follow the water back to you. Something else. When the rig makes a turn, lower the tower. We don't want you flipping out of it when the truck starts bouncing over those ruts. You think you can remember all that?"

Bob nodded.

"All right. It's your turn up there. Wait till I turn into the next row before you get in the cage."

Carl stepped up into the cab and worked the truck over the small embankments lining the furrows where water ran during irrigation. When he had gotten it so it was aimed straight down the next lane, he signaled to Bob to get in the tower and Bob climbed up onto the top of the truck and into the cage. He turned the knob and took the tower up to its full height. He guessed he was thirty or thirty-five feet above the ground.

"You don't need to be up that high," Dick called. "Take it down a little."

Bob lowered the tower a few feet and Dick nodded his head. He and James turned on their spray guns and Carl put the truck in gear. Bob turned on his spray gun and began to spray the tops of the trees on either side of the lane below him.

"I thought you would call or come over last night after you got off work," Jen said. They were eating hamburgers in a Denny's. She was treating him with money she had saved from her allowance.

"I was too beat by the time we finished up. And then I had to go out and buy lunchmeat and a thermos and stuff."

"So how was it? Tell me about it. Did you meet anybody interesting?"

"Oh yeah. Everybody's interesting. Carl runs the crew. He's an older guy, but he's not heavy-handed. He and this other guy, Dick, kind of watch over me. Dick showed me how to hold the spray gun and how to spray so you get both the tops and the undersides of the leaves. Today we got a new guy named James. New to the company, at least. He used to work for another company, but had a falling-out with his boss. A guy named Alberto runs the nurse truck. The nurse has a tank on it where they mix—where Alberto mixes—water with the chemicals we're spraying and then he pulls up alongside the rig we're working off of and fills our tank with the stuff from his tank. Usually he does this when the rest of us are taking a break or eating lunch. My first day, I thought he had kind of a lazy job, mostly sitting in the nurse and eating these snacks he brings from home. But I realized today that he's almost constantly moving. While we're spraying, he's going back to a water hydrant and filling his own tank with water, and then he drives out to where we are and transfers that water and poison solution to our tank. Then he drives back to the hydrant to get the nurse ready for the next fill. He doesn't eat lunch when we eat, although he sits down with us for a little while and has a sandwich or a piece of fruit maybe. I think he doesn't eat with us because he doesn't have time. We take thirty or forty-five minutes for lunch and I don't think he has that much time to spend away from the nurse. I think he's constantly munching on his snacks because he doesn't take time for lunch."

"Wow," Jen said.

"What?"

"That's a lot. You said a lot. I didn't know you were that interested in your job. I thought it was just a way to make money."

"Well, it is. But it's interesting too. The people I work with are. And the job itself—it isn't anything I ever heard about. I didn't know this kind of work existed."

"But didn't you know Vern, or whatever his name is, in school?"

"Yeah, but he never described it to me. All he said was that it's hard work. And it is."

"Are you going to have any time left for me?"

"What do you mean?"

"I thought you were going to call me last night. I was really disappointed that you didn't. And I didn't know what to tell my parents. They were worried that something had happened to you. I was too."

"You could have called me."

"I should have. But I waited for you to call and then it got too late."

"I didn't know your parents were that concerned about me."

"I didn't either. I was surprised that they were so worried."

"I'll call from now on," Bob said. "If I say I'll call, then I will, if only to let you know I'm okay. But you can call me too."

She picked up his left hand with both of hers and brought it to her lips and kissed the back of it. "Thank you," she said. After working with men for two days, he was surprised at how small her hands were.

"How many girls you had?" Alberto asked.

"I don't know," Bob said.

"You don't know? You had so many you can't count?"

"Six," Bob said.

"You're eighteen? That's pretty good for eighteen." Alberto's mouth and eyes took on a look of appreciation. James nodded as though he thought six was pretty good too.

"How many you had, Alberto?" Dick asked.

Alberto thought. He said, "Maybe two hundred."

The others laughed.

"Okay, maybe one hundred," Alberto said.

"'Maybe,'" Carl repeated. "Does that include your nieces?"

"Hey, you leave my nieces alone. They're in a special class."

For a minute Bob thought he meant a special class in school, but then he realized Alberto was talking about the way he thought of them.

"How many nieces you got?" Dick asked.

"About a hundred," James put in before Alberto could answer.

Everybody laughed, Alberto too. Then he said, "Not so many. Maybe only ninety." They laughed again.

Bob liked the tower. He had watched James ride it like a bucking horse when Carl turned into another lane, the tower whipping back and forth as the rig bounced over the sun-hardened irrigation walls, James gripping the cage rail, his knuckles white with tension, a frozen grin taking up the lower part of his face.

After completing the turn, Carl got out of the truck. "Just checking to make sure you're still with us!" he called. James hadn't lowered the tower at all.

"I'm still with you!" James shouted. "Head 'em out! I got some sprayin' to do!"

"Cowboy," Carl muttered, climbing back into the cab.

When it was Bob's turn in the tower, Carl stopped the truck just before beginning a turn and called up to him, "Lower that tower! There's no room for two Bronco Billys in this outfit!"

Dick and James laughed and Bob lowered the tower.

Squat

On Saturday Bob rented a motel room. He was tired and Jen did the work while he lay passive until he could feel the knot of semen rising toward the head of his penis. His hips began to move in spite of his exhaustion and Jen stopped her own movement, allowing him to establish his rhythm. She leaned forward, the palms of her hands on his chest. Suddenly he visualized his penis thrusting into her anus and in an instant he gave out a loud groan as he released. It seemed to pulse out of him for minutes, though it could not have, and he clutched Jen's back and held her to him as he groaned again.

She was kissing his face. "Are you okay? Are you hurt?"

He couldn't speak, but nodded that he was okay. She said, "You're okay or you're hurt? Oh, Bobby."

"Okay," he said. "I'm okay."

"What happened? I've never heard you make that sound before."

"I don't know."

"Was it good?"

"Yes, oh yes, it was good. God, I love you."

She pushed away so that, still straddling him, she was smiling at him as from a height.

"Say that again," she said.

"I love you," he said, testing it, tasting it on his tongue.

"You've never said that to me."

"I know."

"It's the sex," she said. "It's that big orgasm you just had. I thought you were in pain."

"It was so good, I couldn't contain myself."

"Contain yourself? Oh, my Bobby, what have you been reading?"

"*Lady Chatterley's Lover.*"

"Really?"

"No. Do something for me?"

"Anything."

"Squat over my face. I want to see my come inside you."

"I'd be embarrassed."

"You don't have to."

"I will. I'll do anything you want me to do. Are you getting hard again?"

"Yes."

She raised herself off him and moved forward so that her vagina was directly above his face. He grasped her buttocks with both of his hands.

"Do you like it?" she asked.

"God, yes." He raised his head and pressed his lips against the black hair.

"Will you do something for me?"

"Yes."

"Put your tongue inside me."

He tried to but succeeded only in sliding it past her labia. She rolled off him and onto her back and he followed her. "Lick me," she said. Then she said, "Oh, oh…" Her hips made those small involuntary movements that indicated she was lost in pleasure. She gripped his head as though to stuff it inside her and he thrust his tongue at her again and this time he felt it slip inside her as she opened. She came, flooding his mouth as she had in the park a couple of weeks before. He licked her again and she came again and he continued licking. But now she was moving her legs and pushing at him with her hands and, confused, he raised his head.

"Stop. I can't stand any more."

"What's wrong?"

"It hurts. It's so good, it hurts."

He moved up beside her and put his arms around her.

"I've never experienced that before," she said.

"You came at least twice, maybe three times."

"I did? It seemed like it was just once, but it went on forever."

"I'm glad I can give you pleasure."

"What a night. You tell me for the first time that you love me and then you make me come so much I thought it would never end. You don't know how much you mean to me."

"Because I said the magic words or because I gave you pleasure?"

"Both." She held his hard penis in her hand. "Poor guy. You're just going to have to wait."

The Quality of the Room

If they were going to a motel, Bob would call in the afternoon to make a reservation for, say, six o'clock. Then they would drive over and he would park off to the side so no one could see Jen from the office. She would wait in the car while he registered. Sometimes he registered for Mr. and Mrs. Bob Givens and sometimes he registered using only his name.

When they first began going to motels he would take a small bag with him into the office, but he soon realized that the clerks didn't care whether or not he had luggage. Once, after he had registered as Mr. and Mrs., the clerk asked him where his wife was. He said she was coming in by bus and he was going to pick her up at the bus station later. Fortunately, the room was in the back, so the clerk did not see Jen get out of the car.

She was always nervous about walking the few feet from the car to the door of the room. She was afraid that someone passing by or looking out the window of another room would recognize her, perhaps someone who knew her father.

Often the motel room was seedy because Bob could not afford a more expensive one. Sometimes they could hear the TV from the room next to theirs and sometimes they could hear voices. Sometimes a couple would be arguing. Sometimes the voices were of boys who had chipped in to rent a room so they would have a place to drink.

Although it was unpleasant listening to people who were angry with each other, Bob did not look at them as a danger. Drunken boys, though, were another story. Bob had been beaten up when he was a junior by some guys who had been drinking and he knew now not to trust a drunk. A drunk was capable of anything. He might, in a rage, punch through a wall, or knock a stranger to the ground where he could kick him. Coming back from a lounge or a bar, he might confuse Bob and Jen's room with his own and try to get in. This happened once. Bob always used all the door locks once they were inside their room. Bob's fear was that something would happen and he wouldn't be able to protect Jen.

But sometimes, when Bob had the money, they would get a place higher up on the scale of motel quality. Here the rooms were larger, and if they heard the people in the room next door, the walls were thick enough to prevent their hearing them clearly enough to understand what they were saying. Here there were no drunken boys. Here the room heater was large enough that they didn't have to get the extra blankets from the closet to keep warm. Here their lovemaking was without care and they could allow their imaginations free rein.

He liked to look at her—her adolescent figure, her flat stomach, her rib cage whose outline he could see beneath her skin when she raised her arms, her breasts that hardly fell when he removed her bra, the black vee, what Tom called "the little goatee," that was revealed when she straightened up after stripping off her panties, and he liked the smell of her vagina, especially after he had been inside her. Sometimes she would walk around the room naked for him, or perhaps for herself.

Once, as she bent forward to change the channel on the TV, he saw the wet hair on her labia hanging like threads between her thighs and, without thinking, he began to stroke himself. She saw him when she turned and an odd smile appeared on her face. "What are you doing?"

"I guess I'm masturbating."

"I can see that. But why? Aren't I enough for you?"

"Looking at you excites me."

He left off touching himself.

"Don't. I want to watch."

His hand moved back down to his groin. He was erect again in an instant. He became aware that he was breathing heavily.

"This is really exciting," Jen said. "Why haven't we done this before? Can I do anything to help you?"

"I don't know."

"Do you want to look at my pussy?"

He felt a sudden hardening in his penis.

"Yes. Move closer so I can touch you."

Her labia were swollen and, as he petted them, they opened and his fingers went inside. She had been watching what he was doing with his other hand but when he went inside her, she closed her eyes and that "unh" sound she sometimes made issued from her throat.

His hips began to move and he abandoned the last bit of shyness he felt and he closed his eyes and imagined his hand was Jen's vagina and he thrust up into it and he felt Jen move his hand off his penis and substitute her own, and then he felt something he hadn't felt before and he opened his eyes and saw his penis disappearing into her mouth and then becoming visible again, disappearing and then reappearing. He worked his fingers in and out of her vagina in rhythm with his penis going in and out of her mouth, but then he could think only of his own pleasure and his semen burst out of him.

She gagged and began to cough. He ran into the bathroom and got her a glass of water and came back and handed it to her. By this time her coughing had subsided and she gave a tentative laugh. "I'm so fucking proficient," she said. "I wanted to surprise you."

"You did."

"I wanted to do something for you that nobody else has done."

"You did."

They left the motel about eleven and got a sandwich at a Pearson's before he took her home. She was supposed to be home by one and they tried to honor their commitment to her father to be back by then. Bob wanted to help him deny to himself his knowledge of what he and Jen were doing.

Leaving the motel room, Jen turned to look at the disheveled bed. "Fucking was born here," she said.

I Can Dream, Can't I?

Carl hadn't shown up. They waited. Both the nurse truck and the tank truck were filled. Finally Marion came out of the office.

"His wife says he's got the flu."

Dick made a sound like a snort. James and Bob looked at him. Alberto walked over to the nurse and got in behind the wheel but didn't turn on the engine.

"Dick, you'll have to fill in as crew leader," Marion said.

"All right."

"When Carl comes back, I'll put him on a different crew."

"We're gonna be short a man. We won't have anyone to work the tower," Dick said.

"Damn, I forgot. Goddamnit. Tell you what, go on to your next job. You should be able to knock it out today. Then tomorrow come back to this one. I'll find someone to work the tower for you tomorrow."

"All right. Thanks."

The dirt was soft and black and gave under each step like something willing. It was a pleasure to walk on compared to the adobe-like furrows they had been walking.

"Carl would like this ground," Dick said at their morning break. "I'll have to tell him what he missed."

"Do you think he'll be coming back?" Bob asked.

"Yeah. He's done this before. He's done it every year, at least once."

"You'd think Marion wouldn't hire him back if he does it so much," James said.

"Well, he does. It's always the same. Carl goes off on a bender, he comes back, Marion takes his crew leader job away from him and puts him on a crew as a regular sprayer, and Carl gets through the rest of the season just fine."

"One of these days, I'll bet Marion doesn't let him come back," James said.

Dick shrugged. "You want his job? 'Cause if you do, you can have it. I'll tell Marion. It's five cents more an hour than what you're getting now."

"Is that all?"

"Yep. You can have the headaches. A nickel more an hour."

"No thanks," James said.

Dick stood up. "Let's get back at it."

Gerry and Kevin were over, playing poker with Tom. Harold wasn't around. Bob had just showered. Gerry asked him to sit in.

"No thanks. I'll just watch."

"Come on. It's just penny-ante."

"Another time."

"Are you going to see Jen tonight?" Tom asked.

"Tomorrow night. Why?"

"No reason. I like her. You ought to marry her."

"Jeez, don't do that," Gerry said.

"Why not?" Tom said. "They make a nice couple. I like watching them together. She just walks along like she doesn't have a care in the world and he's looking at everything as if it's getting ready to jump on her."

"You should marry her," Gerry said, dealing five-card draw. "At least you're old enough."

"She's in love with Bob or I would, if she'd have me."

"What is this thing with you and other men's girls? You sound like you did when you used to talk about Lisa." Lisa was Tom's brother's wife.

Tom reddened. He looked down at his cards but didn't pick them up.

"Uh oh," Kevin said.

Tom got up and went into the living room.

"Hey, man," Gerry said. "Hey, Tom. I'm sorry, okay? I shouldn't have said that. Shit." Then he said to Kevin, "Come on. Two-handed."

Bob took a chance on Harold not coming back tonight and went and lay down on his bed.

They were spraying the grove they had started earlier in the week. Carl hadn't returned and they had a man from another crew. Neither Dick nor Alberto knew Nathan, but James told Bob when they were spraying together, "Don't leave your billfold in the truck. You'll never see it again."

After Nathan's turn in the tower, he asked Dick if he could stay up there. "I like to work alone," he said. James and Bob didn't care. "Okay," Dick said, and Nathan began to raise the tower again.

"There's some power lines up ahead!" Dick called. "You'll have to come down in a minute!"

Nathan put his thumb up. James climbed into the cab and put the truck in gear. "Watch out for those lines," Dick told him. James nodded. But as he got closer to them, James kept his speed steady.

"Hey!" Dick yelled. "Hey! Stop the truck!"

Nathan looked at Dick and Dick made a quick, downward motion with the flat of his hand. Nathan began to descend. "Turn your gun off!" Dick shouted. Nathan aimed it at the ground as he turned the nozzle.

Dick handed Bob his gun and ran up to the cab. "What the fuck are you doing! Stop this thing now!"

James braked and turned the ignition off.

"Sorry," he said. "I must have been daydreaming."

They were directly below the three high-tension lines. Bob heard the tower thunk as it came to rest.

Dick was shaking. His face was livid. "Get out of that cab."

"Are you going to hit me?" James asked.

"Come out of that cab and you'll see."

"I think I'll just sit in here until you calm down."

Dick stepped away from the door of the cab. He walked out in front of the truck and kept walking. The others watched his back recede.

Alberto appeared at the cab. As much noise as the nurse truck made, Bob had not heard him drive up.

"Pull up a ways," Alberto said to James. "I don't want to fill it with these lines here."

Bob looked at Nathan who was still in the cage. Nathan gave a thumbs-up.

James started the rig and inched it forward about ten feet and stopped. Alberto was in front of him, walking backward. "More!" Alberto called. James moved another forty or fifty feet, stopping again when Alberto raised his hand. "Turn it off," Alberto said as he passed the cab on his way back to the nurse.

James climbed out of the truck. He didn't look at Nathan.

Dick came back. "I want you to get your stuff out of the truck and go back to the barn with Alberto."

James turned toward the cab. Dick went over to the nurse where Alberto was monitoring the flow of poison into the truck's tank.

When Alberto was finished, he dropped the hose on the hooks on the side of the nurse and James slid into the passenger seat. They drove off.

Nathan came down out of the tower.

"We've got enough juice to get us through the rest of the day," Dick said. "I'll drive, you work the spray guns in the back. When we've gone a ways, I'll stop and we'll go back and get the tops. I'll talk to Marion when we get back to the barn."

Nathan nodded. Bob said, "Okay."

"He might have killed all of us. Himself too," Dick said.

Tom was listening to a recording of Hitler giving a speech. You could hear the adoration of the crowd in the background. Bob had seen films of some of Hitler's speeches on TV and in school, and he could visualize the gestures he used to punctuate his sentences, his arms and head moving mechanically, as though on a wind-up doll, the poses feminine and disdainful. How different the Germans must be from us to have worshipped this man, Bob thought every time he saw Hitler speaking. Yet Tom, though he did not speak or understand German, appeared entranced. After a while he took the record off the player.

"Is this for a class?"

Tom shook his head. "I wanted to see if I would respond to him the same way the krauts did."

"Did you?"

"A little maybe. I'm not sure. Maybe you had to have been there to get caught up in it. Be one of the horde."

"Was your dad in World War Two?" Some people said "the war," as though the one in Korea had not happened, but Bob always tried to specify which war he meant. One of his uncles had been in the Navy in World War Two and another uncle had been an infantryman in Korea.

"Yes. Was yours?" Tom asked.

"No. He was on the Manhattan Project. That group that made the atom bomb."

"Really?"

"Yeah. He helped make history, but I don't think he knew it at the time. Maybe he did. He probably did. Sometimes he has a sense for things that are more important than other things. Did I just say that? I wonder what I meant."

Tom laughed. "My dad was a Marine. He's never talked about the war, at least to me. I know he doesn't like Japs though."

"In high school they said we should say 'Japanese' instead of Japs. But we had a couple of teachers who had been in the Pacific during the war and they said 'Japs' and none of the other teachers corrected them, as far as I know. Not in front of us kids anyway."

"Yes. You can forgive them if they were Marines. Were they Marines?"

"Yeah. Now that I think about it, only one of them said Japs. The other one didn't say anything about the war. The way we found out he was a Marine was that the chemistry teacher told us. He taught physics—the one who didn't talk about the war. The other one was a coach and taught history. When we got to World War Two in the book, he told us stories about what it had been like to fight them. The Japanese. You could see he was trying not to show it, but he hated them."

Tom nodded. "When you lose your friends, it makes a difference."

Bob wondered how Tom knew that. Bob's uncles had never said anything to him about that. Maybe Tom's father had told him some things. Or maybe men Tom knew in the Air Force had said something.

"I'm going to put on some Wagner," Tom said. "You like

Wagner?"

Bob's father despised Wagner.

"No," he said.

"I love Wagner."

They were parked outside Jen's house. They hadn't made love or even touched each other under their clothes, but were feeling very tender nonetheless.

"There's an older couple who live somewhere near here. They're probably retired. Sometimes I see them walking together in the evening. They always hold hands. She's little, like me, and you can see the veins in her hands. She's wizened. I like that word. I'll be wizened too, when I'm her age. And he looks very alert, very aware, like he's seen a lot of life and remembers it. He wears a leather jacket sometimes, like the one you have, but without the sheepskin lining. I think he's a little shorter than you, but people shrink when they get older. God, if I shrink, there won't be anything left of me. That's how we'll be when we're old. Taking a walk together around the block, or to the park and back. Holding hands, like we've known each other all our lives. By the time we're that old, we will have. At least that's how I think of us. Growing old together, weathering storms together, loving each other every step of the way."

"You're only seventeen. I'm only eighteen."

"So? I can dream, can't I?"

Carl returned and Nathan went back to the crew he had come from. Carl looked grim. He took his place beside Bob behind the tank truck. They were working a lemon grove with young trees and they didn't need to use the tower.

Carl didn't speak to anyone all morning. At the break he sat alone, sipping coffee and eating a sugared doughnut. But at lunch he sat down with Dick and Bob while Alberto filled the tank.

"So, how goes it, Carl?" Dick said.

"For shit," Carl said.

Dick and Bob waited.

"She found a younger guy. I come home and there she is, riding him like he's some kind of horse. May have been, for all I know."

"Marion said he talked to your wife," Dick said.

"Yeah. Moved back in with her. That was a mistake too, probably."

"She had no problem, you moving back with her?" That was Alberto. He had just sat down with them.

"Nah. Never actually got divorced. Never got divorced from my second wife either. Yeah, she had a problem, but she got over it."

"You just keep marrying them, but you don't divorce them," Dick said.

"Divorce costs money. Besides, I wasn't married to this one, the twenty-year-old. We were just shackin' up."

"Well, at least you got some twenty-year-old pussy, an old man like you. You should feel lucky," Alberto said.

"I do."

They all laughed, Carl too.

"You shouldn't be eating doughnuts though," Alberto said.

"Lots of things I shouldn't be doin', but I do them anyway."

They laughed again. It was good to have Carl back.

"Well, time to get back at it," Carl said, and got to his feet. "Oops. Sorry, Dick."

"No, you're right. Not a problem."

Alberto and Bob rose, following Dick.

Freedom

They went to a jazz club in Hollywood, Bob and Jen, Tom and Linda. Linda was older than the others: twenty-nine, she said. She was a librarian where Tom went to check out records and the biographies of high-ranking Nazis he had taken to reading. She had a direct way of speaking and seemed able to tolerate small talk only until she could direct it to something more substantive. Her previous lover was missing in Laos, she said when Jen asked her how long she and Tom had been seeing each other. When she said this, the muscles in her left cheek contracted and Bob thought she had a tic, but he did not see it again. Tom was a welcome change, she said, because with him she didn't have to worry when she didn't receive a letter she was expecting. She hadn't answered Jen's question.

"Where's Laos?" Bob asked.

"It's one of those little countries in Southeast Asia that nobody but the CIA gives a damn about."

"Was your boyfriend in the CIA?" Jen asked.

"He may still be, if he's alive," Linda said. She smiled, the smile appearing as an act of courtesy. "And he wasn't my boyfriend. He's thirty-five years old."

Neither Jen nor Bob said anything. Tom looked uncomfortable. Bob couldn't imagine him and Linda in bed together. Tom had, in fact, told Bob that although they had been sleeping together for only a couple of weeks, he was looking for a way out.

"Tom said you discovered this place, Bob. Wherever did you hear about it?" Linda said.

It was a coffee house that was able to allow minors in because it didn't serve hard liquor.

"I read about it in *Playboy*."

Jen looked surprised.

"You told me you only read the stories," Tom said.

"This was in one of the stories," Bob said.

"Well, I don't see any naked women, so maybe he's telling the truth," Linda said.

"I'm shocked," Jen said.

"Are you really?" Bob asked.

"Yes. I didn't know you read *Playboy*."

"But only for the stories," Linda said. "He can't help it, honey. He's a man."

The musicians walked out onto the floor. The drums and the piano and the bass were already in position. John Coltrane carried his sax. After he had blown a few notes and the others had warmed up their instruments, Miles Davis walked out, his trumpet in his right hand. None of the other musicians had spoken and Miles Davis didn't speak either, but simply began to play, Philly Joe Jones picking it up on drums, Coltrane on his sax, Paul Chambers on bass and Red Garland at the piano. They had walked out so unobtrusively that many of the customers, engaged in conversation, hadn't noticed them, but now everyone was quiet. You could not talk when Miles Davis was blowing; he was talking to you, telling you what you felt, making you feel it even if you didn't want to, and if you spoke you would miss what he was saying. He bent the sound as if he were wrapping it around your emotions and squeezing them out. He drew out individual notes until they sobbed like the wail of mourning, like someone who couldn't catch his breath for his anguish. Bob had not ever heard anyone else do this; he didn't think anyone else could.

It was a short set, Bob thought, but when it was over and

the musicians had left the floor and the applause had ended, he looked at his watch and saw that it had gone for almost an hour. Throughout, except for Miles Davis gesturing with his horn toward each of the other jazzmen and announcing his name, none of them had spoken.

Bob was exhausted. He felt as though he had been beaten up.

Jen whispered to him, "He could have any woman in this room."

Linda said, "Is it just me, or… It didn't do a thing for me."

"It's just you," Bob said.

"How can you say that?" Jen said to her.

"Let's not talk," Bob said. He wanted to retain the spell for as long as he could. He didn't want to piss it away in talk.

After a minute or two, Tom asked, "Have you heard them before?"

"On the radio. And I have a couple of LPs of Miles Davis with Gil Evans. Gil Evans' arrangements. I left them at my parents' house. I hope they don't throw them away. I'd like to get them back someday."

"I take it you're not on good terms with your parents," Linda said.

Bob ignored her.

"I had no idea you liked jazz," Jen said. "Hell, I had no idea I liked jazz. It's free-ing. It's freedom."

"I love jazz. And I love Miles Davis and John Coltrane most of all. Coltrane was the one on sax."

"Do you know who the others are?" Linda asked.

"Yes. If you're an aficionado, there's a late-night jazz show on FM almost every night. It's low on the dial, but I don't remember the number. It's a San Diego station. Chuck Cotilla is the DJ. He's a drummer himself. Plays at a jazz club in Tijuana. He's the one who introduced me to Miles Davis. His music, I mean. I take that back. My cousin introduced me to Miles Davis, but Chuck Cotilla introduced me to the album of his I like best."

They were staring at him.

"What?" he said.

"I had no idea," Jen said. "What else don't I know about you?"

"I wear my socks when I swim."

"You do not. I've been to the beach with you and I never saw you wearing socks."

"That's because you were looking at my feet. I was wearing them inside my trunks."

"What? No you weren't."

"How do you know? Did you check?"

Tom was laughing silently.

Linda seemed not to know what to believe. "Do you really wear socks when you go to the beach?"

Bob nodded. "Sometimes my ears get cold, so I like to have them handy."

"My god," she said. "I think I'm ready to go."

They stared at her. There was another set coming up. The waiter was working his way toward them.

"I'm not," Tom said.

"I am," Linda said. "I don't think I can handle any more. And I don't like the music."

"I do," Tom said.

"I thought it was wonderful," Jen said.

"Then it must be me," Linda said. "I'm sorry, but if I have to sit through any more of it, I'm going to be sick."

"Meaning you'll make a scene," Tom said. He stood up and Linda stood up. Bob shrugged and he and Jen got up too. They had come in Bob's car.

Walking to the parking lot, Linda was chatty and slipped her arm inside Tom's.

"Didn't you want to go to another club?" Jen asked Bob.

"Yes. Les McCann is at The Bit."

"Oh please! Not more jazz!" Linda said.

"She would just ruin it for you," Tom said.

"Do you have enough money to put her in a taxi?" Bob asked.

"I don't see how anybody could like it," Linda said. "It's just noise. Where's the melody? Not that it has to drown you with melody, but—"

"Shut up," Tom said.

Linda stopped talking. Tom walked away from her. In a moment, Bob could hear her heels as she ran to catch up.

In the car, they were silent. Soon after they entered the freeway, Bob heard Linda behind him, "I thought you might want to cuddle."

"No," Tom said.

"Not tonight?"

Tom didn't say anything. Bob heard the friction of clothing against upholstery, then nothing. He looked in the mirror. Tom was cramped in a corner and Linda was lying against him. As Bob watched, she raised Tom's arm and draped it across her shoulders.

Bob took Linda home first. Tom got out of the car with her and walked her to her door. She kissed him and went inside and he returned to the car and climbed into the back seat.

When Bob took Jen home, he stopped the car in front of her house and they kissed for a couple of minutes. He walked her to the house. At the door, when he leaned down to kiss her again, she whispered, "Give me. Give me."

On the way to the apartment, Tom said, "I envy you."

"I envy me too."

"Do you think you're going to get married?"

"We've been talking about it. Hinting at it. Seeing how the other responds when one of us brings it up."

"What do her parents think?"

"I don't know. I don't know if she's said anything to them about it."

"Your parents?"

"I haven't had any contact with them in months. Not since I left."

"It might be better if she just moved in with us."

Bob looked at him. Tom was wearing an exaggerated grin.

"Hmm," Bob said.

"Harold is hardly ever there." Tom's grin widened even more.

"Let's talk about something else," Bob said.

Justin and Phil came by. Bob had not seen Justin since summer, and Phil since before that.

Justin was very thin, his face gaunt. It took Bob a moment to notice that three fingers on Justin's right hand were gone; the skin flap folded over the remainder of the hand was a deep red. It was the first time Bob had seen evidence of mutilation on somebody he knew and he was horrified. He tried not to let it show.

Justin said he had been cutting branches on a buzz saw in the wood yard and, his attention distracted by a sound from the street, he ran his hand into the blade. He collapsed in shock, but Fred saw him fall and ran over and made a tourniquet with his belt and heaved him over his shoulder and got him to a doctor in the medical complex across the street.

"My brother saved my life," Justin said. His eyes filled.

Bob didn't know what to say.

"My father was fine with it. He's seen a lot in his life. Mutti"—Justin used the German word—"didn't take it so well."

"How are you doing with it?"

"Well, I'm learning to write with my left hand. I may go back to my right hand once the soreness goes away. I haven't missed very many classes. Only a few days."

"I wish I had known. I would have called."

"That's okay. Say, do you have a beer? Oh, wait. Phil brought some."

"That's pretty slick, the way you moved the conversation away from yourself," Bob said.

"Thanks. I thought so too."

Phil was sitting on the sofa, a cracked can of Coors in his hand. "I'm here too. Why don't you ask me about me? Hey, where's Tom?"

"I don't know. At the library maybe."

"I'm going to start painting again," he said.

He had not done any painting during his first year in college. He didn't know why. Perhaps anxiety about his classes had inhibited him, or maybe there was something else about UCLA that had blocked him. But now he felt the urge again. The problem was that his paints had dried up and he had no money to buy more.

"The junior college is walking distance from here," Bob said. "It has a bookstore and the bookstore sells art supplies as well as books. We can get in through the roof."

Phil's face lit up as though he were a child and someone had unexpectedly given him a box filled with toys.

"How would we get out? My arms aren't that strong. I don't think I could climb a rope."

"There's a ladder inside that goes to the roof. I've seen it. Or we could just walk out the door and run like hell."

"Have you looked at the roof?" Justin asked.

"No, but if we can't get in, there's nothing lost. We'll just turn around and go home."

"How do we get on the roof?"

"There's got to be a ladder in one of the walls. Workmen have to get up there. I don't think they'd want to move an extension ladder every time they have to go up to the roof."

"Wow. That's really Zen," Phil said. "Let's do it. When?"

That was new, using "Zen" as an adjective. Bob hadn't heard anyone do that before. But he said only, "Let's do it tonight. Ten, eleven o'clock. Nobody will be around on the weekend."

"Tonight," Phil said. He appeared to mull it over. "So soon. I usually like to think about things before I give in to my impulses. But sure, why not?"

"I don't think I can do it," Justin said.

"Chickenshit," Phil said.

Justin was silent.

"Sorry, man. I forgot," Phil said.

"I just don't think it's for me," Justin said.

"That's okay," Bob said. "I'm just doing it for the kick."

"You don't want any books or anything? I don't want to be the only one who steals something," Phil said.

"Maybe I'll grab a book. One thing though. We figure out in advance what we're going to get, we get that, and then we leave. I don't want to get caught because we got greedy and hung around too long."

"All right," Phil said. "That's a good plan."

"We go in, get what we came for, and get out. No easels, no canvas, just tubes of paint and we're gone."

"Okay. I agree."

"If you walk out through the door, you should figure out first where you're going to go after you leave the bookstore. Or, if you get separated, where you're going to meet up," Justin said.

"This is like a movie," Phil said.

"We don't have to meet up. It isn't as if we're going to have to divide up any loot. We're not going to rob a bank," Bob said.

"Not yet," Phil said. "Maybe this is just the beginning of

something."

"Holy shit!" Bob and Justin said.

"I'm only kidding," Phil said.

"When we see you on TV when you come up for parole, I can tell my kids that I knew you when you were just a little burglar," Bob said.

They had some time to kill so Bob opened a couple of cans of chili and beans and heated it and laid a slice of American cheese over each serving.

"You should be careful not to fart when you're in the bookstore," Justin said. "They can trace farts back to the person who farted."

"Really?" Phil said.

"Only if they have a record of your farts," Bob said. "Something to compare them to."

"How would they get a record of your farts?"

"They've put fans in public restrooms," Justin said. "They just suck in the gas from whoever is in there. They're fart activated. The restrooms at UCLA are perfect for that."

"But how would they know who laid a fart? They don't ask you if you farted when you leave the restroom. Oh, I get it. You guys are bullshitting me."

"No we're not," Bob said. He and Justin laughed.

"I can't believe I fell for that."

"You've spent too much time at UCLA," Justin said.

"You're probably right." Phil looked at Bob. "Where's Jen? Don't you usually spend Saturday night with her?"

"She went with her parents to see her uncle in Beverly Hills. He's a lawyer. He lives next door to that guy who plays the sly Mexican on TV. Bill somebody."

"The sly Mexican?"

"You know, the guy who pretends to be stupid but always ends up getting what he wants."

"Have you met him?"

"Who? This Bill somebody?"

"No, the lawyer. Is he an entertainment lawyer?"

"Yeah, he is, and yeah, I've met him. He has two walls full of books in his living room. Philosophy. Russian novels. Histories. His wife told me it's all for show, to impress his clients. He hasn't read any of them. He has another bookcase full of thrillers in his bedroom. That's what he reads. He said Jen and I should get married."

"What? Why did he say that?"

"I have no idea."

"What did Jen say?"

"She was as surprised as I was. Her folks, too."

"Wow."

"That's really Zen," Justin said.

"No, that isn't Zen," Phil said.

"Everything is Zen," Justin said.

"Have you been smoking grass?" Phil said.

"Not lately, sweetie," Justin said.

Phil turned back to Bob. "What did her parents say?"

"Her father wasn't too pleased. Her mother hardly ever talks."

"So are you going to get married?"

"Why? Because her uncle thinks it's a good idea? But the subject does come up."

"Wow."

"Let's go rob a bookstore."

The bookstore had a flat roof. They found the shaft that led into it. Bob went first. When he came to the end of the ladder set into the side of the shaft, he lowered himself from the last rung so that he had only to drop a couple of feet before he was on the floor.

Phil followed him, doing what Bob did. Phil had brought Bob's canvas duffel bag.

"There's a utility closet over there." Bob aimed his flashlight in its direction. "There may be a ladder we can use to reach the bottom of this one when we leave."

"How do you know so much about this place?"

"I was in here once and saw some workmen going up to the roof."

"Okay. Where are the paints?"

"That way. Look around."

Bob went over to the reference section and picked out a hardcover dictionary. It was the same as the one he had when he lived with his parents. Then he found an *Old Man and the Sea* that Jen needed for one of her classes. From the Steinbeck books, he took a *Sweet Thursday* and a *Cannery Row*. He had left his copy of *Cannery Row* at his parents' and Tom had told him about *Sweet Thursday*.

He found Phil. He had located the art supplies and was going through the tubes of paint, occasionally tossing one into the duffel bag. Bob put the books in with the paint.

"I'd like to take it all," Phil said. "I'll probably come back."

A light from outside swept across the windows. They froze. Bob turned off his flashlight. "Kill your light," he whispered as though someone else was in the store, alert for trespassers.

"We'd better get out of here," Phil said. "I'll just grab these."

"I'll see if there's a ladder in the utility closet."

Bob came back with a folding ladder and placed it below the access shaft in the ceiling. At the top of the ladder he slid the one in the shaft down to where they could step onto it. He followed Phil up. Almost to the roof, Bob pulled the sliding ladder up after them, but left the hatch in the ceiling open, unable to reach it now. Maybe the people opening the store on Monday will think the maintenance men had been careless.

On the roof, they crept to the side where they could see the street in front of the bookstore. A police car was patrolling, spotlighting the doors and windows of the buildings on the campus.

Phil giggled. "I can't believe how easy it was. I never would have done this on my own."

"If we get caught, I'm going to tell them you made me do it," Bob said.

Carl didn't come to work. His wife didn't know where he was. Marion said he wouldn't hire him back again. They were nearing the end of the season and they were laying people off anyway.

They took their lunch break at the end of an irrigation ditch. Just beyond the grove was a schoolyard with monkey bars and tetherballs and slides and other equipment for children to use during recess. It was recess now and they could hear the screams and laughter of the children and the sharpness in the voices of the teachers.

"I wish I was a kid again," Alberto said. "Then I wouldn't have to work."

"I've been working all my life," Dick said.

They would finish the grove on Wednesday. After that, there would be one, maybe two more. Small ones. Then it would be over. Marion had told them that three hundred and fifty acres of this grove would be gone next year. Housing.

Bob asked Dick if he was going to come back next season.

"I don't know," Dick said. "Probably."

"If I was a kid again, my parents would support me," Alberto said.

"Shit. I wouldn't want to have to do anything over again," Dick said.

Phil and Bob Sniff Gas

Jen had started her classes at Fullerton. She had applied to Berkeley and UCLA and the new university in Riverside and had been accepted at all of them, but had decided to go to the junior college so she wouldn't have to be away from Bob. He wasn't sure he wanted the responsibility that implied. He told himself it was her decision, but he couldn't help feeling a vague sense of obligation.

Her father was disappointed. He had thought it would be good for Jen to live away from Bob for a while; it would be a test, he told her, to see if her feeling for him was something more than infatuation. But beyond voicing his disappointment to Jen, he said nothing. He said nothing at all about it to Bob.

She was taking the required English class, a history class, and a couple of electives. For P.E., she had signed up for a class in modern dance. She was happy that she would be able to build on what she had learned in high school. It meant a lot to her: the movement, the discipline, the improvisation that was one of the things that distinguished it from ballet, the sense of freedom— "It's like jazz," she said—all contributed to her love of the form. And she knew that dance had given her her body, which attracted attention and which had introduced her to so much pleasure.

In class one time, midway through the semester, she did not wear a bra beneath her leotard because she wanted to feel free of its restraint. Afterward, her instructor cautioned her not to come to class that way again—it had disturbed the other students. Her teacher was right, she said. She had been embarrassed when she was dancing, knowing the other girls were angry with her and the boys did not know what to think. She was grateful to her instructor for waiting until class had ended before speaking to her. He could have humiliated her if he had wanted to. He could have rebuked her in front of everyone.

She was glad her breasts were not larger, she said, although if they were, she probably would not have foregone her bra. But except during dance, she would have liked them to be larger; they were the one thing about her body she was dissatisfied with. Bob liked them: they were responsive and they gave her pleasure and they gave him pleasure. Her dissatisfaction had to do with her relationships with other girls.

Once when Jen was over and Tom was at Linda's and Harold was who knew where, Justin came by the apartment with a girl Bob had known in high school. She had large breasts that she knew pleased Justin, and when he was in the bathroom, she told Jen that they had gone to dinner and a movie last Saturday and she had worn a low-cut top. She was on her period and her breasts were swollen and when she bent over, they podged out of her bra and Justin loved it. Later she let him unfasten her bra. She really liked him.

Jen masked her anger until after Justin and Karen had left. Karen had talked about her breasts just to humiliate her, Jen said. "You're the one she really likes. Saying all that as if you weren't sitting next to me. She was telling me that she could take you away from me if she wanted to."

"I didn't catch any of that," Bob said.

"You weren't supposed to. She was saying it to me. She was trying to frighten me. She did, too."

Bob moved beside her on the sofa and put his arm over her shoulders, but her body was rigid.

"Did you ever make love to her?" she asked.

"No."

"Okay." She allowed herself to lean into him. "But I can't stand her. And you are the one she wants."

After a moment, she said, "When she said she let Justin feel her up, did that excite you?"

Bob didn't say anything.

"It's okay if it did. I just want to know how your penis works. I mean how your mind works." She laughed. "Talk about Freudian slips."

"I just wondered why she was saying it in front of me." It was true, but now he wondered if he hadn't been a little aroused too.

"When I tell you about what Michael and I used to do, how does that make you feel?"

"You've asked me this before."

"Really? What did you say?"

"I don't remember, but I want to do the same things to you so you won't feel that you're missing out."

"Really?"

"Yes."

"Oh, Bobby, you do so much more. Come here."

After she kissed him, she said, "I suppose it's inevitable that you always retain some feeling for people who used to be important to you."

Bob thought she was going to ask him about Sara, but she didn't. Instead, she said, "Hey, is it true that you and Phil robbed the bookstore at the college?"

"It wasn't a big robbery. Just some books and paints."

"But why? You guys aren't that poor. Phil isn't anyway."

"I'm not sure why. It was exciting. And Phil was out of paint. And I wanted some books. That's where that Hemingway I got you came from. *The Old Man and the Sea*."

"Really? You stole it to give to me?"

"Yep. You received stolen property. If you turn me in, you go to jail with me."

"Jeez. I still don't understand why you did it."

"You sound like my mother. I did it because I wanted to."

"I don't sound anything like your mother."

"Sorry, but you did."

"At least I learned something about you that I didn't know before."

"What?"

"I don't know if I can put it into words. But it's something."

"But you can't say what it is."

"Are you angry? Don't be angry with me."

"I'm not angry."

"Yes, you are. We're fighting, aren't we? Why are we fighting?"

"I don't know. Are we fighting?"

"It's because of Karen and those big tits of hers. Are you sure you didn't ball her?"

"I'm sure."

"Would you tell me if you did?"

"I don't know."

"What if I slept with someone else? Would you want me to tell you?"

"I don't know. Yes, I would." He felt his stomach knot up.

Jen leaned into him again. "Hold me." He put his arm around her and stroked her cheek. He inhaled the scent of her hair.

"I think we're both mature enough to handle it if it happens," she said. "But don't let it happen to you." She punched him in the ribs as if she were playing. Then she kissed him through his shirt where she had punched him. "Okay?" she asked.

"Okay."

"It's all right if it happens to me though."

He pushed her away.

"I'm only kidding. Let me cuddle. By the way, I'd already bought that book. I took it back for a refund. I told them my boyfriend surprised me with a copy for my birthday."

"Ho, ho, ho."

"It's true."

Phil asked Bob if he wanted to join him in another raid on the bookstore.

"Have you used up all your paints already?"

"No, man, I just want to get into the bookstore again. I'll find something I can use."

"I knew this would happen," Justin said.

"What would?"

"That you'd want to do it again. I know you."

"You don't know me. Or maybe you do."

"Leave me out," Bob said. "I did it once. I don't need to do it again."

"Okay. I know you're not chickenshit. Hey, where's Tom? He might do it. Or Kevin. I know he would. Oh, he's working. Where's Tom?"

"He's at Linda's," Bob said.

"Who's Linda?"

"His girlfriend."

"Tom has a girlfriend?"

"You've been spending too much time at UCLA," Bob said.

"I thought he had broken up with her," Justin said.

Bob shrugged. "He changed his mind."

"Hey, have you ever sniffed gas?" Phil asked.

"What's that?"

"I've heard of it," Justin said.

"Oh? What did you hear?"

"It's a really quick high. And it makes everything really funny. And it leaves lead in your brain."

"Yeah, that's what I heard too. But it doesn't always make things funny. But it never makes anything sad."

"Have you done it?"

"No, but I've talked to people who have. So, do you want to try it?"

"I'd rather sniff girls' bicycle seats," Justin said.

"Weren't you going to raid the bookstore?" Bob said.

"There's plenty of time. I can do both," Phil said.

"Okay," Bob said. "I'll try it. How do you do it?"

"First we get some gas."

"That sounds reasonable," said Justin.

"We need a container with a narrow neck to put it in."

"Gerry Crowe. He has a narrow neck," Bob said.

"A gallon jug," Justin said.

"Yeah, something that you can put your mouth around and suck in the fumes."

"That sounds pleasant. I'd rather suck in the fumes from girls' bicycle seats," said Justin.

"It works really fast."

"I have gas in my car," Bob said.

"You'll need a hose," Justin said, "unless you're strong enough to tip the car over on its side. Of course, if you want to drive it again, you'll have to tip it back."

"I have a hose in the trunk. But I don't have anything to put the gas in."

"You can buy a bottle of apple cider at the market," Justin said.

Justin watched. They were behind the apartment in the lot where Bob's car was parked. Phil went first, inhaling the fumes from the

bottle and then holding his breath for a few seconds before letting
it out.

"Are you supposed to do it like you're smoking a doobie?"
Justin asked.

"I don't know," Phil·said.

Bob inhaled, held it for a second, and then exhaled. He didn't
feel anything, so he did it again.

Phil began to laugh.

"What's so funny?" Bob said. He started to laugh too. Seeing
Phil laugh, Bob couldn't help himself. Watching him, Phil
laughed all the harder and, watching Phil, Bob laughed harder
too. The laughter seemed to have nothing to do with anything,
yet everything seemed genuinely funny: the expression on Phil's
face, the movement of his hands when he went for the bottle
again, the shadow of the chain-link fence, a street lamp behind
it as it posited small squares on Phil's button-down shirt, the
buttons poking through his collar. Bob felt everything as if it were
all one, and he felt elation as he had not experienced it before. The
muscles of his abdomen were sore from laughter.

Then, in a moment, it was gone, leaving only a residue of
contentment. Bob looked at Phil; it seemed to have left him too.
Suddenly Phil stood up, looked around, and took off running.
He ran into the alley between the parking lot and the garage the
apartment rested on and disappeared behind a small grocery store.
Seconds later he reappeared, running on the sidewalk along the street
at the opposite end of the parking lot. He was running very fast.
"He's like a cat on Benzedrine," Justin said. "I once saw somebody
give a cat some Benzedrine. In high school we called him the mad
genius. Phil, not the cat."

"Poor cat," Bob said. He started to laugh, but the impulse
passed.

Phil had disappeared again. Bob sat on the asphalt, leaning

against the link fence. Justin sat down next to him.

"What was it like?"

"It wasn't like anything else."

"It deposits lead in your brain."

"I didn't know that," Bob said, although he remembered Justin saying it earlier.

Phil came into sight at the far end of the alley, running at top speed. Soon he was on them and he put his hands up and ran into the fence. He bounced off it, caught his balance, and sat down. He was breathing hard.

"You have a weird neurological system," Justin said.

"That was pure Zen," Phil said.

"For me, maybe. I don't know about you," Bob said.

"I saw the undifferentiated cosmos," Phil said.

"You saw it?" Justin said. "What did it look like?"

"I felt it. It's the same thing. And everything is okay. I could feel that, too. No matter what happens, everything is okay."

"Sure, if you're the cosmos. But what about for us humans?" Bob said.

"What's going to happen?" Justin asked.

"I don't know," Phil said. He laughed and then he stopped. It was a laugh he might have given at any time.

"It's cheap, too," he said. "Pot is a lot more expensive than sniffing gas, and it doesn't make you nearly as happy."

"It leaves lead in your brain. It doesn't go away," Justin said.

"Who cares?" Phil said. He eased himself back on his elbows and then lay flat on the ground. "I don't think I'll raid the bookstore tonight. I'll save it for another time."

Bob Felt Sentimental

The spray season was over at mid-afternoon on Friday, at least for black spider. Dick and some others from other crews would stay on, possibly until December, to spray a few groves for gray spider or red spider or whatever it was, but everybody else was out of a job. Bob wished the season could have lasted forever. He liked the men he worked with. He said goodbye to Dick and Alberto and he asked Dick to give his regards to Carl if he saw him. Bob left his phone number with Marion for next year. He didn't see Vern; he would have liked to thank him for getting him hired. He felt very sentimental. Marion told him to be sure to file for unemployment. It won't be much, but anything is better than nothing, he said. That evening, Bob had supper with Jen and her parents.

"How does it feel to be a nonworking man?" Jen's father asked. He wasn't being mean; Bob knew he liked him and was concerned about him. His name was David.

"It feels pretty good, but I'm going to miss the people I worked with."

David nodded. "The jobs I've had that I liked most were always the ones that paid the least. I don't know why that should be."

Bob didn't say anything. He didn't know enough to risk an opinion.

Carol, Jen's mother, recalled how as a girl in Biloxi she had had a job as a sales clerk in a five-and-ten-cent store that she hadn't liked because her boss had favored another girl and always gave her the best hours and more of them than anybody else. Carol had always suspected that the other girl was letting their boss do what he wanted with her.

"What's that got to do with anything?" David said.

"It was just something I remembered," Carol said. She didn't seem abashed; she didn't appear to have perceived that David had been short with her.

"What are you going to do now?" David asked.

"I don't know. I'll start looking around next week," Bob said.

"You could be a paperboy," Peter said.

They all laughed, but then David said, "That may not be a bad idea, at least as a way to get some income, even if it's only a little. Peter makes what? A hundred a month?"

"A hundred and ten," Peter said. "But I have a big route. Most of the kids don't make that much."

"You have to get up early," David said. "About four o'clock?"

"Yeah."

"But you're used to that," David said to Bob.

"I thought I would sleep in for a few days," Bob said.

Carol said she had enjoyed going back to bed after she got married and David had gone to work. But then she had Jen and after Jen was born she never was able to sleep late again.

"There might be something at Lockheed," David said. "I could ask around, if you'd like me to."

"My father got me on at Hughes right after I graduated, but I quit after the first day. I don't know what there was about it, but I felt like I couldn't breathe."

"Maybe it was because it was your father who got you the job. What were you doing?"

"Draftsman trainee. I had drafting in high school."

"A good way to start," David said.

"I didn't mind the work. I just couldn't stand being there."

David nodded.

After supper, Jen and Bob said they were going to a movie. He had reserved a room at a nice motel.

"He really likes you," Jen said.

"I like him too."

"He cares about you."

"I know. I can't make out your mother though."

"Oh, she just likes to tell stories."

"I mean I can't tell what she's feeling, except confused and maybe afraid sometimes. Did I tell you that I saw her in that little bookstore on Chapman, and she went and hid in a corner when she saw me?"

"You didn't tell me. But I can understand why she did that. She's afraid, of everything, at least everything outside the house and the stores she's used to going to. But, you know, we all went back to Mississippi once to see mom's family, and after we got there she was just fine. She was open and lively and she laughed at the right times and people really loved her. She fit right in, even after being away for so long."

"How did she and your dad ever get together? He's from New York, isn't he?"

"He was stationed in Biloxi during the war. She was a local belle. 'A demur southern belle,' my father always says. He met her at a dance. He knew he was going to marry her the minute he saw her. That's what he told Peter and me."

Bob pulled into the motel's parking lot. Jen waited while he went into the office and filled out the registration form and got the key. Their room was in the back and he drove around and got a space almost in front of their door and he and Jen walked in together.

"You're sure you're not too tired? You worked today, remember."

She sat down on the bed.

"I'm not too tired. I feel really energized. Let me undress you."
He hadn't done that before.

She watched his hands unbutton her shirt. He kissed her
breasts through her bra. She turned and he unfastened it and
watched from the side as her breasts fell. He slipped the straps
past her shoulders. Now she was naked above her hips. He knelt
in front of her and kissed her right nipple, then her left. Her hand
came up behind his head.

"I've missed you," she said.

"What do you mean? I've been here."

"Not like this. You've been so tired, because of your job."

"I couldn't help it," he said.

"I know, but I missed you. But you're back now."

"Stand up."

He unzipped her jeans and worked them past her hips and
down to her ankles and she stepped out of them, her hand on his
shoulder. He pulled her panties down and she withdrew one foot
from them and then the other. He was directly below her vagina.

"Aren't you going to take your clothes off?"

"I will," he said.

He kissed her pubic hair just above her cleft. He ran his hand
up the inside of her leg and put one finger between her labia and
made a small circle with it. He had never moved his finger this way
with her before. He heard her breath go in in a quick rush. Her
vagina lubricated and he went inside her with the same finger and
the one next to it. Both of her hands were on his shoulders. He
made the circular movement between her labia with his tongue.

"Oh God. Catch me."

He caught her in his arms and laid her on the bed. He lay
down beside her.

"What did you do to me? My legs wouldn't hold me up."

"I tried something new."

"I've never come standing up before. If you're not going to take off all your clothes, at least take off your pants."

He undressed, laying his clothes on a chair, and returned to the bed. Jen went between his legs and took his penis in her mouth, then took it out.

"I don't know how to do it. I want to suck you off."

Instead, she rubbed his penis over her cheek, her forehead, her nose, pressing it against every part of her face. Her eyes were closed.

"I love its smell," she said. She placed it between her lips. "It's mine. Is that clear stuff your jizz? I thought it was white, like mayonnaise."

"It's something else. It comes out before I come."

"I never noticed it before. I want you to come. I want to see your face when you come." She was running her hand up and down the shaft. "Give me. Come on, pretend you're inside me. Give me, give me. Come, my lover, my Bobby, come on me, give me your jizz. I've never seen it so big. Look at it. Open your eyes." She squeezed it and it came flooding out of him in a scalding wave.

He opened his eyes. Jen was turning her hand this way and that. His semen was oozing between her spread fingers. She moved her hand closer to her chest and, with her other hand, raised her breast to catch his come. "I've never seen so much at one time. If we ever need money, you could join the circus."

"Come one, come all," Bob said.

She put her index finger in her mouth. "It's sweet. I'm surprised."

"What did you expect it to taste like?"

"I didn't know. I didn't expect it to have any taste. Do you want to taste it?"

"No."

"But you swallow my juice. What does it taste like?"

He thought about it. "I don't know. The taste is all mixed up with your smell, with the way you move when you're coming, or getting ready to come."

"Do you like my smell?"

"I love it," he said.

"Doesn't it smell like fish? Michael used to tell me I smelled like a fish when I got excited. Not very flattering."

"To me, it smells like the sea. Not like fish, but the sea. It makes me want to cover myself in your juice."

"That's the way I feel about your jizz."

"I like swallowing your juice," he said. "I like the taste, or the smell of it in my mouth, on my face."

"I'm hot again."

"So am I."

She looked at his penis.

"What shall we do?" she asked.

"What do you want to do?"

"I want you to fuck me in the ass."

"Are you sure?"

"Let's try."

"I can't get it in. You're too small."

The odor excited him so that he wanted to plunge into her, regardless of the resistance.

"Rub your penis against me again. That felt good."

He did. The smell permeated the room.

"God. I had no idea it would feel this good."

"Touch yourself."

"Do you think that will help?"

"I don't know."

"Okay, I'm touching myself. Push, just a little."

He could see her eyelids scrunch up as he pushed, and he withdrew. "I don't want to hurt you."

"Just rub it against me while I do myself. There. Like that. Be quiet now."

She spasmed and his penis slid inside her. She moved and he held back until he felt himself fill and he pushed hard into her and released.

"Oh God, oh God, oh God, that was everything. More than everything," she said.

"Did you come?" She was in his arms and he was kissing her face, her hair, her face again.

"Hell yes, I came! Couldn't you tell?"

"Everything was happening at once. I lost track of what was going on."

"That's how it was for me too. Everything was happening at once. But I think I'm going to be sore tomorrow. My ass really burns. I'll be right back."

When she came back from the bathroom, she said, "There was blood mixed in with your semen. I assume it came from me, not you."

"There's a smear of blood on the sheet. I noticed it when you got up."

"Not very much. I think I'll be okay. Don't you want to wash yourself?"

"Okay."

"There's got to be a trick to this," she said when he crawled into bed again. "How do homosexuals do it? It must hurt them, too."

"Maybe they get used to it."

"Build up calluses on their anuses? How would they ever take a shit? Or hold it back if they needed to?"

"I don't know." He was very tired.

"Hey! Don't go to sleep!"

"I won't."

"I'll bet. Okay, go ahead. I'll wait. I'll give you five minutes."

He opened his eyes.

Jen said, "That was six minutes. I was very generous with you."

"You were. You're generous with everything."

"If only I could learn how to give a blow job. Then I'd be a triple threat."

"I don't know what to tell you."

"If I could give a decent blow job, I'd be ready."

"What do you mean?"

"I'd be ready, you know, for you to put me on the street."

"What the fuck are you talking about?"

"I'd turn tricks. You know, if we ever need money. Michael used to tell me I was sitting on a gold mine. Although I'm not a virgin anymore."

"Uh uh," Bob said. He stared at her. Finally the corners of her mouth began to lift and she gave a full smile.

"Did you think I was serious?"

He didn't say anything. He still wasn't sure.

"You did. I fooled you. Hah!"

"That wasn't funny."

"Yes it was. I enjoyed it."

We're Supposed to Make It Look
Like We're Trying to Help You

Waiting in the line to sign up for unemployment compensation, Bob saw ahead of him a man in his mid-twenties wearing a worn Army fatigue jacket. It was Elliot. His hair was longer than Bob remembered it and it was tied behind his head with twine. He was performing for two other men around the same age as himself. He was enacting the effects of a pill he had taken or had seen someone else take. His body mimicked convulsions and he rolled his eyes and laughed, and the others laughed.

Not certain what he wanted to do, Bob remained still. The line was made up entirely of men and it stretched outside the building for thirty or forty yards. Some of those approaching old age talked, as if reassuring one another, of a depression that would be arriving any day now. Young people, they agreed, would not know how to handle hardship whereas they themselves would survive it because they had learned what to do during the one in the Thirties.

Elliot noticed Bob staring at him and before he could get embarrassed or angry, Bob introduced himself and reminded him of the trip they had talked about taking—when Bob said "trip" Elliot laughed again and looked at the other men who laughed with him—and asked about Earl because he could think of nothing else that they both might know something about. Elliot's face lost its liveliness and he said he had not seen Earl. The last time he saw Earl, Earl was throwing up in front of a bar, drunk on sloe gin and pills. Bob was surprised that the story about Earl had not changed since he had last seen Elliot.

Elliot was somber now and asked Bob about himself. Bob said he was thinking about going into the Army. Elliot said he had hated being in the Army. Then there was nothing else to talk about and they each said how well the other looked and Elliot returned to his friends and became lively again and Bob stood behind them in the line. He wondered why he had said he was thinking about enlisting. He wondered, too, if Elliot and the girl he was with the last time he saw him were still together, but he didn't ask.

Once inside, Bob sat down on a blue plastic chair among many other blue plastic chairs on which sat many other people, filled out some forms that a clerk gave him, and waited for his turn to see another clerk. Finally a man at a desk called him up. He asked to see Bob's DD214. Bob told him he didn't have one and that he didn't know what a DD214 was.

The man looked at Bob as though he were something alien and then he held out his hand. "Well, let's see what you do have."

Bob gave him the forms he had completed. The man looked through them. "Weren't you in the service? Army, Navy, something?"

"No. I was just laid off from an agricultural job." Bob categorized the job as agricultural because one of the forms he had filled out had a box that said "Agricultural" and none of the other boxes seemed to apply to spraying orange trees.

The man was appraising him. He was in his thirties and he had sand-colored hair and wore glasses in rectangular black frames. "You got in the wrong section," he said. "I handle the military service cases."

"There's only one section."

"Well, maybe I can do something for you. I could use a break. I just had a guy here who had a Less-Than-Honorable discharge.

Like there's anything I can do for him. The DD214 is the document the military gives you when you leave service. There's a code on it that tells us what kind of separation you got—Medical, Bad Conduct, et cetera. If you have anything but an Honorable separation, you're shit out of luck, unless it's Medical. We're not supposed to help you, but we're supposed to make it look like we're trying to help you. On the other hand, even if you have an Honorable, there's not a lot we can do for you, because there's not a lot of work around these days. Well, let's pretend you have an Honorable and see what's available."

He riffled through a shallow wooden box filled with index cards, occasionally stopping at one, then moving on.

"Nope. I'll file your application for compensation—that's this form—and we'll see what happens."

Bob read the want ads. He applied for a job as a reporter-copywriter at a small, twice-weekly newspaper. He might have had it, had he been to college or at least taken some journalism classes. The editor advised him to try *The Register*. It was a larger paper and they might be willing to train him on the job.

He got an interview with the managing editor at *The Register* and, after having Bob take a test to determine his writing ability, he offered him a job as a copywriter. But then he asked Bob how old he was and when Bob said eighteen, the managing editor froze. When he spoke next, he said that actually he had no openings for a copywriter. Bob could start as a copyboy and work his way up to copywriter or reporter, but he couldn't hire him as a copywriter now. He encouraged Bob to take the copyboy job.

The managing editor talked about journalism as a career, and how important it was to have a sense of integrity, which he could see Bob had, as well as an ability to write well. Curiosity, too.

Curiosity was as important as integrity. But at the same time, you had to know who buttered your bread. Ads paid for the newspaper. It made nothing from circulation; it was ads that brought in the money. The reporters might resent the constraints on them, on which stories they were allowed to cover, but if the ads went, so would their jobs.

After listening to him talk about journalism as it was rather than as Bob had imagined it, having read about Hemingway's and Steinbeck's and Dos Passos' careers, he decided that he did not want to be a copyboy. He had seven hundred dollars in a savings account and he had time before he would have to worry about money.

It's All About the Next Performance

He took a Greyhound up to San Francisco. They picked up 101 in Los Angeles and followed it north through the San Fernando Valley to Ventura where Harold's future father-in-law had his walnut groves. He hadn't seen Harold in a while and wondered what he had been doing, other than going to school. Then along the coast to Santa Barbara. Bob had a cousin who lived there, or near there. They had been good friends when they were in junior high school, and then she moved. He had another cousin who lived in the Valley—he had almost forgotten him. The three of them—Paul, Marlene, and Bob—were close five or six years before when they all lived within twenty or thirty miles of one another, but then Paul moved and a year or two later Marlene moved even farther away, to a town north of Santa Barbara whose name Bob couldn't remember.

They drove along the coast and then turned inland, putting the coast range between the ocean and the bus. They drove through ranchland where there was hardly a cow and only occasionally a horse grazing on brown grass, and then, later, through harrowed farmland, eucalyptus trees and poplars running along either side of the highway, mile after mile, an infinite windbreak protecting infinite, barren acreage.

They drove through Steinbeck country and Bob remembered scenes from Steinbeck's stories of ranchers and farmers and remembered, too, the sense of connection between people and between people and land and people and animals that ran through the stories. He had thought of looking for agricultural work, but looking at this country at the onset of winter, so long and broad and sad and gray, he knew he didn't want to harness himself to it.

They went through San Jose where a friend of his father lived—Pete somebody; Pete Sampos?—and he remembered how when they were all younger—his father, his mother, his sister and he—they had driven up here to see Pete and meet his family, and his father had introduced them, his own family, to Pete and his. His father had not seen Pete since the war, since 1942, since shortly before he met Bob's mother. It had been six years now—no, five; no, six—since they had seen Pete, since they had moved to California. Of course his parents could have driven up here and visited Pete and his family without Bob's knowing, but he doubted they had. His father was too tied to the routine of his job and his mother was bound to their house and to the intricacies and dynamics of the doings of her parents and her brothers and her sister and their families. That was not a life for Bob either.

From the bus station in San Francisco he took a cab to North Beach. Harold Seaver country, then cousin country, then Steinbeck country and Pete Sampos country, and now beatnik country. Bob knew where he wanted to go: the Columbus Hotel where, he had read, some of the beatniks rented rooms.

It was a nearly decrepit building with high ceilings and wooden wainscoting on thick plaster walls. The worn carpeting may as well not have been there, for all the warmth and color it provided. He paid for a room on the second floor for three nights, then remarked to the manager that he had heard this was a place that was popular with poets and musicians. The manager gave him a short smile and said, "That's what they call themselves." He said they were all over North Beach.

His room was cold. It was about five o'clock. The heat did not come on until six and the chill seeped in through the window and seemingly through the walls. He decided to look for a place to eat and he left the hotel and began to walk around North Beach. At a number of coffee shops he saw men only a little older than he was in black turtleneck shirts and black jeans and black berets, sitting at a table with a book in front of them, or a notebook and pen, and a coffee cup at their side. All had a cigarette burning between the first and second fingers of one hand or in an ashtray, and all had a sallow complexion. They reminded him of the James Dean lookalikes he had seen in Schwab's Drugstore just after he and his family moved to California: the straight, blond-brown hair combed back, just a little too long for the day's fashion, the cheekbones slightly pronounced, the cheeks sucked in or the molars removed to accentuate the malar bones, the glasses with tortoise-shell frames, the black motorcycle jacket left unzipped.

So who did these guys in North Beach want to notice them? Women? But the women at the other tables ignored them and the waitresses only took their orders. Who were these guys, these youngsters with their unmarked, unlined faces, their unlived-in bodies, looking as though they knew less about life than Bob did. Were they really beatniks? Were they disaffected students?

They did not look like people he could learn anything from. He was more comfortable with men like Elliot and Dick Miles and Tom and Harold than he thought he could be with these guys with their affectations of thought and suffering. (And who was he pretending to be, with his bomber's jacket and his asking after poets and musicians?)

He went into a café on Jackson and had a sandwich with fries. It was still early when he finished eating and he went back to his hotel room and lay down on the bed wearing his jacket and fell asleep.

When he woke, it was dark. He went outside again and found the Purple Onion and the hungry i. A comedian was going to be at the Purple Onion, but Thelonious Monk was going to play at the hungry i at nine. Bob had an hour to kill and he went to City Lights Bookstore. Other than a couple of used-book stores in Long Beach, he had not been in a bookstore this large before. But there were few people in it and nothing of moment seemed to be going on, and he wondered what had happened here to give the place its reputation. He wandered through its stacks and among its tables, feeling overwhelmed by the abundance of written words.

He flipped through several books, stopping at the odd page. He remembered Justin showing him a book he was reading for one of his classes and saying he was a better writer than the author. Justin was talking about his own ability to make words into sentences and sentences into paragraphs; he was not talking about what the sentences and paragraphs meant. He said they should try to sell their writing—Bob was a good writer too, he said. But Bob knew he had run out of things to write about by the time he graduated from high school, and he was sure that Justin, only a year and a half older than he was, had no more to say than he had. Bob left City Lights without buying anything, walking out as a short man standing beside the cash register stared at him.

At the hungry i people were standing outside or leaning against the building, listening to the music flowing through the doorway. A man came out of the club and said the place was at capacity, but they didn't mind if people hung around outside to listen. A few minutes later a different man came out and told everybody they had to leave; they were blocking the door and if the fire marshal came by, as he sometimes did, he would fine the club for creating a fire hazard. They could come back at eleven for the next performance.

"That's what it's all about," someone said. "The next performance."

Bob returned to his room and lay down, telling himself he would get up in an hour and go out again. He had not asked about a cover charge and did not know if they served liquor. He did not have a fake ID, so if they did serve liquor and they ID'd him, he would not be able to get in. He sat up and undressed and slipped into bed. The room was warm now and he fell easily into sleep.

In the morning he went to a state employment office. There was almost no line. He told the interviewer that he had been doing seasonal agricultural work and that he had already applied for unemployment compensation. He had come up to San Francisco to try his luck because there wasn't any work in southern California.

There wasn't any work here either, the interviewer said, especially not agricultural work, not at this time of year. He didn't have anything to add to this and he looked at Bob as though puzzling why he was still sitting in front of him. Bob got up and left the building.

He walked around the city for a while until he realized he was hungry. On Market Street he saw a café called Mary's. He remembered Nelson Algren's dictum about never eating at a place called Mom's and looked again at the hand-painted sign above the door to be sure he had read it correctly the first time. He went in and took a seat at the counter. An old man, a derelict, followed him inside and sat down on the stool next to his.

It was lunchtime and the place was crowded with women in white blouses, plain skirts, stockings and heels—secretaries, he thought—who were sitting alone, reading novels as they ate, and men who might have been salesmen sitting with other men who might have been salesmen, talking about what was going on in the office and who was making it happen. Bob had never noticed a secretary reading a novel in a restaurant in Orange County and he wondered if secretaries here were better educated or if something else was going on. He had seen plenty of salesmen before and those he saw here were much like those he had seen in other places.

A stocky, middle-aged waitress asked him what he wanted and he said a bowl of chili and a cup of coffee. She asked if he wanted crackers with the chili and he said yes, please.

The old man beside him said he would have a cup of coffee too. The waitress stared at him. "Can you pay for it?"

The old man stood up. He appeared very weak, so that standing up was a struggle.

"I'll pay for it," Bob said.

The old man sat down again. The waitress made an expression of disgust. She brought two coffees and then she brought Bob a bowl of chili with two packets of oyster crackers. The old man was trying to pour milk from a stainless steel container into his coffee but it was splattering on the countertop. Bob took the milk out of the old man's hand and poured it for him. "Thank you," the old man said. The waitress wiped up the milk with a white cloth. Her face told nothing.

The old man tried to get his coffee cup to his lips. He was using both hands, but they were shaking so badly that he had already slopped half the cup onto the countertop. The waitress was there with her towel and opened her mouth as if to say something, but Bob took a straw out of a jar at the far edge of the counter and peeled the paper off it and stuck one end of it in the old man's coffee and the other end in his mouth. The waitress refilled his cup and Bob heard him laboring to suck the coffee into his mouth; he had crushed the end of the straw between his lips. Bob peeled another straw and set it on the counter beside the old man's cup. Then he turned away to eat his chili.

Bob felt the old man leaning against his shoulder. He thought the old man was going for his wallet and he moved quickly to face him. The old man fell backward off the stool and onto the floor. Bob heard his head hit. The old man groaned and then was silent. He was lying between two tables. He wasn't moving. Bob looked around, but nobody appeared to see him, not even the people at the tables he lay between.

Bob squatted down and straddled the old man's hips and pressed on his chest just above his sternum. He had learned to do chest compressions in health education when he was a sophomore. He pressed again and then again, setting up a rhythm. He shouted, "Call the police!" though everybody was pretending not to see either the old man or Bob. He noticed that when he pressed on the old man's chest his face would become ruddy and his eyes would roll forward and stare at him, but every time he eased off, the old man's eyes would roll up into his head, showing only the whites, and the color would leave his face. Bob thought he was trying to save a dead man, but he continued pressing on the man's chest. "Call the police!" he shouted again, and the waitress behind the counter shouted back, "I did!"

People had begun to leave, some stepping over the man on the floor, one woman's foot coming down on his outflung arm. "Excuse me," she said, but she didn't stop and no one else did either, and no one said anything except for the one "Excuse me."

Two policemen came in and Bob stood up, expecting one of them to relieve him, but they each grabbed the old man by an arm and yanked him to his feet. He appeared to be conscious or semiconscious now and was muttering something as they dragged him out of the café. Outside, they started punching him, one hitting him in the back, the other in the chest. Then the one who had been punching him in the chest shoved him. The old man staggered but kept his feet, and Bob saw him through the plate-glass window, shuffling away.

Bob paid his bill and the old man's, and left. He walked without direction and soon found himself on Mission Street. There were fifty men, maybe more, who looked like the old man in the café, sitting or lying on the sidewalk. If Bob hadn't turned onto Mission, he would never have seen them. He wondered which of them were already dead, and he wondered how Kerouac could ever have romanticized all of this.

He spent that night reading in his room and the next day he walked through the city until he thought he would be tired enough to sleep through the night without waking. It was not a large city in terms of miles—it was not Los Angeles—and he thought he could cover all of it, or almost all of it, in two or three days if he wanted to. But all he wanted now was to see enough of it to get the taste of what happened in Mary's out of his mouth and the disappointment of his first day here out of his thinking. And he was successful, because on the day he took his long walk the sun was out and reflected brightly off the pastel houses and created contrasts of shadow and light everywhere. The bay was blue with small whitecaps and the Golden Gate Bridge was engulfed in an orange aura that, along with the sun and the bay and the houses in variegated colors, lent cheer to the day.

He thought about staying another day to walk more, but he had told Jen that he wouldn't be gone more than four or five days and he wanted to get back to her. Although he would tell her about Mary's café, he might be able to turn the story into something funny or something more tragic than it was, so that it was not simply something else that was dismaying about the trip. Maybe the whole purpose of traveling anyway was to be able to tell stories about your journey when you went home.

In the morning he checked out of the hotel—"Did you find
any poets?" the manager asked—and took a taxi to the bus station
and bought a ticket on a Greyhound going south.

All These Esses in Your Life

"How do you feel afterwards?"

"Tired. Exhausted. At least for a little while."

"I feel full. Filled up. As if every part of me has been filled with your stuff. I like feeling it seep out of me. But I want to keep it inside of me too. It reminds me that you've been there. My lover's come. Do you remember that photograph Justin showed us where the woman is being penetrated by one man and she has another man's dick in her mouth and another's dick in her hand?"

"Yes."

"Have you ever thought of trying that sometime?"

"With you, you mean?"

"Yes, with me. Who else would you do it with?"

"I don't know. I haven't thought about it. I don't know. Who would we get?"

"It would have to be friends of ours. People we trust."

Bob didn't say anything.

"We don't have to," Jen said. "It's just something I thought up."

"Let me think about it."

"Would you be jealous?"

"I don't know. That's what I want to think about."

"It's just our bodies."

"That's a lot."

"Okay. Hey, have you ever heard of a woman taking two men inside her at the same time?"

"One in her pussy and one in her ass? Yes."

"Oh, I hadn't thought of it that way. I thought they were

talking about both in her pussy. I don't want it in my ass."

"I thought you liked it the time we did it."

"I did. With you. But if there was somebody else and he wanted to do me in my butt, I don't think I'd want that. It was an experiment. I don't think I'd want it as part of our regular repertoire."

"Where are you getting this stuff? These ideas."

"This book of Victorian porno I found. How do you know what you know? You haven't done it all yourself, have you?"

He thought about it. Where had he learned what he knew?

"Have you?" Jen said again. She looked worried.

"No. I'm just trying to remember where I learned things. Some of it was from listening to older boys when I was younger. Oh yeah, I remember. There was a book in the school library that told about a girl's body, how to get her excited, where to touch her, that sort of thing."

"Really? There's a book like that? Like an instruction manual?"

"Yeah. I don't remember the name of it. I found it when I was nosing through the stacks. I showed it to a friend of mine who showed it to the librarian and she took it off the shelf. That's the last time I ever trusted that so-called friend."

"A girl?"

"A boy. He thought male dogs should have to wear pants or diapers or something to cover their parts."

"You're kidding."

"No, I'm not. We were walking home from school once and there was this little kid—he could hardly walk, that's how young he was—and he was in his front yard and he'd lost his diaper and Dave started screaming at him to go inside, that he shouldn't be outside naked. I mean he was really yelling, and the boy's mother came running out of the house and grabbed her kid and took him inside. Then Dave started yelling at her that she should know better and she was a terrible mother, and like that. Like Dave is all of fifteen and he knows what she should be doing. I thought she was going to call the cops."

"She should have."

"Maybe so."

"His name was Dave?"

"Yeah."

"My father's name. David."

"I know. But he wasn't anything like your father."

Jen was silent. Then she said, "Only you would learn about pleasuring a girl from a book. But you learned well. You must have really studied it."

"What about you and your Victorian novel or anthology or whatever it is?"

"But that's only fantasy. We haven't done any of that stuff."

"That library book—that was only fantasy until I met you."

"Thank you. I think."

"Thank you."

"To you I'm just a pussy."

"You're teasing me, aren't you?"

"What do you think?"

"I think you're teasing me."

"Then I'm teasing you." She asked, "Does it bother you when I talk about Michael sometimes?"

"Why do you keep asking me that? No, it doesn't. I feel something, but I don't know what it is."

"You don't talk about Sara anymore."

"Do you want me to?"

"No. It hurts when you do. She's the only girl you slept with before me, right?"

"Sara and I never slept together. It was somebody before I met Sara."

"Before? You never told me about her. What's her name?"

"Sherry."

"All these esses in your life. Sara, Sherry, Susan, Samantha. Am I leaving someone out?"

"I don't know a Susan or a Samantha."

"You get my point."

"There haven't been so many. And I only slept with Sherry."

"You spent the night with her?"

"I mean she was the only girl before you that I made love with. Had intercourse with."

"What did she look like? How old were you?"

"Are you sure? You said it hurts you when I mention Sara, and Sara and I never screwed."

"I'm not sure, but my imagination is running wild. If I knew what exactly happened, maybe that would help me."

"I haven't made love with anyone but you since we've been together. You know that, don't you?"

"I know, but tell me: was she better than me?"

"Nobody's better than you."

"Oh ho! And how would you know? How many girls are you comparing me to? But thank you for saying so. Tell me about Sherry. What did she look like?"

"She was tall, a little shorter than me. She had red hair. More orange than red. She was eighteen and she was home for the summer. She was going to college in Ohio, but she lived in Fullerton."

"A college girl? How old were you?"

"Fifteen. But I told her I was sixteen."

"So you were only a sophomore."

"I had just finished my sophomore year. I told her I had just finished my junior year."

"And she had just finished her freshman year in college?"

"Yes."

"How did you meet her?"

"Joe and I—I don't think you met Joe. He went into the Navy last summer, about the time Harry went into the Air Force. Anyway, we went down to the beach one night—you know the state park by Huntington where the fire pits are?—and we saw Sherry and another girl walking on the sand ahead of us. They didn't seem to be with anybody so we caught up to them and started talking with them. They were classmates in Ohio and both lived in Fullerton. They had been classmates in Fullerton too. The other girl had a boyfriend in Ohio who had a job back there, but he was going to come down and visit her later in the summer. She was the one Joe was attracted to, so they kind of drifted away from Sherry and me, and after a while I kissed her. Are you okay?"

"Go on."

"So we began kissing. Actually, I was surprised that she kissed me back when I kissed her, because she seemed kind of shy."

"She was looking for a fling."

"So we kissed for quite a while and when Susan and Joe came back—oh, I guess I do know a Susan—I asked Sherry for her phone number. She didn't think I would call her, but I did."

"Did you feel her up?"

"No. I tried to, but she wouldn't let me."

"Was she pretty? Did she have a good figure?"

"Yes. She was pretty and she did have a good figure. She was built more like a woman than the girls I knew. She was heavier. Rounder."

"Ouch."

"I'll stop."

"Just give me a minute. Where did you go on your first date? I assume you had more than one."

"We went to a coffee house in Newport Beach that I had been

to before. I had a friend, George, and he and I used to go there sometimes. He was older than me too, and had come from back east to look for a job."

"How did you meet him? No, don't. You can tell me another time. So you took Sherry to this coffee house. It must have impressed her. It impressed me when you took me to the one in Hollywood."

"Oh, Jen. This was two years before you. Before you and I started...before we got involved."

"Is that what we are? Involved? I thought it was more than that."

"I'm going to stop. I can't stand this."

"I'm sorry. I can't help it. I feel so helpless."

He put his arm around her and leaned back against the headboard with her. The tears stopped and she put her hand on his penis and began to rub it.

"At least I can still get you hard."

He kissed her. His penis was raging and when she squeezed it he could feel the Cowper's fluid ease out of it, and then, only a few seconds later, he came in her hand.

"Who were you thinking about when you came?"

"What? I wasn't thinking about anyone. I wasn't thinking at all."

"Wrong answer, Buckwheat. But not the worst answer. I don't think I want to hear any more about Sherry."

"Good."

"I feel betrayed. I know I shouldn't, but I do. You seem different from the boy I fell in love with."

"Maybe you're the one who's changed."

"I don't know. But I know I love you. I don't doubt that. Maybe that's what growing up is about, if you grow up together and love each other—learning ways to accept changes in each other."

They were driving back to her house when she said, "I think we should get married."

They had talked about marriage before but it had seemed to be something that, if it happened, would be so far in the future that it almost concerned two different people. Now something in her voice made it sound imminent.

"When?" he asked.

"Soon."

"Why soon?"

"I want us to live together. I want to be able to go to sleep with you after we make love and wake up with you in the morning. We spend so much money on motels anyway that we might as well get our own apartment."

"If I could afford it, I'd have my own apartment." In fact, he was worried that he wouldn't be able to pay his share of the rent on Tom's apartment if he did not find a job soon.

"You'll get a job," she said, as though she had heard his thoughts. "I have faith in you."

"I'm not God," he said.

"You're my god."

Then she placed her hands over his eyes so that he couldn't see. They were on the freeway, doing sixty the last time he looked at the speedometer.

"What are you doing!" he yelled. He was afraid to brake; he didn't know what was behind them. He grabbed one of her arms and pulled it away. "Are you trying to kill us?"

"You're my god. You won't let us die." She was rubbing her arm. "That hurt."

"Don't you know how dangerous that was!"

"Oh, don't exaggerate. I was only trying to show you that you need to have faith in yourself."

Kevin Was Nervous

Kevin was nervous, Gerry irritated. They didn't look at each other. When Kevin said something, Gerry focused on him, then looked away. He was more than irritated; he was angry. With the next thing Kevin said, Gerry snapped at him, "Just button it up, okay?"

Gerry asked when Tom would be back. Tom had gone to the liquor store. Bob thought he would be back soon: it was the beginning of the weekend and Tom would want to get his drinking started.

Kevin asked if Bob knew anything about the legal relations between Mexico and the United States. Bob didn't know how to respond. He didn't know anything about legal relations between Mexico and the United States and he didn't know what Kevin was talking about. Kevin said he and Gerry had gone to Tijuana last weekend.

"For Christ's sake," Gerry said. "What's that got to do with anything?"

Kevin ignored him. He asked Bob, "If you do something in Mexico, would they look for you in the United States, if you're an American?"

"Jesus fucking Christ," Gerry said. "I'm leaving."

But he didn't leave.

"I don't know," Bob said. "I guess it depends on what you did." Why is he asking me? Bob thought.

"I'm pretty sure I killed somebody."

"Fuck," Gerry said. He sat down on the sofa. His gaze fixed on the door.

Bob said, "What happened?"

"We were in an alley. We had just come out of a whorehouse and this guy came up to me with a knife and told me to give him my money. I didn't even think. I don't even know how I got the knife away from him."

"You kicked him in the balls and he dropped it," Gerry said. He gave out a small giggle.

"I did? I don't even remember that."

"You did."

"I must have picked it up. I don't remember that either, but I must have. And I stabbed him in the stomach with it. I remember stabbing him."

"Maybe you didn't kill him," Bob said.

"He was bleeding an awful lot. I'm sure he was dead before we left him. I had blood on my shoes when we got home."

"He was dead," Gerry said.

"Okay," Bob said. He still wondered why they were telling him all of this, but now he was interested. "What did you do with the knife?"

"I left it there, next to him," Kevin said.

"Did you wipe your fingerprints off it?"

"No. I didn't think of it. Shit."

"I did," Gerry said. "I wiped off the handle with my handkerchief and I tossed my handkerchief in a trash bin at a gas station before we crossed the border."

"I wondered why you threw your handkerchief away," Kevin said. "We stopped at the gas station so I could wash my hands and get rid of my shirt."

"You had some on your face, too. And in your hair. I don't know how the hell you got it in your hair. Maybe when you were fighting with him."

"I don't remember fighting him."

"After you kicked him in the nuts."

"I was fighting with him?"

"Take my word for it."

"You crossed the border without a shirt?" Bob said. "Didn't Customs say anything?"

"He still had his tee shirt," Gerry said. "There was hardly anything on it."

"I'm worried they'll find me," Kevin said.

"I don't see how," Bob said. "Did anybody see you fighting with this guy?"

"Just me," Gerry said. He gave that little giggle again.

"Then I don't see how they could find you." How do I know to ask this stuff, to think like this? Bob thought. Movies? TV? And why have they told me all of this?

"Are you going to tell Tom?" Bob asked.

"No," Kevin said.

"Probably," Gerry said.

Kevin laughed.

"I feel better now," he said. "Thanks for listening."

"I don't," Gerry said.

"If I were you, I wouldn't tell Phil," Bob said.

"Hell no!" Kevin said. "He'd tell everybody he knows. Are you going to tell Jen?"

"No." She would tell her father. Maybe.

"Thanks."

"The fewer people who know, the better," Gerry said.

Tom said he'd spent the night with Linda, part of the night anyway. After they fucked, he wanted to leave but she wanted to cuddle, so he concentrated on what was on TV while she nestled against him. Soon he realized he was out of cigarettes and he left to get a pack, but before returning to Linda's apartment he stopped in a bar and had a beer. Then he got a Coke for her and another beer for himself and brought them back with him. He had expected her to be angry, but she wasn't. She said she had been worried that something had happened to him, that was all.

"Bullshit," Bob said. "She was pissed off. She just wasn't showing it."

"You're probably right."

She said she appreciated his thoughtfulness in bringing her a Coke, Tom said.

"Sarcasm," Bob said.

"No, I don't think so."

They went back to bed and she drank her Coke and he drank his beer and she started playing with his dick, so he fucked her again and then they watched TV again and when he was certain she was asleep, he got up and went home.

"I hate this," he said. "I hate her."

"Why do you stay with her?"

"She won't leave me alone. I've tried breaking up with her, but she follows me everywhere. She knows where my favorite bar is and she just shows up as if it's a coincidence that we're there at the same time, and she calls me at home until I agree to see her again."

"Is that who calls you so late?"

"That's her. Also, if I do break up with her, I won't be able to use the library again. Not that one anyway. And it's more convenient than the others."

"I'll bet her ex-boyfriend went to Laos to get away from her."

"Or he said he was going to Laos. Who knows where he really went."

"If he really went anywhere. How would she know?"

"If he really worked for the CIA. How would she know if he

was lying about that?"

"Maybe there is no ex-boyfriend who works for the CIA. Maybe she made him up."

"I'll bet you're right. The cunt."

Thanksgiving Turkey

The idea was to sneak into the Moores' backyard from the alley side, locate their turkey, slip Bob's duffel bag over its head, stuff the bird inside, bring it back to the car and take it home where they would chop its head off with a hatchet, let it bleed out, clean it, pluck it, and roast it.

Going after the Moores' turkey was Bob's idea. He thought of the Moores because he knew they had a turkey and he was familiar with the layout of their house and backyard, having once spent a weekend there playing poker when Todd's parents were away. He was not particularly close to Todd, though they had been classmates and Bob lived only ten houses away from him then. He had nothing against Todd, but neither Tom nor Bob had money to buy a turkey at a supermarket and they wanted a Thanksgiving that would match other people's Thanksgivings. Also, they thought it would be fun to steal a turkey. It was the notion of fun that drew Harold and Justin into the scheme.

Harold owned an MG and Justin's car was in the shop and Tom didn't own a car, so Bob drove. He parked in the alley a couple of houses down from the Moores and they let themselves into the yard through the gate in the low, wire fence that marked the border of the Moores' property. The fence was there to keep their dog in, but Bob knew the dog stayed in the house at night.

He heard chickens across the yard near the house. Then he saw something large and white. "There it is," he whispered. He moved toward it with the duffel bag. Justin was beside him.

"That's not a turkey, Bob. That's a goose."

"A goose? They used to have a turkey."

"Maybe he's their Thanksgiving dinner. I'm sure that's a goose."

"I don't think you're going to get him in your duffel bag," Tom said. He and Harold had moved up beside Justin and Bob. The four of them made a dark cluster between an orange tree and a cumquat tree.

"I can't by myself," Bob said, "but I can with some help."

"Geese are aggressive," Justin said.

"Wait!" Tom said. "There's the turkey, in the shadow by that shed. Holy shit! I didn't think he'd be so big."

"That duffel bag looks pretty small," Justin said.

"That's a tom turkey. Sorry, Tom," Harold said. "You're not going to get him in your bag. Let's go for the goose. Did you bring the hatchet? We'll probably have to kill it here."

"Me?" Bob said. "It's your hatchet."

"It's your plan. Jesus Christ," Harold said. "What a goat fuck."

"Do they have goats, too?" Justin asked.

Harold laughed.

"Shhh!" Bob said.

The back door of the house opened, letting a wedge of yellow light into the yard. A dog barked.

"Run!" Bob meant to whisper but it came out as a shout.

They bolted from the yard, Bob and Justin through the gate, Tom and Harold over the fence, and ran to the car. Bob's key was tangled in some threads that had come loose from the seam in his pocket and he couldn't get it out. Justin said, "Get behind the car," and they crouched along the its far side.

"Get thee behind me, Satan," Justin said.

"What the fuck are you talking about?" Harold said. He was squatting behind Justin.

"I don't know. It just came to me."

"Do you have to say everything that just comes to you?"

"Shhh!" Bob said.

They waited silently for the dog or one of the Moores to come out of the yard, but the gate didn't open and they heard no footfalls.

Tom said, "We didn't even get a chicken."

Bob stood up. "We could go back and get one."

A sardonic laugh came from Harold. "Shit," he said.

"Well, I guess we won't."

Bob tore the car key away from the threads that had snagged it and inserted it in the door on the driver's side.

Jen Wonders Why She Hasn't Gotten Pregnant

Tom was back after the long Thanksgiving weekend with the Crowes. Jen had come over with the last of the leftovers from the Thanksgiving dinner her mother had prepared for her small family and Bob. The dinner had been significant in that for the first time Jen had talked openly about the fact that she and Bob were thinking about getting married, although she made it clear that she wouldn't get married without her parents' consent. Bob had not known that she was going to bring this up. He sat silently as she made her announcement and her parents asked questions and she answered them. David and Carol did not even glance at him. They did not give their consent.

Phil was home from UCLA and, after four days with his parents, stopped in on his way back to Los Angeles. Harold, who had gone to Ventura with his fiancée and her family, had not returned. Fog had settled in all along the coast and the Highway Patrol was advising people not to drive if they didn't have to.

"If Harold was killed in an accident, I get his guns," Phil said. Harold owned a number of shotguns and hunting rifles.

"'...the fuck—you don't even live here. Besides, I want his thirty-ought-six," Bob said.

"We'll share," Phil said.

"Are you guys serious?" Jen asked.

"Hell yeah. Those are some nice arms," Phil said.

"Thank you," Jen said.

"I meant the guns. Guns are called arms sometimes. But you have nice arms too. And legs."

Jen pulled the hem of her skirt up so he could get a glimpse of her thighs.

"Although I'm a boob man, myself," Phil said.

"Those you don't get to see," Jen said. She went over to the table where Tom was drinking and sat down next to him. She stood up again and reached across the table to the cabinet and got a water glass, putting one knee on the table, stretching her other leg out behind her and extending her arm forward. For a moment, she appeared as a small animal, a deer maybe, in flight. Bob ached for the beauty of her body and at the same time was proud that only he, of the men in the apartment, knew what it looked like unclothed. She poured herself half a glass of wine from Tom's bottle.

Phil was watching Bob. Phil made a circle with the thumb and first finger of his right hand and put the index finger of his left hand through it.

"I didn't know you were left-handed," Bob said.

Phil grinned.

"Phil would like to ignite Jen's passion," Tom said. "But he's already got a girlfriend."

"What? What?" Jen said. "That statement calls for two whats. I didn't know you were serious about anyone. Is it Beth?"

"Yes. Beth. I told you about her," Phil said.

"They're engaged," Tom said.

"What?" Jen said. "That was worth three whats even if I only said one. How long have you known each other?"

"We're not engaged. Tom's full of shit. We're just sleeping together."

"They're engaged," Tom said. "Kevin told me."

"Oh, pissy, fucky, farty, shitty, damny, helly. I only told Kevin and Gerry and they told the rest of the world. We'll be getting married next summer unless we break up before then, or if she gets pregnant. If she gets pregnant, we'll get married earlier."

"I have a thousand questions. I don't know which to ask first," Jen said.

"I don't want to answer any questions. I'm really nervous about it."

"Phil wishes he hadn't proposed," Tom said.

"I don't wish that. I just regret…having proposed." He laughed but he looked worried.

"That's a problem," Tom said.

"What are you, a fucking Greek chorus?" Phil said.

Jen said, "I wonder why I haven't gotten pregnant."

Everyone was quiet. Jen's face grew red and she came over to the sofa and sat down next to Bob, though not close enough for him to touch her. She had not told anyone that they made love.

"Do you want children?" Tom asked after some time.

"Not now. Not yet. But some day, sure," Jen said.

She didn't look at Bob or at Tom or Phil.

"That was embarrassing," she said. "Somebody say something funny."

They heard a heavy tread on the wooden steps outside and the door opened and Harold came inside.

"Shit."

"I love you too, Phil," Harold said.

"We've already divided up your guns," Phil said.

"They thought you were dead," Tom said.

"They thought you had died in the fog," Jen said.

"Are you sure you're not Harold's ghost?" Tom said.

"O-o-oh. Don't talk like that, man," Phil said. "I believe in that shit."

"I am Harold's ghost, Phil," Harold said. "Give me back my guns or I'll haunt you for the rest of your life."

"That isn't funny, man. Besides, we never took your guns.

They're wherever you left them. Shit, I'm going back to UCLA."

"You're not safe anywhere, Phil. Not from a ghost," Harold said.

"Fuck you, man. I'm leaving."

"Wasn't Phil seeing her before?" Jen asked after he had gone.

"Who? Beth?" Tom said.

"And then they broke up and she started seeing someone else," Jen said. "He was worried she wouldn't want him back."

"He never said anything to me," Tom said.

"Me either," Bob said. "How do you know all this?"

"When I was here a couple of weeks ago, he told me she was seeing another boy."

"I never heard about it," Tom said.

"Maybe he wants her to. Maybe he wants to swing," Harold said.

Tom laughed. "Not Phil."

"Hey, you never know. Some of these bible thumpers are the randiest people you'd ever want to meet."

"Is Phil a bible thumper?" Jen asked.

"He's not a bible thumper," Tom said.

"He's not? Who am I thinking of then?" Harold said.

"How come he confided in you, but not in the rest of us?" Bob asked.

"I don't know," Jen said. "Because I'm a girl and you're not?"

"Nobody's going to argue about that," Tom said.

"Is he really engaged?" Bob asked.

"Not that I know of," Tom said.

"What are you talking about? You just said he was engaged," Jen said.

"I made it up," Tom said, "and Phil went along with it."

"Is he still seeing Beth?" Bob asked.

"I don't think he ever was. I think he wanted to date her, but she was seeing someone else."

"That's not fair," Jen said. "You were just having fun with me."

"Life's not fair," Tom said. He offered a smile.

"I'd expect something a little less banal from you," Jen said. She was angry.

"Wow," Harold and Bob said simultaneously.

Phil Has a Bad Experience

Phil said he'd been looking forward to doing gas fumes again since he went back to school in September.

"Jesus wouldn't like you getting high on his birthday," Justin said.

"How do you know what he'd like? Besides, his birthday was yesterday," Phil said.

They got the bottle they had used before from under the stairs leading up to the apartment and went out to the lot where Bob had parked his car. Bob got the hose out of the trunk and unscrewed the cap from the neck of the gas tank.

"I'll do it," Phil said.

Bob handed him the hose. "To stop it, raise the end of the hose and bend it shut."

"I know how to do it."

He stuck one end in the gas tank and, after wiping it off with his hand, put the other end in his mouth.

"It's erotic," Justin said. "Look at the expression on his face. He's closed his eyes."

"Maybe he'll let you go next," Tom said.

"No thanks."

Phil took the hose out of his mouth. "It's not coming."

"Suck harder," Tom said. Justin and Bob laughed.

Phil put the hose back in his mouth. Suddenly he straightened up, dropping the hose, and backed away from the car, gasping. Gasoline was flowing from the hose onto the asphalt.

Bob ran over and picked up the free end of the hose and held it high above the car fender and away from his body. When he was certain the gas inside the hose had run back into the tank, he pulled the hose out and tossed it on the ground.

"Wasted your gas," Tom said.

Phil's face was a deep red. He couldn't find his breath. He was coughing now and walking in a tight circle, dragging his right foot. The sandal had come off, but one of the straps was hooked on his large toe, and as he made the circle, the sandal scraped along the ground.

Justin went over to him. Did he want to sit down? Did he need a doctor? Should they call an ambulance? But Phil pushed him away and continued making his tiny laps. He had air now and had stopped coughing, but remained speechless.

"You were supposed to suck it, not inhale it," Tom said.

Phil raised his middle finger, but did not stop walking.

Tentative grins appeared on Justin's and Tom's faces. Bob touched his mouth to see if he was grinning too. His fingernail clicked against a tooth.

"You owe me money for the gas you spilled," he said.

Phil raised his middle finger again. They laughed; they weren't going to have to watch him die.

Phil continued making his circles and the others sat down in the shade of a pickup a few yards away and waited for him to do something else.

After twenty or thirty minutes he stopped, bent over and replaced his sandal and walked over to them. His leg seemed okay.

"I want to lie down. Can I use your couch?"

"Sure," Tom said. "But do you think you ought to? Maybe you should work some more of that crap out of your lungs first."

"I'm tired," Phil said.

He walked past them and they followed him up the stairs. Inside, he said, "Do you have any wine?"

"I'm not going to give you any wine, Phil," Tom said. "You need to get your lungs clear before do any drinking."

"Fuck you," Phil said. He lay down on the couch and went immediately to sleep. They watched his chest inflate and deflate.

Bob was late picking Jen up. She was going to eat macaroni and cheese with them this evening. When they arrived Phil was still lying on the sofa, but he was awake. He watched them walk inside, then swung his feet to the floor and sat up.

"How do you feel?" Jen asked.

"With my hands," Phil said. His voice was hoarse. He sounded as though his throat had been scalded. "Can I have some wine?"

Tom had a gallon jug of cheap red on the table and poured some into a glass and gave it to Phil.

"Thank you."

"Can I have some too?" Jen asked.

"Well, I might as well have a glass," Justin said.

Bob took several glasses from the cabinet, including one for Tom and one for himself.

Jen went over to the couch and sat down next to Phil. He turned to her and began to tell her what he had been through. His voice had returned to what it had been before he sucked in the gas, though it sounded a little throatier now.

Justin was saying that he was on an elevator at Long Beach State and noticed that someone had scratched in the paint on the door: "God is dead—Nietzsche". Phil said he had seen the same thing in a men's restroom at UCLA, but someone had written below it: "Nietzsche is dead—God".

They all laughed and Phil turned back to Jen, and Justin and Bob turned to Tom who had read Nietzsche and read about him and was saying now that Nietzsche had died of syphilis, but since he had never been laid, it was hard to understand how he had gotten it. He had gone to a brothel once but had left, horrified, before he did anything. Tom spoke as authoritatively as if he had just written his own biography of him. But then he said, "God gave him syphilis without sex. That's what I call a real miracle."

Justin said, "Like Mary getting pregnant when she was a virgin. All the pain without the pleasure." He and Tom and Bob laughed.

Bob had expected to hear Jen's laughter too and looked to see why she hadn't joined in. Phil's head was between her breasts and, as Bob watched, she placed her hand behind it as she did with Bob when he kissed her breasts. Phil's hand was on her thigh. Bob had seen the expression she wore once before, on a girl nursing a newborn, but he had not seen it on Jen's face before.

He walked over and grabbed Phil by his shirt.

Phil raised his head; he was grinning. Jen looked up. She said, "It's all right." She was coming back into herself.

"Relax, man. We're friends," Phil said.

Bob moved towards him but Justin inserted himself between them and Bob moved back.

"I'd never seen you like that," Jen said. They were sitting in the car a few doors down from her house. "It was scary. I thought you were going to hit him."

"I was going to hit him."

"He wasn't doing anything."

"He had his face in your boobs. He was feeling your leg."

"He was scared. He told me what happened with the gas getting in his lungs. He thought he was going to die." Then she said, "I didn't know he was touching my leg."

The pressure in Bob's chest began to ease. He asked, "What were you feeling when you were holding him?"

It took her a moment to answer. "He reminded me of Peter when he was small and he would hurt himself playing. He would come running to me. He would be crying and I would comfort him. I would make these little cooing noises and he would laugh and tell me I sounded like a pigeon."

"But what did you feel when you were comforting Phil?"

"Oh. I don't know how to define what I felt. I haven't experienced it very often. I just wanted...I don't know what I wanted. I wanted to make him feel better."

"Why didn't Peter go to your mother for comfort?"

"You know my mother. Sometimes he'd go to her, I think, if I wasn't around."

"I keep learning things about you," Bob said.

"Isn't that good?"

"I think so."

"If we're going to spend our lives together, we need to know each other," she said. "For instance, I didn't know you could be scary."

"Damn."

"What?"

"I was going to ask you to make love. But now it doesn't feel right."

She put her hand on his penis.

"Are you always hard? Are you ever not hard?"

"I'm always hard when I'm with you," he said.

"Flattery will get you everywhere. But we can't do it here. People aren't asleep yet."

"We can go to the park."

"Take it out. I want to play with it."

He loosened his belt and undid his fly.

"Little Bobby," she said.

"What?"

"Little Bobby. That's how I think of it. See? Now you know something more about me. Come on, let's go. Oh, look. It's drooling."

Linda had broken up with Tom. She had met someone else. "He has a body like a Greek god," she told Tom.

"Which means," Tom told Bob and Harold, "that he's no good in bed." Tom was very thin.

Harold said, "So everybody who works out is bad in bed?"

"Yep. Wouldn't have it any other way."

Harold and Bob looked at each other.

Tom went into his bedroom.

"I don't think he's very happy," Harold said.

"No," Bob said.

What Does It Look Like?

The room was plain but clean and smelled of disinfectant. He turned on the heater and they went to the Denny's across the parking lot to get something to eat while the room warmed up. Jen brought a paperback book with her. She wanted to show him something. They ordered and then she opened her book.

"Here's one where they lay the heroine on the hood of a car and take turns with her. She loves it."

"Of course she loves it," Bob said. "It wouldn't be porno if she didn't love it. Where'd you get this book?"

"In that bookstore on Harbor. I don't think they know what they've got. It was in the romance section. Although maybe they do know. When I went to pay for it, the guy at the register told me he'd had a young woman in there who'd bought a book by the Marquis de Sade. He figured she'd return it as soon as she saw what was in it. But she came back the next day and asked if he had any more like that. She was very plain, not at all like me, he said."

"He was coming on to you."

"I know. Look, here's one where they make love in the balcony of a movie theater. She takes her panties off and sits on his penis. Whenever someone walks by, she stops moving and they pretend she's just sitting on his lap, cuddling with her boyfriend."

"Remember that time I was feeling you up in the theater and they made us leave?"

"Oh yeah. That was embarrassing. I guess that lets this one out."

"Are you looking at these books to find things we could do?"

"Sure. Why not? Or I could be a prostitute and you could be my pimp. How much do you think I could get?"

"I don't know."

"Well, how much would you pay me if I was a prostitute?"

"I don't know. Whatever I could afford. A million dollars, if I had it."

"Wow. Maybe I'll stop putting out until you get rich. Do you think you could wait?"

"No. Do you think you could?"

"Not on your life. Seriously, how would you feel if I sold myself to another man?"

"Not too good."

"If I gave myself?"

"I don't know, Jen."

"Should I shut up?"

"Yes."

"Okay. One more thing?"

"One more."

"If I gave myself to another man, would you want to be there? There's a scene in the book where the girl's lover watches her make it with another man."

Bob didn't say anything.

"Do something for me?" she asked.

"What?"

The sandwiches came. They were silent until the waitress left.

"When we go back to our room, would you masturbate for me?"

"Is that in this book?"

"No. We did it once before, remember? We did it together."

"I'd like to do it together again."

"I want to watch you while you do it. When I do myself, I can't concentrate on you. After you're done, we can do me."

"Are you ready to go?"

"I've hardly eaten."

"Hurry up."

"We can take it with us. I'll wrap it in a napkin."

"Don't forget your book."

"What does it look like?"

"Like a baby bird's mouth, waiting for worms."

"That's disgusting! Does it really look like that?"

"No."

"And you're comparing your stiffy to a worm."

"Haven't you ever looked at it?"

"How could I? I can't bend that far."

"Use a mirror."

He got her handbag and took out the mirror she used when she brushed her hair.

"I don't know if I want to," she said.

"Why not?"

"Some people think it's ugly. My mother thinks it is."

"It's not ugly."

"You don't think it's ugly?"

"God, no. I could spend my life looking at it."

"Looking at it and jacking off. Okay."

She raised her knees and opened her legs. He held the mirror a few inches from her vagina.

"What do you think?" he said.

"It's not ugly. It's not beautiful either. I hoped it would be beautiful."

He kissed it.

"If it were somebody else's, would you want to kiss it?" she asked.

"I might, but I wouldn't do it."

"Good answer."

"Would you want to kiss another girl's?" he asked.

"I don't know. Maybe. If I knew her and liked her. And wanted to give her pleasure. Does that bother you?"

"No. You know how you feel sometimes after I come inside you? Fulfilled?"

"Filled up. It's not the same thing. But maybe it almost is."

"When I look at your pussy, I feel like that. That this is what I was meant to do."

"Look at my pussy?"

"It's more like adore your pussy. It's almost a religious feeling. I feel something expand inside me, as though I'm looking at something eternal."

"It's only seventeen, the same age as the rest of me."

"I'm not saying it right."

"You're saying it just fine, Mr. Eternal. Here, stop adoring and give me something. I've just gone to the filling station for a top-off. Put your hose in my tank."

"Do you remember when we went to Disneyland that time and we were in one of those places where you just wander around— the Eighteen-nineties display or something like that—and you came in your pants?"

"Yes."

"And everybody was staring at you. You were wearing your khaki pants and everybody could see your jizz leaking through the front. How did you manage to stay so calm, as if nothing had happened?"

"There wasn't anything I could do. We were in the middle of a crowd and there was nowhere I could go. Even if there was a restroom, what could I have done? Go in there and wait until it dried? How long would that have taken?"

"Do you remember the expression on that man's face when he saw what had happened?"

"I think he just wanted to get his family out of there, but he didn't know how to without making things worse."

"Why did you come? What were you thinking about?"

"I was thinking about your butt. And then I was imagining how you look naked. And I was smelling your hair. And I came. It gushed out of me before I knew there was a danger."

"I was so proud. I didn't know what was in your mind, but I knew it had to do with me, and I was so proud—I could make you come without even touching you."

"Fucking is a way of life for us, isn't it? Doing it. Thinking about it."

He got a letter informing him that he had been turned down for unemployment compensation. Justin's father had paid him under the table and had not paid into the insurance fund. The tree-spraying outfit he had worked for had paid, but he could not draw on it until six months had passed since his first paycheck. That's what the clerk at the unemployment office said when he went in to ask for an explanation.

"You'll have to wait till February to reapply," he said. Bob didn't know whether or not to believe him. He remembered what the blond man with the black eyeglass frames had told him about how they misled military veterans and he wondered if they weren't doing the same to him. But it didn't matter. The guy could be lying through his teeth and there was nothing Bob could do about it. "In the meantime, you're welcome to come in and look through our binders to try to find something. These are tough times though. Employers just aren't hiring. Have you tried the classifieds?"

"Yes."

"Well, things will get better eventually. They always do. And then they get bad again." The clerk laughed, pleased with his own wittiness.

Bob left without checking the binders. He still had money, but if it was not flying out of his hands, it was walking steadily and nothing was coming in to replace it.

He was angry and he told Justin the next time he came over that his father was not paying into unemployment insurance.

"He does for the permanent employees," Justin said, "but not for the temporary ones. He doesn't like the paperwork. Also business has been really slow this last year, so maybe he's cutting corners too. In the old country he was a socialist, so you'd think he would be willing to sacrifice a little to help other people. But I think he feels he's doing something for people just by hiring them."

"I didn't know your father was from Europe. Which country?"

"With a name like Muller, which do you think? He left because he was a socialist. When Hitler came to power, Dad figured it was time to get out. Sometimes it's hard to know what's the right thing to do."

"You mean leaving Germany?"

"No, I don't think he ever doubted that leaving the old country was right, especially in the Thirties. I mean now. He was probably faced with the choice of paying into unemployment insurance in order to benefit his employees, or holding that money in reserve as security for his family. If he holds the money back, you get the shaft, but his family can hang in there without too much discomfort until the economy improves. If he pays in, you would have some kind of income now, but we—I mean my family—

would lose, I don't know, something. Maybe I would have to drop out of school and go to work. Assuming there is work out there that I can do. It's an existential dilemma. It isn't as if my dad owns a big corporation, after all."

Tom was at the table, listening, and he asked, "Have you been reading Plato?"

Justin's eyes widened. "Why, yes." He dragged the why out so that it came through as a kind of sprawl. "Why-y-y, yes." Bob thought it was another of the verbal affectations he had adopted since starting college, like stringing out "interesting" so that it became "in-ter-est-ing." Probably one of his professors had impressed him and Justin was aping him.

"How did you guess?" he asked.

"Elementary," Tom said. "I knew you were taking a class in Greek philosophy and that it's still fairly early in the semester and Plato is one of the first philosophers you would study, and you seemed a little detached as you were talking, so naturally I thought—"

"Naturally," said Justin.

"—you had been reading him."

"Of course. And not only reading him, but trying to emulate him."

"Really? How?"

"By trying to be consistent in thought and behavior. By rising above passion."

"Oh? How's it going?"

"Pretty well. Not very well. I've been dating this girl and I thought we had an understanding that it was just a Platonic relationship. But the other night I was kissing her goodnight and the next thing I know we're in her bedroom and she's telling me to be quiet because she's afraid we'll wake up her parents."

"Had you done the deed?" Bob asked.

"Of course. Who could resist those titties?"

Tom asked, "Was fucking her worth violating your ideals?"

"It was at the time. She seemed to enjoy it. At least she said she did. But it's more complicated than I want to deal with."

"Didn't you like it?" Bob asked.

"Oh yes. Yes. But she wants to go out with me again and I know she'll expect me to make love to her again and I don't know if I want to."

"Just think of her titties," Tom said. "That'll ease you past your good intentions."

"All right. Can I use your phone? Never mind, I'll call her from my house later."

"Look at him," Tom said. "Did you ever see such a lascivious grin?"

Bob laughed. Ol' Justin. Always setting standards for himself that he couldn't possibly meet, always happy to fall away from them.

"Now Bob doesn't much care about consistency between thought and behavior. Bob sees himself as part of the natural world," Tom said.

"Are you saying hypocrisy is a part of nature, or that Bob thinks it is?" Justin asked.

"I wouldn't presume. But why don't you ask him?" Tom said.

"Do you think hypocrisy is a part of nature?" Justin asked.

"I have no idea. But I don't see myself as a hypocrite," Bob said.

"Bob's trying to find himself by conforming to what he believes is the natural order of the world," Tom said, more or less again.

"I don't know what you're talking about. I'm not trying to find myself, whatever that means. I just want to understand how the world works." Until he said it, he didn't know he thought it; he certainly didn't know if it was true. But if it was, it was not all that was true. He felt there was something else that was also true, maybe even truer, but he didn't know what it was. Who or what he was was not something he thought about, and maybe was not even the question to ask. But there was something else, he was certain, and he didn't know what it was.

"Your soul then. What's essentially you. You're trying to find that."

"Do you think we have souls?" Bob said.

"Sure. Don't you?" Tom said.

"Do they go to heaven when we die?"

"I don't know. I doubt it."

"Then what happens to them?"

"Souls? How would I know?"

"My head is spinning," Justin said. "My soul just wants to get laid."

"You've been reading too much philosophy," said Tom.

"Why do you think I'm trying to find myself, or my soul?" Bob said. "I sure don't see myself as conforming to anything, at least not intentionally. I see myself as trying to resist conformity." And there it was. Not the resistance to conformity, but resistance to whatever or whoever would try to dictate to him. Later in his life, he would come to see himself as a sort of control freak, but one who resisted other people's attempts to control him rather than one who tried to control others.

"I think you're trying to figure out the nature of the world so you can find your place in it."

Bob didn't know what to say. "Maybe that's true. But why do you think so?"

"I talk with Jen. We talk about you quite a bit."

"He's like Diogenes," Justin said about Bob. "Except he doesn't make love in public."

Tom and Bob stared at each other until Tom looked away.

Jen put her hand over his eyes. They were on the freeway again and moving fast. Bob pushed her hard enough to knock her against the passenger door.

"Why do you keep doing that!" He yelled.

She was rubbing her back. "Ow."

"You're going to get us killed!"

"I won't do it again. Not if you're going to hurt me."

Then she did it again and he shoved her away again. The driver in another car honked; Bob had swerved into the lane on his right.

"You said you wouldn't do that again!"

"I lied," Jen said.

In Mexico

Janice Crowe's father killed himself a couple of years earlier. He was at the supper table with his wife and his younger daughter and he left the table to go upstairs, saying he had something to show them. He was in a good mood and seemed eager to surprise them with whatever it was. He was upstairs for less than a minute when they heard the shot. They never found out what he wanted to surprise them with, unless the suicide was the surprise.

Bob did not know Janice well and when she told him the story of her father's death, she told it without inflection so that he couldn't tell what her feeling was about her father or his death, except that she resented having to clean up the mess he left of himself because her mother and her sister were not up to it.

The occasion of her telling him was a small pre-New Year's Eve party she and Gerry and Kevin were having at their house. They were sitting on a couple of wooden stools at the wet bar Gerry had finished building just in time for the holidays. Jen was at the end of the bar, talking with them and Barbara, Kevin's girlfriend. Tom sat by himself on the sofa in the living room, sipping something from a martini glass, seemingly content, when Linda came in with her boyfriend whom she introduced as Nikos. (So he *was* Greek. But Bob didn't see anything godlike about him. "Maybe his godly attributes were hidden inside his clothes," Jen said the next day on the way back to her parents' house.) Tall and blond, not as tall as Tom, but not as thin either, he was friendly and at ease with Tom, sitting down beside him as soon as Linda handed him a drink. Tom looked unhappy, his face gaunt, his eyes too large and unable to conceal his discomfort, but he managed to smile and respond to whatever Nikos was saying. Linda, standing between Janice and Gerry, observed.

Janice was telling Bob again how angry she was with her mother and sister for refusing to deal with her father's mess, and he began to understand that her father's suicide and the images of cleaning it up were things she lived with every minute of her life. The bits of brain and skull that, in her memory, she picked off the wall and ceiling of her parents' bedroom were something Bob later saw inside an armored personnel carrier in the central highlands of Viet Nam, and years after that, when he occasionally thought about Janice, he wondered if he had placed one of his own memories in Janice's collection. He was certain she told him her father had shot himself and she had to clean up afterward, but the details of it may have been from his own experience to come.

"Once she gets started, you can't shut her up," Gerry said, moving past Linda to stand beside his wife.

"I can't help myself," Janice agreed.

Gerry put his hand on her shoulder and she reached up and placed her hand over his.

"That's okay," Bob said. "I'm interested."

"People talk to you, don't they? I mean, they tell you things," Janice said.

"It seems that way. But I don't mind. I kind of like it."

"I know. I can tell. Thank you." She bent forward and kissed him on the mouth.

"Hey! Whoa! Stop being nice to my wife," Gerry said.

Linda and Nikos left, Linda apologizing for leaving so early, but there was somewhere else they had to be, unfortunately, et cetera.

"I'm sorry, Tom. I thought you and Linda were still together when I invited her," Janice said. Tom forced another smile and waved his hand as if to say everything was fine.

Barbara said she was having trouble breathing—all the cigarette smoke—and had forgotten her inhaler, and she and Kevin left to go back to her house to get it.

Bob looked at Jen and Tom. Should we be leaving too?

"I know," Gerry said. "Let's go down to Tijuana, all of us."

Tom and Bob stared at him.

"What's in Tijuana?" Jen asked.

"Honey, you don't want to know," Janice said. Then, to Gerry, "Are you trying to corrupt this young couple?"

"Who? Me?" Gerry said in mock innocence.

"'Who, me?' Yes, you."

"What's in Tijuana?" Jen asked again.

"We can see a sex show," Gerry said.

Jen looked at Bob. He shrugged.

"A strip show," Tom said. "But more than that."

"A hell of a lot more than that," Gerry said.

"What about the kids?" Janice said.

"We'll get Kevin and Barbara to watch them. We'll be back by the time they wake up. Kevin wouldn't want to go with us anyway."

"I'll have to call my parents," Jen said. "To let them know I won't be home tonight."

"Do you live with your parents?" Janice asked.

"How old are you?" Gerry said.

"Seventeen."

"Oh my god, you're so young," Janice said. "I thought you were married, but you're not, are you? How old are you?"

"Eighteen," Bob said.

"You're babies."

"Good things come in small packages," Gerry said. Then,

acknowledging how small Jen was, he said, "In more ways than one."

"I keep telling him that the meat closest to the bone is the sweetest," Jen said.

"Hell, she's not that young!" Gerry laughed.

"What will you tell your folks?" Bob asked.

"I don't know."

"Tell them you've had too much to drink and you're going to spend the night at our place," Gerry said.

"Oh, right," Bob said.

"How will we get her across the border?" Tom said.

"She can hide in the trunk," Gerry said. "They probably won't look, going down. And coming back, she can sit up front with everybody else. All they ask is where you were born."

"You can't tell them you've had too much to drink," Bob said.

"I know," Jen said. "I'll tell them we're going to play cards, so I'll be late. I may even spend the night here."

"Do you think they'll buy that?" Tom asked.

"I don't know. My mother will. My father may not, but maybe he won't say anything."

"Maybe it's not worth it," Tom said.

"I want to go with you guys."

"Why don't you two just get married?" Janice said. "At least you wouldn't have to worry about making up stories to tell your parents. We were your age when we got married."

"Hell, you can do it while we're down there," Gerry said.

"We're not quite ready," Jen said.

"You should probably find a job first," Tom said to Bob.

"Damn, I wanted to be best man," Gerry said.

"Can I use your phone?" Jen asked.

"Sure. Use the extension in the bedroom." Janice indicated a door.

When Jen came back, she said, "Well, that's done."

"What did they say?" Bob asked.

"I talked to my mother. She just wanted to be sure that I was going to be with nice people."

Everybody laughed.

"I've been called lots of things, but never nice," Gerry said.

"You're nice to me," Janice said.

"How is your father going to react when he finds out?" Tom asked.

"I don't know," Jen said.

"Did you leave them our phone number?" Janice asked.

"I forgot to. I was so nervous. I've never lied to them before."

"You've never lied to them? How could you get to be seventeen without lying to your parents?"

"Remember what you just said when our kids are seventeen," Gerry said.

"I've lied to them, but not like this." Jen came over to Bob and he put his arms around her. "I feel so guilty," she said.

"We don't have to go."

"I want to. It's just that I feel guilty."

"It'll pass," said Tom.

"I know," Jen said.

Kevin and Barbara returned and Gerry told them about Tijuana and asked them to stay with the kids. Barbara said she couldn't. She and Kevin hadn't been together that long and had never spent a night together. Also, she was still living with her parents and she didn't think she would be able to make them understand. Kevin said he would watch the kids, no problem. The others waited while he drove Barbara home again.

Jen said, "She makes me feel like a bad girl."

"Barbara's sweet," Janice said, "and she knows her own mind, like you. Know your own mind, I mean. Oh, oh, what am I saying?"

"You're not a bad girl," Bob said.

After a while, Gerry asked Tom, "You ever go to any of the Rhino games?"

Tom shook his head.

"They're pretty good. Not good football, but entertaining. The last game I saw, they gave up forty-two points to the other team. I don't remember who they were playing. They were okay the first half, then they fell apart."

"What are the Rhinos?" Jen asked.

"A semi-pro ball team. They play their home games at Rhino Stadium. In Anaheim."

"I wondered why they call it Rhino Stadium," Bob said.

"That's why."

"It looks more like a baseball park, with that wooden fence around it."

"They play baseball there too," Gerry said.

"The only time I was there, I went to hear Herbert Philbrick talk about the evils of Communism," Bob said.

"The guy from 'I Led Three Lives'?"

"Yeah. Not the actor, but the guy who wrote the book."

"It was a TV series."

"Yeah, but it was a book first."

"Why did you go? I didn't have you pegged as a right-winger."

"All the high schools in Orange County send their senior classes to listen to him. I think some of them send their junior classes too. Didn't you go?"

"My father refused to give his permission. I'm surprised your parents let you go," Jen said.

"Maybe they were afraid not to. My father works in Orange

County. Your father works in Los Angeles."

"Wasn't it boring?" Tom asked.

"Probably," Bob said. "I didn't stay. Three of us from Buena Park climbed over the centerfield fence. And when the kids from the other schools saw us, they jumped the fence too, some of them. The teachers were running all around, screaming at us, threatening to flunk us. One of our teachers just stood there and watched us go. He was laughing his head off."

"At you guys or at the other teachers?" Jen asked.

"Both, probably. We had a car waiting for us. Dave Hernandez, a friend of ours who had graduated the year before, was waiting for us a block away."

"It sounds like a prison break," Jen said.

"Well, it was."

"So what did you do when you were free?" Tom asked.

"We went to the beach. We went to Balboa and checked out some of the boats in the marina. One of them was pretty big— somebody said it was John Wayne's—and we jumped off the top of the what do you call it? The wheelhouse? I think it's the wheelhouse. We jumped into the water a couple of times. It was a twenty-five- or thirty-foot jump."

"I thought you were afraid of heights," Jen said.

"I am. Then I decided to swim the channel between Balboa and Newport. It's about a quarter-mile, I think. Harry and Joe didn't want to do it, so Dave and I did it alone. Big mistake. I had no idea the water was so cold. I got about halfway when I went deaf. The water was so cold, I lost my hearing. And I got really tired."

"Your body was expending energy just trying to stay warm," Gerry said.

"That's what I think too. I was extraordinarily tired—"

"I like that word," Jen said. "Extraordinary."

"—but I was halfway to the Newport side, so I just kept going. Harry and Joe had driven around to Newport, and by the time I got out of the water they were already there to help me. I could hardly walk. But Dave wasn't there. We had started out together but I had pulled ahead. I had assumed he was fairly close behind me. When I stopped halfway out, I could see him waving to me, but by the time I got to the other side, he was gone. We didn't know what to do. He's a close friend of Harry especially, and Harry was really upset. 'Distraught' is a better word. He blamed me for letting Dave drown.

"Then Dave shows up. He's on a yacht and everybody on the yacht is waving at us and he's in the middle of all these people and he's waving too. And then they put him in a dinghy they're trailing and another guy gets in and rows him over to where we're waiting for him and he climbs out and falls over into the water. Harry and Joe run into the water and pull him out and get him onto his feet and his chest and back are huge, as if they had been pumped up with an air hose. And his skin is really red, like it had been scorched. He said he just couldn't swim anymore, he couldn't even move his arms, so he got onto his back and waited, either to eventually drown or to get back enough strength to make his way to shore. It was the cold. But along comes this yacht, and they see him, and they ask him if he needs help, but he can hardly talk. So they lower a couple of guys down into the dinghy and they get him into it and finally they see us and bring him over to us."

No one spoke, as though they were waiting for Bob to say something more. But he had finished.

"That's my story," he said, "and I'm sticking to it." It was a line he'd heard both Jen and her father use.

"You do like to have adventures, don't you?" Janice said.

Bob almost objected. He almost said, What about Kevin? What about your husband? For that matter, he could have said,

What about Jen? But he didn't say any of those things. He liked Janice and didn't know what she knew and he didn't want to say anything that would lead her to question her life.

Gerry nodded. "I hadn't seen that in you. But now some of the other things you've done make sense."

"Like what? Sometimes I think I don't know anything about him," Jen said. "As much as we've…" She left off and Gerry and Janice laughed.

"As much fun as you've had together?" Janice offered.

Jen's face was flaming. "Everybody knows," she whispered, as though to herself.

"You sure haven't tried to hide it." Gerry's laughter roared out of him. Tom smiled sympathetically. Bob put his arms around her but she pushed him away and Gerry laughed again.

They crossed the border and Gerry drove a few blocks and turned into a residential neighborhood and stopped the car. He and Bob got out and Gerry unlocked the trunk and Jen climbed out.

"That was fun. It's really roomy in there," she said.

"Yeah, if you're four feet eight," Gerry said.

"I'm not that little."

She got in the back and sat next to Tom and Bob slid in and sat at her other side. Gerry drove to the center of town and pulled into a diagonal parking space. A boy offered to keep an eye on the car and Gerry gave him two dollars and said he would give him five more when they came back if he did a good job.

"You've done this before," Janice said.

A look of irritation swept over Gerry's face and then was gone.

"I was only teasing," Janice said.

They followed Gerry to wherever they were going.

"I've never been here," Jen said. "You went to the bullfights here, didn't you?"

"A couple of times," Bob said.

"You did? Did you like them?" Tom asked.

"You have to overlook some things if you're going to enjoy them."

"Or you have to learn to like those things," Gerry said.

"Have you been?" Tom asked.

"Janice and I went once. I don't want to see another one. I'm no Hemingway."

They came to the Blue Fox and Bob thought they would stop there. Judging by the people going in and out, American kids a little older than Jen and him, students probably, and others with their hair cut like Marines', and a man at the door, urging passersby to just take a look inside, it appeared to be the kind of place they were looking for, but Gerry walked past it and they ended up in a nightclub on the next block. It was half-filled with kids who looked the same as those they saw at the Blue Fox, with their evenly cut hair and their clear complexions. They took a table and pulled a chair over for Tom from a vacant table and ordered beer. The stage was empty but for a microphone on a stand and they talked about what to expect, Gerry telling Janice and Jen to be prepared for anything. The two women went to the restroom; as soon as they had gone, two prostitutes came over and sat down where they had been and a third stood next to Tom and pressed her hip against his shoulder.

"Buy me a drink?" the one in Jen's chair said.

"My girlfriend is here."

"Here?" She looked around as though trying to locate her.

"She's in the bathroom."

"Oh. The bathroom. Okay." She squeezed Bob's penis through his pants and stood up. "Maybe next time."

He heard Gerry say, "You're going to get me in trouble," and the woman beside him got up and followed the first to a couple of stools at the bar.

The woman beside Tom was wearing a red blouse made of a soft material that accentuated her breasts. She said something in his ear and he shook his head vehemently and the woman left.

Jen and Janice came back laughing because a woman in the bathroom had asked them if they wanted to meet some men and, as they were walking away, called after them, "Women?"

The lights went out and a spotlight lit a circle on the low stage and a man in a dark business suit stepped into it and took the microphone out of its holder and told the audience how much they were going to like the pretty ladies they were going to see and that, if they stayed for the entire show, they would be able to see the lesbian act.

"Does he mean a performance by a single lesbian or one by two or more lesbians?" Jen asked, but no one responded.

Somebody in the darkness yelled something and the emcee said, "No, we don't have donkeys," and the kid who had yelled, or somebody near him, said, "Aw, shit."

The emcee left the stage and a girl, eighteen or nineteen, stepped onto it and into the spotlight. She was wearing a small, two-piece bathing suit and she walked around the stage, following the light that was blue now instead of white. Some slow music came on and she sometimes made a kind of half-twirl to it, but mostly she just walked, occasionally hooking her thumbs in her G-string and pulling it away from her body and looking down inside it and then looking up again and smiling at the dark tables. She seemed fragile. She did not have enough flesh on her body to conceal the nervous tics in the small muscles of her back.

"I'm going to ask her to go out," a boy at the table behind Tom said.

"Where will you take her?" another boy said.

"I don't know. Are there bullfights tomorrow?"

The girl was naked now. As she walked, her body seemed to become more fluid and the smile did not leave her face. Her pubic hair was dark and glossy and Bob wondered if she had put some kind of lotion on it.

"I could eat her out right now," Janice said.

The girl whirled completely around in a surprisingly graceful pirouette—it was obvious that she had had some kind of training—and stopped and bowed so that her small breasts hung away from her chest and the audience applauded politely. She picked up her bra and G-string from the floor and walked off toward the rear as the emcee came back and the light returned to white. Bob's eyes had adjusted to the scant light and he saw that the tables were almost filled. A waiter came by and brought them more beer and Gerry paid him. The emcee was talking about the beauty of the next performer, who had not yet appeared.

Bob got up and went to the restroom. Walking through the corridor leading to the bathrooms, he saw the boy who wanted to date the girl on the stage standing against the wall. His erect penis was out of his pants and the girl was stroking it. Two other boys stood next to them, watching. The one boy said something to the girl who answered yes. He seemed surprised and he said something more and the girl answered yes again.

"She said she would," he said to the other boys, as if the girl weren't there.

"Where are you going to go?" one of them asked.

"I don't know," the one boy said.

When Bob returned to the table, a different girl was lying on her back on the stage. She was naked and a shirtless boy with a very pale, pimpled back lay between her legs, his mouth against her vagina. Bob sat down beside Jen. He didn't see Tom. Gerry motioned with his thumb and Bob looked toward the back. Light shone from another hallway and a couple walked through it from somewhere off to the side and he realized there were rooms in the back.

On the stage, the boy had sat up and was pulling his pants off. The girl was pushing against the floor with her hands, moving away from him. The emcee came out and told the boy he had to keep his pants on. The boy seemed not to understand him. "How can I fuck her with my pants on?" he said.

"You are not allowed to fuck her," the emcee said. He motioned to the girl who moved forward again. When she was in position, the emcee pushed the boy's head toward the girl's pudendum and the boy resumed cunnilingus. The boy was wearing only his boxer shorts now and the emcee placed himself away from the blue spotlight but remained close enough to be able to intervene, should the boy get too aggressive.

The girl placed her hands on the back of the boy's head and spread her legs wider. She made moaning sounds. Finally she raised her legs in the air and screamed and several people in the audience cheered and applauded and the boy rose, smiling.

The emcee spoke to him and the boy gathered his clothes and walked off the stage. The girl remained on her back, her legs apart, her pubic hair glistening in the light that had become white again.

A dark-haired girl came up out of the darkness onto the stage. She could hardly walk, leaning on the backs of the chairs on her way for support. She had already removed her blouse and her bra. The emcee moved between her and the prone girl, who was laughing. In a moment the American girl had returned to the audience and disappeared among the tables. Her attempt to perform had earned her some cheers.

Tom was back. He was drinking beer. Gerry and Janice were talking quietly. His hand moved up her leg.

Jen leaned toward Bob and whispered, "I'm so wet."

"I heard that," Gerry said. Janice laughed.

Another boy walked onto the stage and took his place between the legs of the prone girl. He kept his tee shirt on.

"Do you want to go to another club or are you ready to go home?" Gerry asked.

Janice said, "We should go back. Give Kevin a break."

"The kids will be asleep," Gerry said.

"Not by the time we get home."

"What do you say, Tom?" Gerry said.

"I'm ready to go."

"I would think so."

"Shhh," Janice said, and laughed again.

"How about you guys?"

They would have liked to stay for another show, but Gerry was driving, so Bob and Jen deferred to the others.

Jen sat between Tom and Bob in the back. Tom was scrunched against his door, as though he were trying to avoid contact with her.

"What's wrong?" she asked.

Tom shook his head and made a small smile. A minute later he closed his eyes and let his head ease back against the doorframe.

Bob put his arm around Jen and she settled in under it.

Janice turned toward them. "Have you ever made it with a woman, Jen?"

After several seconds, Jen said, "When I was younger, a girlfriend and I used to touch each other."

"Did you like it?"

"Sure. Who wouldn't? I mean...well, who wouldn't?"

Janice turned back so that she was facing the highway ahead.

Bob whispered in Jen's ear, "Are you still wet?"

She nodded. "A little."

"I don't suppose you have a blanket somewhere," Bob said to the back of Gerry's head. He leaned forward and saw Janice's hand on Gerry's exposed penis. Bob moved back.

"No, man. Sorry."

"Go ahead," Janice said. "We won't look."

"Liar," Gerry said.

Tom seemed to be asleep.

Bob kissed Jen, letting his tongue go deep into her mouth so that he could feel her tongue, her teeth, even the soft part of her palate. Her hips began to move and he placed his hand between her legs. He felt the muscles in her thighs quicken and she dug her fingernails into his arm. He kissed the top of her head. "Thank you," she whispered.

Janice was watching them. "Sorry. I couldn't help myself." She turned around.

Jen's father put her on restriction. Yes, he knew that her mother had said it was okay for her to stay over at the Crowes, or whatever their name is, but he knew, too, that Jen had avoided talking with him because she knew what his answer would be. Who were the Crowes anyway? Had he ever met them? No. Was he supposed to agree to her spending the night with strangers? Strangers to him, anyway. And where was Bob? Did he spend the night at the Crowes too? He didn't just drop you off, did he?

She was grounded for two weeks. She could go to school and then she had to come home. She couldn't go out at night. Bob could come over for dinner and they could watch television or play Monopoly or cards if they wanted, but that was all.

She was angry. She knew her father was angry too, and afraid of losing his daughter, and that he was reacting in the only way he knew, and she was sorry for him. But he made her feel like a little girl, and given all that she had experienced and the new things that she was experiencing almost every day, it seemed, she resented him for making her feel small again.

What Is Outside and What Is Inside
Can Work Together to Ruin You

The man who owned the apartment Tom and Bob lived in lived across the yard from them. He had built a coop in his attic for his pigeons. On weekends he raced them against pigeons owned by others in his club. He had become concerned that he was losing too many of his birds. He expected to lose one occasionally to a hawk or to weather, but he was losing one almost every week now. He told this to Tom who told it to Bob.

Tom felt bad. He liked the old man. He was kind enough not to insist on full payment of the rent when Tom shorted him. Since Harold had moved out to live with his fiancé and her family, Tom had not gotten anybody to replace him. He knew he should, but he did not want to deal with somebody new just now. It didn't help that Bob wasn't paying what he owed each month. When Tom said this, his tone was not one to accuse or induce guilt, but was the flat tone of acceptance of one of the facts of life.

Tom felt bad about the old man because he, Tom, had been killing his pigeons. The pigeons usually returned from their races on Sunday evening or Monday morning and they would congregate on the telephone lines before flying through the attic window to their coop. It was then, while they rested on the varicolored wire, that Tom would shoot one with a pellet gun he had borrowed from Harold. It was a matter of food. It was free meat, or almost free if you considered the cost of the gas it took to cook the birds. Tom tried not to do it too often, only once every couple of weeks, but obviously the old man had noticed the increase in the losses of his birds.

"How do you know he hasn't seen you shooting his pigeons?" Bob asked. "Why did he tell you about it?"

"We were just talking one day when I went over to pay the rent. If he had seen me, he would have said so."

"Maybe he's afraid you'll leave if you can't shoot his pigeons. Maybe he needs the rent money, even if we don't pay all of it. Maybe he's afraid you'll shoot him."

"I hope he's not afraid I'll shoot him. I like that old guy. I don't want him to be afraid of me."

"Tom Persons. Great White Hunter, Inc. Pigeons Our Specialty."

Tom laughed.

"So, Tom, why haven't you shared your bag with me?"

Bob found a job on an assembly line, putting together bobbers for fishing lines. On his second day, the owner of the shop was away and at noon the foreman turned off the conveyor belt, telling the ten or twelve people who worked on the line that they were all incompetent and he was firing everybody. They were welcome to come back tomorrow and reapply for their jobs if they wanted.

One by one, they punched out and filed through the doorway leading out of the building. One of them, a young blonde woman with a wide face and wide hips, did not leave with everybody else, but leaned against the wall by the time clock and observed them observing her as they passed their time cards through the machine. When the last of them had gone, the foreman locked the door from the inside.

"I'm going to come back tomorrow and tell the guy who owns this operation what a shithead for a foreman he has. This is no way to run a shop," one of the former assembly line workers, a man twenty or twenty-five years older than Bob, said.

"Won't do any good," another man said.

"It might. How do you explain firing everybody and then telling them they can reapply for their old jobs?"

"He'll deny he told you to reapply. It'll be his word against yours. Who do you think the boss will believe?"

Bob found another job, selling vacuum cleaners. The sales director put him with an experienced salesman for the first week.

The office had gotten an appointment for them by promising a gift to the householders if they listened to the entire presentation. The householders were an elderly couple who offered Art and Bob coffee and cookies. Bob sipped his coffee while Art went through his spiel. At the end, trying to impress the couple with the health advantages of this machine, as opposed to any other brand of vacuum cleaner, Art asked them, "How would you feel if you found out one day that you only had six months to live because you hadn't used this vacuum cleaner which picks up and traps almost one hundred percent of the dust in the average home?" It was a question the salesmen were required to memorize and ask as part of the wrap-up.

The couple looked at each other. Finally the man said, "I have six months to live. Less, maybe. I don't think your vacuum cleaner will be any help to me."

Bob set his coffee cup down.

After several seconds, Art said, "I didn't know. I'm very sorry."

He began to gather up the vacuum cleaner attachments he had demonstrated.

"Do we still get a gift?" the woman asked.

"Oh. Sorry. Of course you do."

Art took a small package out of his briefcase. It contained a pair of tiny ceramic salt- and peppershakers.

Art called the office from a gas station pay phone and explained what had happened. He said when he returned to the car, "They don't have any more appointments scheduled. They want us to go door to door. Personally, I'm not up for it. Want to get a beer?"

"I'm not old enough to go into a bar."

"How old are you?"

"Eighteen."

"They won't care."

He drove to a bowling alley on Katella a few minutes from the house where he had pitched the vacuum cleaner. They sat down at a table in the lounge and Art went up to the bar to get a pitcher. When he came back he was followed by two women in slacks and tops that stopped a little above their waist. Both appeared young and athletic, but as they got closer, Bob could see that they were older than they looked from a distance.

Art introduced them. "Bob. Sharla. Lorene." Sharla sat down across from Bob, Lorene in the chair at his right. Lorene's cheeks were marked with scars from acne. She had attempted to smooth over the pocks with pancake make-up. She had bleached her hair. Sharla's hair was dark brown and she had a round, clear face. Bob shook Lorene's hand, then Sharla's, and said hi to each.

"He's a writer too," Art said. "And he doesn't believe in God either."

"I don't remember saying that," Bob said.

"But you don't, do you?"

"No."

"So I got it right."

Lorene was staring at Bob intently. "What do you write?" she asked.

"Stories, mostly. A little poetry. Do you write?"

She nodded. She was searching his eyes for something.

"I write poetry too," she said. She took a steno pad out of her bag and thumbed through it. She asked, "Would you like to read some of it?"

"Sure."

She stopped flipping the pages. "That one," she said. "And the one after it."

The first poem was all tone and description: trash accumulated in alleyways, papers carried by the wind through city streets, the sky pressing down ominously. The second one conveyed a feeling of barely controlled rage. Bob was amazed that she was able to get it on paper. It had to do with something that had happened to somebody, presumably her. He could guess what it was. He had heard about some of the things that happen to women. To some women.

He didn't know what to say. He pretended to be studying the second poem while he tried to make something up.

"How old are you?" he asked.

She hesitated, then said, "Nineteen." She was lying.

"The first one is really effective at creating a mood," he said, recalling Mr. Amos' vocabulary of two summers ago. "It reminds me of my own writing. The second one is really angry. It's unusual for someone so young to be so angry." He didn't know why he said that. Maybe it had to do with the question, almost a pleading, in her eyes. Certainly he knew it wasn't true. He knew from his own writing the anger that resided in him.

But what lived inside her poem went far beyond anger. It disclosed a foundation of hate, of fear—fear of herself, of life. Bob had thought, if he thought about it at all, that rage was about something that happened to you, something imposed by the world outside. It had not occurred to him until this moment that what was outside and what was inside could work together to ruin you.

Bob didn't say any of this. He didn't want to let her know, if she didn't already know, how much of herself she had revealed. He said, "It isn't beautiful, but it's powerful. I'm going to remember it, at least the feel of it."

He handed her the steno pad. He didn't want to read any more.

"Thank you," she said. She seemed sincere; her eyes were glistening.

Bob was upset, by the poem and by Lorene's need. He wanted to change the subject. He said, "What do you do to make a living?"

For a moment she didn't say anything. Then she said, "We're models. Sharla and me. Sometimes we get an acting gig."

"If I were you, I wouldn't show that poem to just anybody."

She nodded. "I don't. But I wanted you to read it." She was staring at him as she had earlier.

Be careful, he told himself.

"Ready to go?" Art asked. He stood up. "We'll be back tomorrow," he said to Sharla.

"I'm not sure we'll be here," she said. "But maybe we will, if we finish early."

When Bob got up from his chair, Lorene stood up with him. She smiled and then she kissed him.

"You should wipe that off before your girlfriend sees it. Do you have a girlfriend?"

"Yes."

"I hope I see you again."

"They're hookers," Art said when they were in the car. "In case you hadn't guessed."

Bob hadn't. He hadn't thought about it. He didn't say anything.

"This is my last day," Art said. "I'm going to turn in my demo kit tomorrow. They don't know it yet. So I probably won't see you again."

"Why are you quitting?"

"I haven't sold anything in almost two months. I had three months where I was selling like wildfire. I couldn't do anything wrong. Clients were tripping over themselves to buy a vacuum cleaner from me. But lately I seem to have lost whatever I had before. I don't feel the connection with people that I had then. I should have picked up on something with that couple tonight. Not that I should have guessed that the old guy has cancer, but I should have picked up on something."

"Does he have cancer?"

"Doesn't he? He's dying of something; I assumed it was cancer. Maybe not. Anything will kill you, you get old enough."

"What are you going to do for work?"

"Something will turn up. But I enjoyed working with you today."

"I don't see you selling vacuum cleaners," Jen's father said. "No offense." He passed Bob the mashed potatoes.

"My problem was that I didn't want to try to sell something to somebody who didn't need it, or who didn't read English well enough to understand what they were signing."

"That's what I mean," David said. "I take it that a week is enough."

Bob nodded. "Maybe if I'd sold one, I would feel different."

"You could get a newspaper route," Peter said. "I'll let you use my bike." Everybody laughed, Peter too. But he was serious. Bob had taken it as a joke when Peter suggested it before, after he had been laid off from the tree-spraying job, but he saw now that Peter was trying to help him. He was touched.

"If I used your bike, what would you use?"

"You could get a morning route. Mine's in the afternoon."

"Do they deliver newspapers in the morning and the evening?"

Carol asked.

"Different papers deliver at different times."

"Oh. So somebody could read one newspaper in the morning and another at night to be sure he knew what was going on all the time."

"If he had the time to read two papers a day," David said.

"Some people take two newspapers. I don't know if they read both of them," said Peter.

Jen and Bob watched TV with her parents until they went to bed. Jen waited a few minutes, then went into her bedroom and changed into a muumuu. When she came out, Peter was coming out of the bathroom and he asked her why she had changed clothes.

"To make it easier for Bobby to feel me up," she whispered. She put her finger to her lips and made a "shhh" sound with her mouth.

"What did he say?" Bob asked when they were in the car.

"Nothing. He just stood there with his mouth open, and then he laughed. I overheard him and some of his friends talking about us the other day. About you and me. They wanted to know if we did it."

"What did Peter say?"

"He said he didn't know. But I think he knows. He just didn't want to tell them. He's so sweet. When you went to Porterville last summer—the first night you were gone—I went to bed and I was crying and he came in and laid his blanket on the floor and slept there. He must have heard me through the wall. He didn't say anything. He just knew I didn't want to be alone. Did I tell you this already?"

"No. And I didn't know you cried when I left."

"I didn't think you were coming back."

"Why? It never occurred to me not to."

"I know. But I couldn't help thinking that way. I didn't realize until that night that I had fallen in love with you. And then you went to San Francisco."

"Oh, Jen."

"It's all right. I was hurting at the time, but I'm all right now. I want to make you come. Are you getting close?"

"Not yet."

"If I talk dirty to you? Come on, baby. Come on, sugar, give me your stuff. Give me your wretched and huddled masses of sperm. Sorry. I got distracted. Think of my pussy. Think of my tits. Come on me, lover. Ooh, you did. It worked."

"Why didn't you tell me before that you were afraid I wouldn't come back?"

"I thought I did. I talk to you all the time in my mind. I must have thought I told you in a real conversation. Am I crazy? You'd better say no."

"You're not crazy. I talk with you in my head too. And I know I'm not crazy."

"Touch me. I want to come too."

"I was thinking about Mexico, that show we saw."

"You got really excited, didn't you? In Tijuana."

"It was as if that boy was eating my pussy. I was imagining myself on the stage with him. I could feel his tongue inside me. Does that bother you, that I could imagine making love with somebody else?"

"No."

"I had an orgasm, watching them. I could barely keep myself from screaming. Did you see me put my hands over my mouth?"

"I thought you did it because you were surprised at what was on the stage."

Jen laughed. "I was surprised, but it was because I was having an orgasm. I so wanted you to touch me."

"I didn't know."

"Would you have made love to me there if I had asked you to?"

"Sure."

"Really? In front of everybody? We've felt each other up when other people were around, but we've never fucked when somebody was watching."

"If you had wanted me to, I would have done it. Would you like to do that sometime?"

"I don't know. I like fantasizing about it, but I don't know if I could do it. Do you want to?"

"Actually, we did do it. On the way home. Janice was watching."

"But we weren't fucking. You were touching me up through my clothes. It would be different if we were doing it while we were naked and people were watching us."

"That time by Newport Beach," Bob said.

"Oh, yeah. But I wasn't aware they were watching us. But we didn't fuck then either, did we?"

"No. Tom may have seen us. In the car. He seemed to be asleep, but he may have been faking. But we had our clothes on."

"He saw us. He pretended to be sleeping because he didn't want to embarrass us."

"How do you know?"

"He told me. We had coffee together at school last week."

"Wow," Bob said.

"Is that important? That he saw us? Or that I had coffee with him?"

"I know you have coffee with him, but it feels strange, knowing that you talk to him about what we do."

"I don't usually. Just that once. And only because he had seen us. I wish I hadn't told you."

"Who brought it up?"

She thought for a moment. "I asked him if he had seen us because I needed to know if I should be embarrassed when I'm with him. No, that's not what happened. I had said that I knew he was embarrassed about making love with that woman in the club. I was trying to reassure him that nobody cared, that we all knew he needed to do it."

"God, he must have felt humiliated, you talking to him like that."

"Like what? I was only trying to reassure him."

"How did he respond?"

"He got really red. You know how light his skin is. He looked like he was on fire. Then he said he'd seen us, you and me, playing with each other on the way home from Mexico."

"He must have been really angry, to say that to you."

"I don't think he wanted to hurt me."

"You don't think he wanted to embarrass you like you had embarrassed him?"

"I didn't embarrass him. You mean by talking to him about the prostitute?"

"Sure. Why do you think he got red?"

"I thought it was because he was telling me he had seen us making love right next to him. I thought he was embarrassed for us."

"I didn't think about that. Maybe you're right. But why did he tell you? He saw us, but he didn't have to say anything about it."

Jen was quiet. Bob's hand was under her dress, resting on her bare hip. He moved it up to the small of her back.

"All right," she said, as though she had made up her mind about something. "He said that watching us had made him envious of us, our having each other, but of you especially. He said he wanted me to know that he thought I was desirable—'a very desirable young woman' is what he said—and that he was attracted to me, but that he wasn't going to ask me to make love with him because if he did, he would feel that he was betraying you."

Bob tried to think about what she had just said, but he couldn't. His thoughts wouldn't come together.

"What did you say?" he asked.

"I told him I was flattered that he thought I was desirable. I had never thought of myself that way. And I said I was glad that he had not asked me to make love with him because I would have had to say no, because I couldn't betray you either. Are you hurt? Your face looks funny."

"I think so. Yes."

"I'm sorry. I wanted to tell you. I've felt so guilty, even though we didn't do anything. I'm so sorry. I'll stop seeing him."

"Seeing him?"

"Meeting him for coffee. That's all we've been doing."

"No, don't do that. I know he means a lot to you. I don't want you to give him up."

"Oh, Bobby, thank you, thank you. I promise we won't do anything."

"Okay."

"Bobby? Let's get married. As soon as we can. If we were living together we could talk about things like this as soon as they came up. I've been living with this for a week because you were working and I was grounded. If we were married, we could talk to each other as soon as something happened and get it all out in the open."

"I need to think," Bob said.

"I know you're afraid we won't have enough money, but we will. Think of the money we'll save by not having to go to motels to make love."

"I don't know. I need to think."

"All right. God, you're hard. You don't always get this hard, do you?"

"I don't know. I feel like I want to jam it in you and drown your insides with my come."

She looked out the side window. "I'll sit on it. I don't think anybody's going to walk by."

She lowered herself onto him. He wondered what her experience was, how it felt to have him inside her. He wondered what her emotions were at this moment. She raised her hips and then lowered herself onto him again, and each time she came down on him he pushed up into her. He felt his penis grow even larger and he dug his fingers into her buttocks and then his penis opened in a burst of light and he was without either thought or sensation.

She was kissing his face—his eyelids, his forehead. "Are you all right? Bobby, my Bobby, tell me you're all right."

He began to breathe again, gasping, taking in huge drafts of air. He felt as though he had drowned, or nearly drowned, and now he was on the surface again, struggling to come back to himself. He could see Jen was panicked, but he didn't know why. He asked, "What's wrong?"

"Oh, Bobby. You made this terrible sound and then you started crying, you were sobbing, and then you just collapsed. I thought you had died."

"I was crying?"

She brushed her hand across his cheek. "Feel."

He touched her fingers with his. They came away wet.

"I don't remember crying."

He didn't say anything to Tom. He didn't know where the conversation would go once he opened it. He suspected Tom and Jen had made love, even though he also believed they hadn't, and he didn't want a confrontation that would force him to acknowledge that Tom was Jen's lover, no less than he was. Also, he wanted his relationship with Tom to be what it had been. He didn't want to carry the weight of distrust. If he put his suspicions out of his mind, it would be as though nothing had happened.

Bob and Jen Fantasize

He had some money from the temp jobs he'd worked, even the vacuum cleaner sales job because they had paid him for the training he'd attended before he went into the field, and he and Jen got a motel room.

"I love it when you come in me. Someday, when I learn how to suck you off, I want you to come in my mouth," she said.

"I'd like to fuck you in the ass again."

"Mm. I don't think I'm ready for that now."

"Okay."

"What do they call that when a girl sucks a boy's dick? It's cunnilingus when a boy eats a girl out, but I've forgotten the word for the other way around."

"Fellatio?"

"That's it. I'd like to get good at that."

"You could hold it in your mouth while you jack me off."

"I hadn't thought of that. Let's try it."

It took a couple of minutes to get the rhythm going between her hand and her mouth, but after she did, he relaxed and gave himself up to her.

She gagged again when he ejaculated. She couldn't stop coughing and he had to thump her on the back. Finally she stopped. "Jesus."

"Maybe you had it too far back in your mouth."

"It was touching the back of my throat. I didn't know you were going to come."

"How did it feel?"

"How do you think it felt? I thought I was going to choke to death."

"I mean how did it feel when my penis touched your throat?"

"Oh. I liked it. I don't know if I liked it because of the way it felt or because I knew I had it all the way in my mouth, but I liked it."

"When I use my tongue on you instead of my penis, it feels more intimate to me. As though I'm learning about you in a way I can't when I only use my penis."

"Me, too. I love the sensation of your penis on my lips. When it's in my mouth, I feel something I don't feel when it's in my pussy. And I feel like I'm the boss over you. I'll bet I know your penis better than you do. When it's in my mouth, it has to do what I tell it, although it did surprise me a few minutes ago. And I love it when you come on my skin. I feel it inside when you come, even if your penis isn't in me. Of course, I also love it when you come inside me. Sometimes, just before, your penis seems to grow so large that it fills my whole body."

"Wow. That's some penis."

"Well, it's yours. And it's mine too."

"Do you fantasize about things we haven't done?"

"Like what?"

"Like anything. Just something we haven't done that you might like to do. Or something that you might not want to do, but you still wonder about it."

"Give me an example."

"You want me to tell you one of mine? Okay. Here's one. We're in a bar or a tavern. Maybe it's in Mexico. I haven't been in a bar in the United States. I'm drunk. So are you. And another man who I don't know is with us. He must be a friend of yours.

Finally we decide to go home. I guess we're not in Mexico. We're married, you and I. And this man comes home with us. When we get home, you undress me while the other man watches. When I'm naked, you get undressed and you open my legs—I'm lying on the bed—and you get on top of me and go inside me without any foreplay. While you're fucking me, the other man takes his clothes off. He plays with himself while he watches us fuck, and I'm watching him. Finally you come and as soon as you get off me, he gets on and he fucks me while you watch. After he is finished, I suck you off and then I suck him off. In my fantasy I am an expert at blowjobs. Also, I never get tired. Okay, your turn."

"In mine, a man I don't know is fucking you from the rear. Maybe he's in your pussy, maybe he's in your ass, I can't tell. You are on your hands and knees on an unmade bed and he is pounding into you. I can see your breasts swing back and forth with the rhythm. I am there, sitting at the side of the bed, and you are looking at me, but you don't see me. You're looking at me, but your eyes are glazed with the pleasure this man is giving you."

"Your fantasy is supposed to be about you, not me. Both of our fantasies were about me."

"They were about me too, in a way."

"Okay. In this one, I am a little girl and my cousin and I are playing in the barn. He is only a little older than me. He is twelve, I think, and I am probably nine or ten. Then he says he wants to play you-show-me-yours-and-I'll-show-you-mine, and he tells me to take my clothes off and he takes his clothes off. He is beginning to get pubic hair—it's dark brown—and he has an erection. I have never seen a boner before, and I touch it without even asking him and almost immediately it spurts out this creamy stuff. I get some on my finger and I taste it. I think it was salty, but I don't remember for sure. Afterward, whenever we had a chance, we would go into the barn and play with each other."

"You don't remember if it was salty? Is this a fantasy, or did it really happen?"

"It really happened and I've fantasized about it."

"What happened to him?"

"He's still in Mississippi. He's a farmer. He writes me every once in a while. Okay, now you tell me one that really happened."

"Are you sure? I tried to once, but you told me to stop."

"Oh, yeah. We can try it again. Maybe I'm more mature now."

"All right. This is about Sherry. She had a girlfriend who went to college with her and also lived in Fullerton. There must have been something about the way we were making out, Sherry and me, that she was unhappy with or not satisfied with. Maybe she was worried that she wasn't satisfying me, because she asked Susan to watch while we made out. I thought that was weird, but I didn't really care. So we started kissing—we were in this old Buick that my parents used to have—and Sherry straddled my leg as she usually did and began to rub herself against me."

"Rubbing against you like a dog?"

"I hadn't thought about it like that, but, yeah, I guess so. I looked at Susan but she looked away as soon as Sherry got on my leg. After a minute or so—it was probably only a few seconds—Susan said she'd call her later, and she left. I must have said something because Sherry said, 'That's okay,' and she just kept rubbing herself against me. I could tell she was close to climaxing—that was what we called it, 'climaxing' instead of 'coming'—and I slid my hand down to feel her. I had never done this before and I expected her to tell me not to, but she didn't, she just kept going. She was wet all the way through her shorts—she was wearing Bermuda shorts. Finally she stopped. She just kind of collapsed against me. She kept saying my name."

"She came."

"Yes. It was interesting. After that, she let me touch her there whenever we made out—"

"Touch her pussy."

"Yeah—"

"Did she ever come before that? With you, I mean."

"I don't know. For sure, not as strongly, if she did. So afterward, when we made out, I would touch her between her legs, but she never let me feel her breasts with my hands, not even after we had intercourse, not until the last time I saw her, and then only for a minute or two."

"With your hands?"

"She used to let me kiss them through her bra."

"So what was the thing with Susan? Did she ever come back?"

"Not to watch us. I'm not sure what it was about, but the next time I saw Sherry, after she climaxed she asked me if there was anything she could do for me. She had never asked before, so I assume Susan had been there to kind of critique her."

"Was she there when Sherry came?"

"No. She left before that. I think she saw more than she expected to see."

"I'll bet she did. What did you tell Sherry when she asked if she could do something for you?"

"I said no. I didn't know what she was talking about."

"Was she asking if she could jack you off, or if you wanted her to suck you?"

"I think she was probably offering to jerk me off, but at the time I didn't realize it. I had never masturbated, so I didn't know—"

"What? When did you start masturbating?"

"Not until you and I started going out. I learned how to do it from you."

"I don't believe you."

"It's true. Oh, wait. Sara did me once. I forgot."

Jen slapped his arm. She started to cry. "Not fair! First you give me something, then you take it away."

"What? What did I take away?"

"First you tell me that I was the first one—the only one!—to bring you off, and then you tell me, 'Oh, wait, Sara did it first.' Can't you see how that would hurt me?"

"I'm sorry."

"You should be. Oh God, I'm never going to grow up. This shouldn't be bothering me. You're so much more mature than I am. I'm so afraid of losing you, and you can just assume you'll always have me. And you're right."

Does Anybody Know What He's Doing?

Harold came by to remind them that he existed, or himself that they did. Tom told him Bob was thinking of getting married.

"To Jen?"

"Who else?" Tom said.

Harold nodded as though he had been asked for his judgment and now he was giving it: "I like Jen." Then he asked Bob, "Are you working?"

"No."

"Do you love her?"

"I do."

Harold began to berate him about love. Bob did not know anything about love, Harold said, not even what it was, because he was too young to know. Bob challenged him to define love. Harold said love is when a man accepts the responsibility of providing for his wife and their children, when they had them. That is love. That and the ability to provide for them. Responsibility and ability. Together they comprise love.

Bob didn't think that a sense of responsibility or the ability to hold a well-paying job had anything to do with love. Love, he said, is an emotional experience and that's all, though that's everything. Love can be experienced by anybody; it doesn't matter what his abilities are. "Love is irrational," Bob said, recalling Fred Muller's saying so.

"No," Harold said. "Love is rational."

"I agree with Bob," Tom said. He had sat down at the table and was nursing a cup of black coffee. "Love makes no sense, but there it is."

"Maybe it makes no sense to the two of you, but to the rest of the world, it makes perfect sense," Harold said.

Tom ignored him. "Love is lust," he said. "There's no difference. Ask Bob."

"I think love makes sense," Bob said, "but at a real primitive level, not at the level of trying to rationalize it."

"Without lust there would be no children," Tom said. "The species would die out. Without love, I mean."

"So you believe that love is a way of understanding how evolution works?" Harold said.

"Hell, yes! Without love we wouldn't exist!"

"Are you drunk?"

"Yes, I'm drunk. Do you think I'd be talking like this if I wasn't drunk?"

Harold laughed, and Bob did too.

Bob called Karen. They met for coffee at the Copper Kettle where she had been a waitress the summer after they got out of high school, before she started college. She was thinner now and seemed to have confidence in herself that she hadn't had before.

They had been good friends in high school, but it had been a while since they had talked and the conversation was awkward. As they fumbled with reminiscences and observations about how each of them had changed, a guy in his twenties passed the table and smiled at her, but also shook his head.

"I went out with him last Saturday. I was wearing this sweater." She looked down at her pink angora sweater. "When we got back to the car, we made out, and it shed all over his jacket." She laughed. It was a funny memory.

He was her boss when she worked here. There was a cook who

also worked here then. One day, during her break, he pulled her into the kitchen and kissed her, thrusting his tongue into her mouth. She found herself responding. It was as though he could see inside her in a way other people could not, as though he saw something in her that she did not want people to know was there. Bob thought he knew what she was talking about. They had been drinking when she told him; that was a couple of years ago.

She told her boss what the cook had done and he fired the cook that day after his shift ended. She had not intended for the cook to be fired. She had not thought what her boss' reaction would be when she told him. At first she felt bad, but then that feeling was replaced by one of gratitude toward her boss. That was why she went out with him when he asked her. But she did not think he would ask her out again.

If he did, would she go?

Probably, she said.

Bob asked her to come over on Thursday night. Tom had a night class then. "I'll make dinner," Bob said.

Karen laughed again. "I'll bring a pizza."

Her breasts tasted of vanilla. The nipples and aureoles tasted and smelled the same as the fleshier parts of her breasts, even though, so much darker, they looked as if they should taste stronger. Her breasts were heavier than Jen's and sat in his hands like soft vessels. When he took one of her nipples in his mouth, she placed her hand on the back of his head and stroked his hair as Jen sometimes did with him, as he had seen her do with Phil.

Her neck tasted of salt and the sun's heat, and he licked it, though his tongue tickled her and she giggled and moved her shoulder to try to protect her neck from him. Her hair smelled of sweet herbs from the shampoo or conditioner she used, but beneath this smell was another that made him feel sad as he kissed her head.

She was naked and she sat beside him, naked too, on the edge of the bed and held his erect penis while he slid his finger between her labia. After a while he heard her gasp and he asked her if she had come. She shook her head.

"Can I come inside you?"

She nodded and kissed his neck.

"I don't have a rubber."

"That's all right."

She moved back on the bed and opened her legs so that he could see the shining black hair between them, and she held out her arms and he slipped between them and between her legs. Afterward she said, "Come again sometime," and he nodded yes and emitted a small laugh.

She was in the bathroom and he was only half-dressed when Tom came home. Karen came out of the bathroom and Bob introduced them and then she left. Bob thought for a moment of asking Tom not to say anything to Jen, but then decided not to. He thought Tom would do what he would do, regardless of what Bob might ask or what Tom might promise. And he did not want to abase himself by further indebting himself to Tom.

Later that night, Tom asked, "Are you sure you know what you're doing?"

"Does anybody know what he's doing?" Bob said.

He's Hooked a Cottonmouth!

Bob had parked his car and was going back to the apartment when he saw Tom walking with a bag of groceries. Bob stopped and waited for him.

"There's a guy following me," Tom said. "An old man. He started talking to me in the market and he thinks he hasn't finished yet."

"Here he is," Bob said, watching him approach Tom from behind. He was a small man in his sixties or seventies, wearing a dark blue baseball cap with an insignia Bob didn't recognize, a light blue long-sleeve shirt, and a tie the color of his cap. High up on the left sleeve of his shirt was the same insignia that was on his cap.

"He's a rent-a-cop," Tom said. "He works at the bank, right?"

The old man said, "Bank of America. Yes sir. But I'm getting ready to retire. Going home."

"He's from Arkansas," Tom said. "He thinks everything is going to be like he left it."

"How long ago did you leave?" Bob asked.

"Thirty years almost. I haven't been back, but my sister's still there, and her kids and grandkids."

"It's not going to be like you remember it," Tom said.

"It'll be exactly like it was the last time I saw it," the old man said.

"Your sister's been lying to you."

The old man did not flinch and his expression did not change. He said, "The creek's still there. It still has catfish. Turtles. I caught a water moccasin there one night when I was a boy. Hooked him by the tail. At first, before I got him out of the water, I thought I'd got a turtle, it was so heavy. That's what the big people were saying. 'You've got yourself a snapping turtle.' But then I got it out of the water and it swung over the fire they'd built to fry the fish we'd caught and I didn't know from nothin' until I heard my uncle yell, 'He's hooked a cottonmouth! Got him by the tail!' and then I could see all that white in its mouth as it swung back and forth over the fire, and my daddy said, 'Drop him in the fire!' and he come running over and grabbed my rod away from me and the next time the snake swung over the fire, he dropped it in, and my uncle had his machete and just started chopping it. The snake was trying to get out of the fire and my daddy was throwing rocks on it and Uncle Charles was chopping it with his machete that he brought back from the Philippines when he was in the Marines. And they were both laughing."

The old man stopped talking. After a minute, Tom said, "They're all dead now. Your father and your uncle and the snake."

The old man again did not flinch, but he said with determination, "That's so, but the creek is still there."

"It probably got paved over for a shopping center," Tom said. "Or it's been rerouted so it's nowhere like how you remember it."

"No sir," the old man said. "It's exactly where it always was."

"Fuck you," Tom said.

That was when Bob knew he'd been drinking. Tom could drink a lot, and he liked vodka, and you couldn't always tell when he was drunk. But sometimes something extravagantly cruel would pop out of his mouth and then you knew.

The old man walked away in the direction of the market, and Tom and Bob went up the stairs to the apartment. "Somebody push the button," Tom said when they were inside.

Part Two
(1962)

We Can Drive Down to Mexico

Jen called from school at midmorning. Last night, she said, her father had given his okay for her to get married. She had rebutted every argument he had against it until finally he had none left to offer. How would they live? he had asked. Bobby's always been able to find something in order to get by, and the economy is improving; everybody says so. Where would they live? There are always cheap places to rent if we're willing to live in them, and we are, at least for now. What about Bobby's wanting to travel? Is he going to give that up, or will he take you with him? He just went to San Francisco without you, for Christ's sake. I think he's given up on that. He's talking about going to college now. Oh? And what about your college? How will you be able to afford it? Everything's paid for this semester and I have the books I need, thanks to you. What if you get pregnant, Jen? That would change everything. Other people manage it; look at you and mom. We would, too.

"Did you tell him we've been screwing for months and you haven't gotten pregnant yet?"

"No, I didn't tell him that. He was being very nice, even though he was upset. Why would I want to upset him even more?"

"What about your mom? What did she say?"

"She didn't say anything. She was just smiling all the time Dad and I were talking. I think she was remembering when she was my age."

"How old was she when she got married?"

"Eighteen. So, what do you want to do?"

"Let's do it," Bob said on impulse. Or maybe it was not impulse, or not only. Maybe he had just grown tired of talking about it over the last months, as her father had. Maybe he had simply grown dissatisfied with his life and wanted a change. Or maybe he was hoping for some stability. Thinking back on this moment fifteen years later, he could not remember what had prompted him to decide as he had. Certainly he loved her. And the prospect of making love with her as often as they wanted was appealing. But if anyone had asked him at the time why he did what he did, he would not have known what to say.

Still later, he realized that he had wanted to marry Jen because he didn't want to lose her. You're drawn to someone because of the shape of her smile and the cant of her breasts or the way she walks or because she's slightly pigeon-toed, and then none of that matters because you've fallen in love with her for other reasons altogether, for reasons you can't even identify. You marry because you don't want to lose her, you don't want to lose the love she brings or the experience of loving her. You marry because when you imagine your life without her, there is emptiness. By the time he had learned this, he had learned also that the women he was most attracted to always wanted something from him that he could not give, or did not want to give.

"We can drive down to Mexico and do it there," Bob said. "Tom can be our witness. I'll ask him."

"When should we do it?"

"We can do it today. I'll ask Tom if he'll do it. I think he's at school now. If we can't do it today, we'll do it tomorrow."

"I have a class in a few minutes. I'll come over after that. I'll skip my afternoon classes."

"Okay."

"Bobby? I thought you would come up with a bunch of reasons why we shouldn't get married now."

"I guess I can if you want me to. Do you not want to do it?"

"I guess I won't be having a big wedding now."

"I didn't know you wanted one. We never talked about the kind of wedding we'd have. We can wait."

"It's okay. Just as long as you're there."

He laughed. He felt giddy.

Jen and Tom arrived at the apartment at the same time. They walked up the stairs together, smiling and laughing.

"I already asked him," Jen said.

"I'll be glad to," Tom said.

"I assume we're talking about you being our witness," Bob said.

"Yes. Do you want to do it today?"

"Why not?"

"Okay. Let me make a sandwich. I'll eat it on the way down."

"Are you hungry?" Bob asked Jen.

She shook her head. "I'm too nervous to eat."

"You're sure you want to do this?"

"Don't you?"

"I do. I'm just asking."

"It's what we've been talking about."

"Your lives are going to change," Tom said.

"Tonight I'll be an honest woman," Jen said.

"I have other news," Bob said. "Just after we talked, a place where I applied months ago called. I'd completely forgotten about them. I've got a job. Warehouseman. It pays two-fifty an hour. I start Monday. I'll be able to pay you the rent I owe in a couple of weeks," he said to Tom.

"You got a job. And on the same day we're getting married. I can't believe it. It's a sign that we should do it," Jen said.

"Everything's coming together for you guys," Tom said.

On the way down to Tijuana they stopped at a shopping center and found a department store and Bob bought a gold band that was only a little too large for Jen's finger. The clerk said they could have it resized later, if they were in a hurry now. It was apparent that they were.

Bob picked a storefront and they went inside and he asked the man there if he was the lawyer and he said he was and Bob said they wanted to get married. The lawyer asked them to sit down and he gave them a form to sign. Bob signed it and Jen signed and then Tom and the lawyer signed and the lawyer said, "Now you are married. It will be fifty dollars."

Bob paid him. He asked how this worked—wasn't there supposed to be a ceremony or something? As soon as he registered the documents there will be a proxy wedding in Mexico City, the lawyer said, and then everything will be legal, but they should think of themselves as legally married now because they had already signed the registration form and paid the required fee. He would send the form in this afternoon. He gave Bob an embossed certificate on which he had typed his and Jen's names.

On the sidewalk, Bob asked, "Do you want to get a drink?"

Tom shook his head.

Jen said, "Let's just go home."

Neither Tom nor Jen nor Bob spoke again until they had passed through Border Control. Finally Jen said, "That was fast."

"It was kind of sterile," Tom said.

"I don't know what I feel," Jen said.

"Do you feel married?" Tom asked Bob.

"I don't know. What does feeling married feel like?"

Jen didn't say anything.

They stopped at a Denny's north of San Diego and after they had eaten a little they began to feel better. They joked about the officiousness of the *abogado* or *licensiado* or whatever translated to lawyer, and made fun of his obesity.

"A lot of couples must go to him to get married if he can afford to eat so much," Jen said.

"Marriage must be a growth industry down there," Bob said.

"Oh jeez."

"A girth industry," Tom said.

"Not you, too," Jen said.

Bob had the gold band in his shirt pocket. He took it out now and slipped it over the ring finger on Jen's left hand. There had been no occasion in the lawyer's office to allow for giving it to her. He kissed her.

They dropped Tom off at the apartment and then they rented a motel room for the night. Bob registered them as "Mr. and Mrs. Robert Givens."

"Did he ask to see proof that we're married?" Jen asked when they were in the room.

"No. They don't care. Wait. Come here."

He led her outside and picked her up in his arms and carried her back inside and set her down on the bed.

"Like a sack of potatoes," she said.

"This is our wedding night. I'm trying to be romantic."

"Would you just hold me for a minute?"

He lay down beside her and put his arms around her.

After a while she said, "I need to call my parents."

She spoke to her mother first, and then to her father. She told them where she and Bob were and that they had gotten married in Mexico. After a few minutes Bob could tell she was talking to Peter. She promised to see him tomorrow.

"I feel better now," she said after she hung up. "I want to take a shower."

She went into the bathroom. In a moment her head appeared at the edge of the jamb. "Hey. This will be the first night that we actually sleep together. I like that," she said.

"I'm sorry," she said. "I don't know why I can't."

"It's okay."

"Would you lie on top of me? I just want to feel your weight on me. Thank you."

His penis was stiffening and he began to push against her. "Tell me if you want me to stop."

"It's like the first time we tried to do it," she said.

Her eyes were closed. She smelled like a little kid again. It had been a long time since he had noticed that smell on her. He was inside her. He felt as though he were violating her.

"What's wrong?" she asked.

He shook his head. When he was close to ejaculating, he made himself think of something else until his thrusts became less frenetic and he returned to a steady rhythm. After he did this twice, she asked, "Don't you want to come?"

"Yes," he said, although he didn't want to until he was certain that she was feeling pleasure too.

"Do it. I want you to come in me. Do you want me to talk dirty to you? Do you want me to hold your balls? Ah, ah. There it is. Sleep now, my darling husband. We'll wake up together in the morning."

At breakfast in the restaurant on the other side of the motel parking lot, she said, "You raped me."

"What? When?" He thought she might have meant in a dream.

"Last night. When do you think? I didn't want to do it. You

forced yourself on me."

She didn't appear angry. And the way she phrased it—"You forced yourself on me"—was she recounting something, maybe a piece of dialogue from a book? He didn't know what to think.

"It's okay. Once you were inside me, I liked it."

He had stopped eating.

"Can I have your bacon?" she asked. Then she said, "I said it was okay. It's just something more that we can add to our repertoire. It only hurt until I was lubricated. I knew you weren't going to hit me or anything."

He dropped her at her parents' house. Her mother opened the door.

He went back to the apartment. Tom was gone. He took a nap because he couldn't think of anything else to do.

When he woke he went out to the market a couple of blocks away and bought a newspaper.

Jen came over and a few minutes later, Tom returned. Perhaps because he had been with them when they eloped, Bob felt Tom was part of their marriage.

"There's an apartment about four blocks from here," Bob said.

"So fast," Jen said. "I thought I'd be living at home for a while."

"We ought to look at it before we make up our minds."

She nodded. "Maybe we won't like it."

But they did like it. It was a second-floor, furnished flat in a very old building. It had a high ceiling and windows on one side that let in the morning light and it offered a glimpse of the shops on Harbor Boulevard a block and a half away. It had a large, tiled kitchen and a large living room into which opened a Murphy bed, and it had a bathroom with a claw-foot tub.

The landlady asked Bob where he worked and he told her and she said they looked like a nice couple so she wouldn't ask them for the last month's rent, only the first month's and the security deposit. She said they would be the youngest people in the building and she hoped they wouldn't have noisy parties. Bob assured her that they would be quiet, that Jen was going to college and he was working and they didn't have time for parties. The landlady looked pleased and took ten dollars off the rent. She said if they needed more furniture, another chair maybe, she had some in the basement they could choose from.

Bob said they could move in tomorrow. He would go to the bank and withdraw some money for the rent and begin moving their clothes and stuff in while Jen was in school, and then they would spend their first night there. The landlady was agreeable.

They had dinner at Jen's parents'. Peter was glum. Finally David asked him what was wrong. Peter said he couldn't believe Jen was moving out.

Jen made a small "oh" sound and rushed around the table to where Peter was sitting and hugged him. She assured him that she would visit often, and he could visit her and Bob whenever he wanted.

David appeared to be in a light-hearted mood, especially after Jen told him Bob would begin his new job on Monday.

"So you'll be able to take care of my daughter in the manner to which she would like to become accustomed?"

When Bob did not immediately respond, Carol put in, "He's not kidding."

"Yes, I am," David said. "So, what kind of job?"

"Warehouseman. I'll have to join a union."

"'Warehouseman' can cover a variety of sins. Did they tell you exactly what you'll be doing?"

"All he said was that it requires some physical strength. But I'm pretty strong."

David nodded. He changed the subject. "Well, what did you think of Tijuana?"

For a moment Bob thought Jen was going to tell him they'd been there before, but she said, "It's really dirty. It looks as if they never sweep the sidewalks."

"That's how I remember it too. And the crowds of tourists. It's been a long time since we've been there. Your mother and I went there after we moved to California. We left you kids with the neighbors. We spent the day down there and when we got back you didn't even know we'd been gone. All you could talk about was riding your bike with the neighbor kids."

"I didn't have a bike," Peter said. "I was too little. I remember riding after Jen on my trike and her riding away without me."

"But I came back," Jen said. "I wasn't gone for very long. And you had Mr. and Mrs. McPherson to look after you."

"You remember their names," Carol said. "I've been trying to think what their names were."

"They probably still are," David said.

"What do you mean?"

"They probably haven't changed their names. So, where are you going to stay tonight? The same place as last night?"

"We're going to Bobby's apartment. We'll spend the night there and then move into our new place tomorrow. Or Bobby will while I'm at school."

"We'll get you some things this weekend," Carol said. "Don't buy anything until you see what we get you. Take some sheets and pillowcases and things to tide you over the next couple of days."

"I'm going to take your bedroom," Peter said. "It's bigger than mine."

Bob parked in the lot behind the apartment and was about to get out of the car when Jen said, "I don't think I can do this. Can we get a motel room?"

"Do what?"

"I don't think I can sleep with you, knowing Tom is on the other side of the wall."

"He knows we make love. He's seen us, for Christ's sake."

"I know, but I just can't."

"Could you go to bed with him if I was on the other side of the wall?"

"That's not fair."

"It is fair."

"Oh, Bobby, let's not argue. Especially not tonight. Won't you just take me to a motel?"

He closed the door and started the engine.

"Are you angry with me?"

"What do you think?"

"I'm sorry. I wish I could explain it to you, but I don't understand it myself."

"What don't you understand? You've fallen in love with him, that's all."

"Not the way I love you."

"How not? You went to bed with him, didn't you?"

"I did not! I wouldn't. I told you that."

"Uh huh."

"If you thought I was sleeping with Tom, why did you marry me?"

"Because I love you and want to live with you. That's what you said you wanted too."

"It is what I want. Oh God. I can't believe we're fighting."

They were in the motel lot. Bob went into the office to register. Back in the car, he said, "We can leave your clothes and things in the trunk." Then he saw that her face was shiny; she had been crying.

"What do you want to do?" he said.

"Let's go inside."

She opened her door.

They lay on the bed in their clothes. After a while, they took their clothes off down to their underwear and slipped under the blankets. Jen took off her bra but left her panties on. She looked at him, then crept under his arm. Her hand found the fly of his shorts and slipped inside and grasped his penis. Bob watched her until her eyes closed and she began to breathe with a slow rhythm. Then he went to sleep too.

The room was filled with thin morning light. Jen was staring at his face as she stroked his penis. "Wake up." There was an urgency in her voice. "I want you inside me."

He took her head in his hands and kissed her mouth. She sucked on his tongue, not allowing him to withdraw it, while she continued to grip his penis. Finally she pushed him away and turned and raised herself on her knees and elbows.

He entered her from behind.

"Not there," she said. "Or there, but not only there."

"I don't want to hurt you."

"I want you to. Talk to me. Tell me what you want to do to me. Tell me you want to fuck me in the ass."

"I want to fuck you until you scream. Here, put your hand there. After I fuck you in your pussy I'm going to fuck you in the ass. Rub yourself. I want to hear you come."

"I can't," Jen said. "I'm sorry."

Bob withdrew. He inched up behind her and placed the head of his penis against her anus.

"It hurts."

"Should I stop?"

"Yes."

"I don't think I can get it inside. I don't want to hurt you."

"Yes you do. But stop."

She faced away from him and, gripping his penis, lowered herself gingerly onto it. She rose, then lowered herself again. Each time, as he watched, she took more of it inside her. It seemed as though his penis were not his, but hers, and that she was pushing it into him. And then it seemed that it was neither hers nor his, but was something independent of both of them. Her breath was coming in shallow measures. He began to move his hips. "Wait," she said. She took her hand from his penis and swiveled slowly around. It fell out of her. "Damn it," she said. When she was facing him, she took it and placed it inside her again and sat back on it. "I want to look at you," she said. He started to move again and she removed her hand from his penis and leaned forward, and he pushed slowly into her.

"Can you come?" she asked.

"Yes."

He moved faster, then faster still, grasping the flesh of her hips. Her scent filled the room. At last he released. He lay back, trying to catch his breath. Jen straightened, his penis still inside her. She raised her hips so that he could see his semen easing down the shaft of his softening erection, and then she lowered herself back down on it and sat without moving until it slipped out of her.

She lay beside him. He kissed her eyelids.

"We should shower," she said. "I'll go first."

When she came out of the bathroom, she asked, "Did all of that smell come from me?"

"Most of it, I think."

"Do I always smell that way?"

"Sometimes when we do it anally. Sometimes, too, when we've done it doggy style, even if I haven't touched your butt. Usually you have other smells."

"I know those. Those are the ones we make together when we fuck in the regular way."

You Ever Been Locked Up?

The foreman was called Ace. He walked Bob around the floor of the warehouse, pointed out the time clock and showed him how to punch in and out, warned him to be careful of the forklifts—"The drivers might not see you if they're carrying a load"—took him past the machines that poured a hundred and six to a hundred and twelve pounds of white trinity powder into reinforced paper bags, and pointed out how the men handled them by gripping the bags' diagonally opposite corners and tossing them onto a pallet with a swinging motion so that they offered only minimal resistance. But even so, Ace warned, it was a hundred and six pounds, each one.

Be careful how you breathe, he said. It's like lifting weights; you need to exhale with the effort. "We don't want you herniating yourself." He pointed out that some of the men working the machines were wearing air-filtration masks, but others were not. "Everybody on the machines or in the boxcars is supposed to be wearing a mask." He told a man without a mask to put one on and he and a couple of others who were not wearing them got some off a shelf beside the water cooler and slipped them over their faces. The masks covered their nose and mouth. Bob noticed that everyone had heavily muscled arms and shoulders.

Ace asked, "What do you weigh?"

"One sixty-five."

Ace nodded. "You'll be on probation for your first month. This is a closed shop. After your first month you'll have to start paying dues to the union. We'll start you in the boxcars. Get yourself a mask and I'll introduce you to the crew."

A railroad track ran along the far side of the warehouse. The forklifts brought the pallets of trinity to the dock and the boxcar crew unloaded the bags and restacked them in the boxcars. When they could, they used the same swinging motion to restack the bags that the men at the machines used to palletize them. But the first bags into the boxcar were placed in the corners and against the sides, and these had to be lugged in by brawn. Some of the men carried two bags at a time. The man Bob worked closest to, John, carried only one because he had a bad back, he said.

Ace watched them for a few minutes and then he went back inside the warehouse. When he was gone, several men pulled their masks down so that they hung off their neck. "It's too hard to breathe with these on," John said. Bob removed his too.

A man who continued to wear his said, "You do this long enough without a mask, your lungs turn to cement."

"Then I'll sue 'em," John said.

"Your widow will enjoy the settlement."

Bob had brought a couple of sandwiches and a small bag of potato chips and an apple for lunch, but when he had eaten them he was still hungry.

"A sandwich truck will be by in a minute," one of the men said. "It's late. It'll pull up over there." He pointed to a spot on the other side of the railroad track. When it came, Bob bought a burrito and a cup of coffee.

By mid-afternoon Bob didn't think he could continue, but he did, although he lagged behind the others.

In the morning his arms were sore and his body was reluctant to move. At lunch John told him that some of the others had thought he wouldn't be back. John personally was glad Bob had decided to gut it out. By next week he would be in condition, John said.

The afternoon was better than it was on Monday: Bob's body continued to obey him where by midday the day before, it had begun to rebel. He had eaten a larger lunch and did not feel as tired as he did yesterday. Still, at the end of the day he was too exhausted to make love, or even to talk with Jen before falling asleep.

Some time before dawn he awoke tremendously aroused. Jen was naked beside him, lying on her stomach. He slid his hand between her legs. "Raise your hips," he whispered.

He plunged into her without restraint and she emitted a small groan. He pushed in again, but slowly. Her hand went down to her mound. She came and Bob withdrew and turned her onto her back and returned inside her. She hooked her ankles on the backs of his legs. He could feel her nails dig into his buttocks. He felt like a machine, as though his penis were a piston driving into her in an unvarying rhythm. She came again, but a moment later she put her hands against his chest and started pushing him. He didn't know what she wanted, and continued on. He was approaching frenzy. "Stop. It hurts too much."

When he stopped, she said, "I came four times."

"Four?" He remembered only two.

"Do you want me to suck you? Give me a minute to rest first."

He crawled up until he was straddling her chest and he began to stroke himself.

"What do you want me to do?" she asked.

He didn't know what to ask for. He said, "Touch your breasts. I want to watch you enjoying your body."

In a moment, he ejaculated on her breasts.

"That was so exciting, Bobby."

He was lying beside her. "What time is it?"

She turned toward the alarm clock. "It's five-fifteen."

"I have to get some sleep."

"I was dreaming that you were fucking me, and then you were."

"I really do need to get some sleep. I'm sorry."

It was hard to get out of bed and he was late to work. He punched in and went out to the boxcars and took his place with the crew he had been working with. He knew Ace had noticed, but he didn't say anything. A short, barrel-shaped man named Bruno said, "Couldn't resist knocking off a piece, huh?"

The others grinned, but kept moving.

"You don't want to be late too often. Ace sees everything."

Bob still felt strong when they broke for lunch. He found a place to sit on a palletized stack of trinity next to Bruno.

"You got a life outside of work?" Bruno asked.

"I do some writing when I can. It's been a while though."

"Yeah? What do you write?"

"Stories, mostly."

"No shit? I used to write poetry. Still do, occasionally. Mostly I work with wood now. Sometimes clay. I sculpt. Keeps me sane."

Bob nodded. "I know the feeling."

"Yeah? You ever been locked up?"

"In jail, you mean?"

"Well, maybe. But I meant in a facility for crazy people. For people who are nuts."

"No," Bob said.

"Then you probably don't know how it feels to be crazy. Psychotic. Actually," he laughed, "it can feel pretty good."

Bob didn't say anything.

Bruno said, "Sometimes you can't tell if you're being nuts or not, until you see what you're doing. You know, like you're standing outside of yourself, observing yourself? One time I was up at Big Bear, working on a piece—sculpting, I mean; I'm not talking about a woman—and I stayed an extra day because I wanted to try to finish it, and it snowed that night. The road was slick as shit and I slid off almost as soon as I started down the mountain and I couldn't get out of the ditch. I was so pissed off, I ripped the windshield wipers off the fuckin' car. Trying to finish that carving before I left, everything had gone to hell and I felt like everything I'd ever done in my life—everything artistic, I mean, maybe everything else, too—it was all worthless. Worse than worthless." He sighed. "That's when I knew I'd gone crazy again, when I tore the windshield wipers off. So I figured I might as well go all the way and I got my axe out of the trunk and smashed the headlights. Fuckin' car was lookin' at me, you know? Then I chopped off the mirrors on the sides. The sideview mirrors. So it couldn't hear what I was doin'. Then I figured, what the hell, I might as well go back to the cabin and finish the sculpture I was working on, and I walked back and chopped it up. Probably if I hadn't already had the axe in my hand I wouldn't have done it. But…" He shrugged. "It got pretty cold that night, so I needed firewood anyway. Although I already had a couple of cords outside. I spent six months of weekends working on that piece. So in the morning I called the sheriff and he sent a deputy over to get me. They knew me from other times they had to pick me up. They knew I wasn't dangerous. Not to people anyway. Not to other people."

The other men were beginning to move about. It was time to get back to work. Bob stood up. Bruno remained sitting on a bag of trinity. Then Ace was there. He said, "You need to load two thousand bags today. You only did seven hundred this morning, so you have your work cut out for you."

"One of the machines was down," a man said.

"I know," Ace said, "but you still need to load thirteen hundred bags by five o'clock."

Bruno remained where he was and Ace sat down next to him and talked to him. After a minute or two, Bruno stood up and walked over to the boxcar. Bob thought that when he saw Justin again, he would tell him about Bruno, about Bruno's standing outside of himself, watching himself, like the guy who worked for Justin's father had done. The guy who cut his own nuts off.

John whispered to Bob, "Ace cuts him a lot of slack."

They were close to finishing when Bob realized that he and John had gotten into a rhythm, heaving the bags from the pallet at the edge of the loading dock to the inside of the boxcar. The bags were stacked close enough to the door now that they did not have to walk to get the next one, but had only to swivel to grab one by its corners from the stack outside and swing it onto the stack inside. It was as if they had become part of a musical score that regulated the speed at which they moved and even the movements themselves, as though they were dancers in a dance that had been choreographed ages before the afternoon in which they were working. When they ran out of bags, Bob felt the impulse to grab John by his crotch and shoulder and toss him on top of the pile, but held himself back. He wondered if John had felt the same impulse.

They were finished. It wasn't five yet. Ace was pleased and told them they could leave early.

"Saved the company a few bucks by having us punch out early," John said.

Bruno picked up a bag from one of the stacks in the boxcar and threw it back on the dock, splitting it open, dusting the air and the concrete dock with trinity. Then he left the boxcar without speaking.

"I haven't seen that before," someone said.

Bob was nearly home when he realized he felt good. He knew he was tired, but he did not feel tired. And the aches he had felt at the beginning of the week were gone. He felt wonderful. He had even kept his mask on all the time he was in the boxcar.

Jen wasn't home. He took a shower, dried off and dressed. Jen hadn't returned. He thought she might be at her parents', or maybe she was delayed at school, but then he thought that she was at Tom's. He went out to a Denny's and had a tuna melt with fries. He was still hungry afterward and had a slice of Dutch apple pie.

The lights were on—he could see their glow behind the shades on the windows as he drove up—and he wondered what she would say and what he would say in return. She was in her terrycloth robe when he came in. It ended at mid-thigh; she wasn't wearing anything under it.

"Where were you?" she said.

"You weren't here when I got home, so I took myself out to eat. Where were you?"

"I was here. I must have been in the basement. I was doing laundry."

Bob looked at her. He didn't think she was lying.

"I didn't think to look there."

"I was worried," she said.

"So was I."

He embraced her and kissed her head. Her hair was damp.

"I just took a shower," she said.

"Have you eaten?"

"I was waiting for you."

"If you want, we can go out for dinner. I'll get a cup of coffee."

He watched her dress. First her bra, reaching behind her back with both hands to fasten it. He thought for a moment of helping her, but he wanted to look at her as she put her clothes on, her arms and hands, her breasts, her shoulder blades as they hid themselves in the muscles of her back and then angled out again. Then her panties, up past her knees and thighs, her pubic hair, like a shaded forest, and her buttocks—he recalled their coolness in the palms of his hands and the contrasting heat of her vagina.

"I'm just going to wear a muumuu," she said, taking one out of the closet.

He could slide his hand up her leg as they drove. He could put his finger in her vagina. He could do anything he wanted with her. Why, then, did he feel so sad?

What did another man's semen feel like when it was in your wife and you touched her vagina? How would he know what it was when he felt it? What if she wouldn't let him feel her vagina when they were in the car? What would that mean?

He was sitting on the edge of the bed. She stood at the door of the closet, staring at him. "What's wrong?"

"Just tired."

"We don't have to go out. I can fix something here. Some soup or something."

"No, that's okay. I don't mind."

At the restaurant he talked about Bruno and about another man John had told him about, Jake, whose wife had had a baby by someone else, but which Jake was raising as though it were his.

"It must be hard to raise a child that your wife got from another man," Jen said.

"He must be bound to her in some way," Bob said.

"Do you think he loves her?" She was being sarcastic.

"I hope so."

"You thought I was with Tom earlier, didn't you?"

"Yes."

"I wasn't."

"I believe you."

"No you don't. But I don't know what I can do to make you believe me."

"I think it will go away eventually, my suspicion."

"I think my dad had an affair when he was younger."

"He was younger yesterday."

"All right, smart-ass. Earlier in his marriage then. Don't say yesterday was earlier in his marriage."

"How do you know?"

"I don't know. I just think so. A few years ago he seemed to change. That's when he started putting my mother down all the time. I love him, and my mother too, although I agree with my dad that she's incompetent when it comes to most things. Except for cooking. She's a wonderful cook. But she's not very smart. Peter knows it too. And my dad is very smart. What was I talking about before I started talking about my mother?"

"You said your father had an affair."

"Oh, yeah. He started acting differently all of a sudden. And then, just as suddenly, he changed again. He was back to who he had been, except that he seemed to resent my mom more than before. If he resented her before."

"But why do you think it was an affair? It could have been something else."

"What else could it have been? What else does a discontented suburban man with small children do to distract himself from his marriage except have an affair?"

"Do you think your mother knew?"

"I don't know. I doubt it. She lives in her own world."

"I can hear your father saying that."

"What? That she lives in her own world? I think he probably has. I probably took it from him. I think he made up his mind not to leave us."

Her hands were around her coffee cup and Bob placed his hands over hers. Tears were slipping down her face, though her expression did not change.

"I think I thought even then that he might leave us. I remember one morning when he was on his way out the door to go to work, I grabbed him around the legs and begged him not to go. I must not have even started school yet. Or maybe I was in kindergarten. No, I remember, I was home, sick. I was in first or second grade. Poor man. He didn't know what to think.

"I'm afraid you're going to leave me. I'm always afraid you're going to leave me."

"I won't. You know I won't."

"Maybe if you hadn't gone to San Francisco that time. Or Porterville. Maybe I wouldn't be so afraid now."

"I wish I hadn't."

"Let's go home."

They lay beside each other. He had an erection. Jen mounted him.

She had been riding him for a couple of minutes when she said, "Give me a baby, Bobby." She said it again. It became a chant. He was not certain she knew what she was saying.

Bruno did not come to work. "He'll come back. Probably next week," John said. "He's on a bender."

Bob thought of Carl from when he was spraying orange trees, and wondered if every company had its Carl.

By the end of the week Bob felt as if he were as strong as anyone in the warehouse, though he knew he wasn't. He hadn't gained any weight and the others, all fully grown, mature men, outweighed him by at least twenty pounds and most outweighed him by thirty or forty. Still, he felt he could do anything that would be required of him.

The only thing he had to complain about, if he wanted to complain, was that he had developed small ulcers on his hands and forearms. He assumed they were from bumping into things at work.

At a supermarket with Jen on Friday night he bought a *Time Magazine*. It had a story about Green Berets rappelling out of a window on the twenty-somethingth floor of a hotel in New York. It was obviously a stunt to make a point about something, but it was the stunt itself that caught his attention. He had never heard of Green Berets. Jen had never heard of them either. The story didn't mean anything to her, and to him it was more a curiosity than anything else.

On Monday he felt rested and the bending and lifting of the work came easily. His body moved smoothly, as if it were a kind of hydraulic machine. He searched for the rhythm that had so enthralled him in the boxcar last week, but he couldn't find it.

Somebody noticed the sores on his arms. "You need to take care of that. It'll eat its way to the bone if you don't do something about it."

"What is it?" Bob asked.

"It's from the lime in the trinity. The dust mixes with your sweat and it makes a kind of acid."

"It doesn't need your sweat," John said. "It'll do that even if your skin is dry. That's one of the ways to get rid of a body. Put it in a pit and pour lime on it. After a while, all the flesh is gone."

Bob and the other guy looked at him. "The voice of experience?"

the other man asked.

"Nah, I just heard about it," John said.

"What do I do for them?" Bob asked.

"Put vinegar on them. They'll go away," John said. "Catch it early, they won't leave scars."

"Imagine what that stuff does to your lungs," the other guy said. "Always wear a mask."

Jen's parents had them over for dinner. David asked him how he liked his job.

"It pays well. And I like the people I work with."

"That's important," David said. "Ninety percent of a job is the people you work with. You don't even have to like them, but you have to respect them. Excuse me, I didn't mean to lecture."

"Dad's teaching now," Peter said.

"Really?" Jen said. "What are you teaching? Are you still working at Lockheed?"

"I'm still at Lockheed. I'm teaching math to some of the new hires. They all graduated from high school, but not all of them should have, if you understand what I mean."

"I'm not sure," Jen said.

Bob wondered how she felt now as one removed from the intimacy of the family she had grown up in and hearing about the changes in its life. But nothing in her expression revealed unhappiness.

"These kids aren't stupid. They're capable of learning, or they wouldn't have been hired. But they weren't taught some of the most basic things when they were in school. They ought to be suing the schools they went to for graduating them without teaching them."

"I notice you call the evening meal 'dinner,'" Carol said to

Bob. "Where I was raised, we called it 'supper' and lunch was called dinner. And if we were there now, I would have said 'reared' instead of 'raised.'"

"Mom grew up in Mississippi," Peter said. "But she calls it 'Mizzippi.'"

"We've heard all this," David said, "I don't know how many times."

"I think Bobby's heard about mom calling Mississippi Mizzippi, but I don't think he's heard about calling dinner supper. This is the first time I've heard it," Jen said.

"Really?" Carol said. "I'm sure I've mentioned it before."

"Jesus," David said. He put a hand to his forehead. Then he laughed and Jen and Peter and Bob laughed too.

"The noonday meal was dinner," Carol said.

I Need to Find a Way to Think About This

Another couple was there when Bob and Jen arrived, and John introduced them first to Shannon, his wife, and then to Don and Leslie who lived in the apartment next door. The complex was in a development on Fullerton's east side, near where they had broken ground for the new state college. John and Shannon and Don and Leslie were all in their late twenties, maybe thirty, and they talked to Jen and Bob as though they were the same age.

They ate steaks and potatoes that John grilled on a hibachi on the patio, and salad that Don and Leslie had brought, and drank beer that Don had also brought. It had not occurred to either Bob or Jen to bring something. Jen apologized to Shannon who told her not to worry about it, they had too much anyway and some of it was going to go to waste.

It was a warm day and everybody wore shorts but for John and Bob who wore Levi's. "They're the only kind of pants I've ever worn," John said. Bob didn't own any shorts.

"Except when we got married," Shannon said.

"Except when we got married. I forgot about that."

Sharon slapped him affectionately on the shoulder.

"How long have you two been married?" Leslie asked Jen.

"A month," Jen said. It was an exaggeration by a week and a half.

"A month! You're innocents! Babes in the woods!"

"How long have you and Don been married?" Bob asked.

"About three years. But this is the second marriage for both of us," Don said.

"And the last," Leslie said.

Don leaned down and kissed her on the cheek. "Thank the Lord we found each other."

"And Shannon and John," Leslie said.

"Amen," Don said.

"How do you like being married?" John asked Jen.

"Well, everything is legal now," Jen said.

Everybody laughed.

"They'll fit right in," Don said.

"I'm going to change into something to get some sun," Shannon said, and went into the apartment.

"Uh oh," Leslie said.

When Shannon came out she was wearing a dark two-piece bathing suit and carrying a beach towel. She spread the towel on the grass at the edge of the patio and lay down on it. In her shirt and shorts, before she changed, her figure had seemed ordinary, perhaps a little boyish. But now, with the swell of her hips and the plumpness of her breasts revealed by her bathing suit, the impression of boyishness was gone.

"I thought you might put on the one you wore the other day," Leslie said.

"The showy one?" Shannon said.

"That's one way of putting it."

Leslie, John and Don laughed.

"Sharon has a one-piece she wears sometimes. No top," John said.

"It has straps that cross between my boobs," Shannon said. "I was going to wear it, but I thought it might embarrass you."

Not knowing what to say, Jen and Bob were silent.

"Why should they be embarrassed? You're the one who would be wearing it," John said.

"Do you ever model for Bob?" Leslie asked.

Jen searched for a response but couldn't find anything. Finally Bob said, "Only her body."

The other couples laughed. Then Leslie said, "Well, we should go. It was nice meeting both of you."

After they had gone, Bob said, "We should go too."

"Oh, don't go. Have another beer. Or would you like coffee?" Shannon said.

Bob looked at Jen.

"I'd like to stay a little while," she said.

"Okay. I could go for another Coors," Bob said.

"I'd like one too," Jen said.

"It looks like you're elected," Shannon said to her husband. "I'll have a Coors too."

John went into the apartment and came back with three Coors and an Oly. He took a long drink from the bottle and then belched.

"John says what he thinks," Shannon said. She rolled onto her stomach. "Would you put some lotion on my back? It's in my bag in the kitchen." She reached back and unfastened her bra.

John rubbed the lotion into her skin, once allowing his hand to stray so that it brushed the side of her breast. "Hey," she said.

"What do you do for entertainment?" John asked.

"They've only been married a month. What do you think they do? What did we do?" Shannon said.

"Do you ever go down to Tijuana? See any of the shows there?" John asked.

"We saw a sex show there once," Jen said.

They stared at her.

"Have another beer, sweetie," Bob said.

"Did I say something wrong?"

"No, no. I just didn't expect... I don't know what I expected," Shannon said.

"What did you think of it?" John asked.

"Some parts of it were interesting. But other parts were boring. It depended on the woman," Jen said. "Whether she seemed engaged or not."

"What did they do? Did they use animals?"

"What? No!" Jen said.

"They do, in some shows."

"With human beings? With women?"

"Uh huh. Donkeys. I've heard of them using chickens, but I haven't been able to figure out what they do with them."

"That's sickening, just to think about it."

"Have you ever seen something like that?" Bob asked John.

"Only in a movie. They used a donkey."

"It's degrading," Shannon said. "For women, at least."

"You saw it too?" Jen asked.

She nodded. She raised up on her elbows so Bob could see her breasts. Her aureoles were brown and very large. "We have the movie. Do you want to see it?"

"No," Jen said.

"We have some other movies that are more fun. I can show one of those," John said.

"How are they fun? You mean stimulating?" Jen said.

"The actors seem to be enjoying themselves. Sometimes they're laughing."

"If you're talking about the one I think you're talking about, I don't think they're actors. I think they're just a couple of couples who got somebody to film them," Shannon said.

"You're probably right."

"Go put it on. I think Jen and Bob will enjoy it. It's lighthearted."

John went inside.

"What do you think?" Bob asked.

"I don't know," said Jen.

"Let's look at it."

"Be adventurous," Shannon said. "If you don't like it, we'll stop it."

"Okay," Jen said.

Shannon sat up and shrugged into the bra of her bathing suit. "Would you fasten me?"

Jen knelt behind her and hooked the bra.

John came out. "You can look at these while I set up the projector." He handed Bob a stack of black-and-white photographs showing people in various sex acts. Most of the pictures were of couples, a man and a woman, many apparently teenagers, but some were of trios or of two couples together, linked by mouth, hand, and sex organ.

They were arousing, particularly those that showed kids Jen's and Bob's age. As Bob finished looking at each photo, he passed it to Jen. She was studying them as though each were a work of art. Two of the pictures showed a couple reflected in a mirror that had been set up behind them; he and Jen had never used a mirror. For a moment he wondered what had become of the kids he was looking at; these were old photographs, some so worn that the slick paper had dulled and softened.

Sharon was observing them. She saw Bob glance at her and she smiled warmly.

"All set!" John called.

Jen gave Bob the photos she had been looking at and he stacked them with those he had and gave them to Shannon and the three of them went inside.

The projector sat on a small coffee table in front of the sofa. John and Shannon sat on the couch to the left of the table and Bob and Jen to the right. John turned off the floor lamp and Shannon reached over and pulled the cord to draw the window curtains. The film, silent but in color, played on a collapsible screen set up against the far wall. It began with a twenty-something couple walking around an apartment in bathrobes. As the flaps of their robes parted, they revealed that the man was wearing boxer shorts and the woman panties. They talked and smiled at each other and then they kissed and the man slipped his hand inside the woman's robe and caressed her bare breast. They seemed very comfortable with each other. The camera showed the man's erection at the fly of his shorts.

Then the man went to the door and opened it and another couple, perhaps a little older, came inside. They were smiling and the man was carrying a bottle of wine. Both he and the woman with him were wearing long coats. When they took them off, they were shown also to be wearing short robes under their coats. As they moved, it could be seen that they were naked under their robes. ("I hadn't appreciated your little robe until now," Bob whispered to Jen.) Everybody in the film laughed and the two women embraced. One of the men, the second, stepped toward the first woman with his palms raised breast high, but she pushed him away, laughing again. They sat down on the sofa together and he began groping her, touching her breasts, trying to get his hand between her legs. She resisted, or pretended to resist, but then, apparently aroused, she returned his kisses and took his penis in her hand. The other man and woman were doing more or less the same thing; sometimes one pairing would stop and watch the other.

Bob kissed Jen.

"I don't know if I can do this," she whispered.

"Look."

Shannon's bra was off and John was kissing her breasts. One hand was inside her swimsuit bottom.

Jen grasped Bob's penis through his pants. He unbuttoned his fly and her hand went inside. He kissed her again and began unbuttoning her shirt.

"Wait," she said. "I should have worn a muumuu." She took off her shirt and bra. Bob kissed her breasts and slipped his hand inside her panties. Her labia were already swollen. He was very excited. "I love you," he said.

He looked at John and Shannon. Shannon was completely naked now, her legs apart, John's hand between them. Bob could see the shadow of her pubic hair above John's hand. The fly of his Levi's was open and his penis was visible in Shannon's hand.

Jen was watching too. "Come in me," she said. Bob rolled her panties down her legs and took his shoes and pants off and pulled her down on the carpet. Her legs opened and he went between them and inside her in a single movement. She made an "unh" sound and in a moment her hips began to work to meet his thrusts. He heard the film run out of the reel and then the end of it flapping and John got up and turned the projector off. He and Sharon moved closer and watched Bob and Jen in the dim light. Jen raised her legs and Bob imagined another penis thrusting into her anus while his was in her vagina. John nestled between Shannon's legs and his face disappeared between her thighs. She gripped his hair with both of her hands. Bob wondered what Jen could see, but when he looked at her, her eyes were closed. He was trying to keep from coming, but Jen said again, "Come in me. I want to feel your wet," and he came. He couldn't keep himself from crying out and he heard Shannon say, "Oh, honey," and then as he settled himself on top of Jen he felt someone touch his face. "That was so good," Shannon said. She was looking at him. He felt himself getting hard again.

"Everybody's come but John," Shannon said. She inserted her head in the space between Jen's and Bob's and kissed Jen's mouth. Jen responded immediately, grabbing at Shannon's shoulders, trying to pull her down on top of her. Bob moved aside and

Shannon, without breaking the kiss, took Jen's nipple between her thumb and index finger and pulled on it. Jen's hips began to move again and John took her ankles and raised them and spread her legs and slipped inside her.

Bob didn't know what to do. He felt vaguely sick, but he was also still aroused. Jen's eyes were closed and John was pumping in and out of her as her hips rose to meet his and then withdrew with his rhythm. The sounds "oh" and "uh" came from her. Shannon's mouth was on one of Jen's nipples. Bob saw Shannon reach back and grasp her own buttock, digging her nails into it, and he moved up behind her and placed the head of his penis against her labia and went inside. He found himself following John's rhythm, and then he set his own. Shannon's hips were wide and he could feel the bone of them under his hands as the flesh of her buttocks rippled with the thrust of his penis. He felt her hand against his testicles and he realized she was rubbing herself and he could hear the guttural sounds that were coming out of Jen and then he heard John's cry and, almost at the same time, Shannon's.

He watched John's penis withdraw from Jen, coated with her lubrication and the semen both he and John had left, and he withdrew from Shannon's vagina without coming.

Jen lay on her back, her forearm over her eyes. Bob moved between her legs and kissed her labia. A shudder passed through her and she placed a hand behind his head.

Shannon brought her a towel. "Here. You're leaking." Jen raised her hips and Shannon placed the towel under her. Then she kissed Jen's mound. "God, I could eat you right here, you get me so hot."

"Is anybody hungry?" John asked. "Speaking of eating. I'm going to fry some eggs."

"He's always hungry after sex. Some people smoke. John wants to eat," Shannon said.

"I'd like to take a shower," Jen said.

"Right through there, honey. On your left." When Jen had gone, Shannon asked, "Is she going to be all right?"

"I don't know. We haven't done this before."

"You're a lucky man," John said. "You have a very sweet lady." He was scrambling eggs in a large skillet.

"She's lucky too," Shannon said.

Jen came out of the bathroom wrapped in a towel. She gathered her clothes from the floor and went back into the bathroom. When she came out again she was dressed. She said, "I'd like to go home."

John was naked under an apron. Shannon had put her panties on. Bob had his pants on and now he put on his shirt.

On the drive home, Jen said, "I don't know what I'm going to do with this."

"What do you mean?"

"I need to find a way to think about this. I feel like they used me. I don't want to feel this way. Did you know this was going to happen?"

"No. How would I know?"

"Are you lying?"

"Why would you ask me that?"

"I'm sorry. I'm just feeling afraid."

"Afraid? Of what?"

"I don't know. This is new to me." She gave a bitter laugh. "Well, I'm not a virgin anymore."

"What do you mean?"

"Until today, you were the only man I had ever made it with."

Bob didn't say anything.

"Were you watching?"

He nodded.

"Didn't it bother you?"

He nodded. "But it excited me too."

"Did you fuck Shannon? I thought I saw you, but I wasn't sure."

He was silent.

"Well, you're not a virgin anymore either. Of course, you weren't a virgin before you fucked her. Did you come in her?"

"No."

"Be honest with me. That's all I need from you right now."

"I didn't come in her. I didn't come at all with her."

"Why not?"

"I couldn't. I think because I was upset, watching you. Did you come with John?"

"You know I did. Not that I had anything to say about it. I wish I could stop thinking about it. They raped me and you watched it and you didn't do anything."

"You're twisting things."

"I know I am, but I can't help it. I need to twist things. Just tell me you love me, won't you? If you do, I mean."

"I love you. I'll always love you. Did you hear me tell you earlier that I love you?"

"When?"

"When you were taking your clothes off."

"I didn't hear you. What made you say it?"

"You were being so brave. I could see how frightened you were."

She let out her breath. "Could we stop for something to eat? I'm hungry."

"We're almost home."

"Let's stop anyway. I don't want to fix anything."

At the Denny's, she said, "It was as if my body wasn't mine, as if it belonged to whoever was using it at the time. And then when I was washing myself, I looked at the stuff that was coming out of me and I thought, 'This is Bobby's. No, this is John's. No, this is Bobby's.' What if I'm pregnant? How would we know whose baby it is? I'm asking a real question. I'm not being rhetorical."

"We might not. But the baby would be mine."

"Really? You would want to raise it as if it were yours?"

"Yes. Don't doubt it."

"Well, that's a help. Thank you. Wait. Would you want to help me raise it because you love me, or—"

"Because I love you."

"All right. Thank you. Bobby?"

"Yes?"

"If I wanted to do it again, would you let me?"

"Do you want to do it again?"

"I don't know. But if I did, how would you feel?"

"I don't know. Do you mean doing the same thing? The four of us?"

"I'm not sure what I mean. What if I just wanted John and Shannon to fuck me? I couldn't stand to watch you fuck Shannon again."

"Would you want me to be there?"

"I don't know. Would you want to? Would you be able to watch me again?"

"I'd rather be there than not."

"Even if it hurts?"

"I think it would hurt worse imagining it than seeing it."

"All right. It was just a question. I wouldn't do something without asking you first. I don't want to do anything that endangers us, endangers our marriage. I'm just trying to find a way to think about myself. But if I wanted to make love with somebody else, not John and Shannon necessarily, but somebody, would you want to watch me?"

"I don't know. I don't think I can talk about this any more now."

"Are you in pain?"

"I think so."

"You think so?"

"I'm in pain."

"One more thing? Please. I want to ask you for something."

"Go ahead."

"When we go home, would you make love to me?"

"Yes."

"Look at my hands." She held her hands out. They were vibrating as though they were made of wire instead of bone and flesh, and somebody had strummed them.

"Why are they doing that?" Bob said.

"I don't know. Let's go now. I'm not hungry anymore."

Lying against him, she asked, "Do you think about anybody else when you're fucking me?"

"Do you?"

"Not fair. You first."

"Sometimes. My mind drifts. Things pop in and out."

"You're not bored with me, are you?"

"No, no. But my mind drifts. What about you? Do you think about somebody else when you're fucking me?"

"Hey, who's doing the fucking here? Are you fucking me or am I fucking you when we fuck?"

"Sometimes I feel like I'm fucking you, other times like you're fucking me. I think it might depend on the position."

He felt her head move. "Maybe," she said.

"Are you going to answer my question?"

"Do I think about someone else? Not usually, but sometimes. I always feel guilty when I do. But I don't think I will now."

"Think about somebody else or feel guilty?"

"I don't think I'll feel guilty now. I don't think I can afford to."

"I don't know what you mean."

"I don't think I can explain it. How did you feel when I said that?"

"When you said you sometimes think about someone else, or that you feel guilty when you do? Or that you won't feel guilty anymore?"

"All of it."

"I don't want you to feel guilty. I don't want you to feel anything that makes you unhappy."

"What if something makes me feel happy and unhappy at the same time?"

"I don't know. You asked me how I felt when you said you feel guilty when you think about someone else when we're making love. I answered that, mostly."

"When we're fucking. The other parts, the touching, the kissing, the exploring of each other's bodies that we do, I don't think about anything then. I just let myself feel."

"Okay."

"So how did you feel when I told you that I think about someone else sometimes?"

"Tom?"

"I'm sorry."

"Are you in love with him?"

"In a way, I think. I'm so sorry. I don't want to hurt you. We haven't made love."

"But you will."

"We won't. Oh, Bobby, I'm so sorry." She was weeping quietly. He became erect. She noticed it and positioned herself so she could take his penis in her mouth. He turned her and slid under her and pulled her on top of him so that he could reach her vagina with his tongue. He looked at her, where the hair was on her labia, where it thinned and then disappeared, leaving her anus and the lower parts of her labia bare. He breathed in the aroma from her anus and began licking her vagina, searching for her clitoris, imagining Tom doing what he was doing. Then that vision was replaced by the memory of John's penis withdrawing from her vagina, coated with his semen and Bob's. Bob kissed her labia and spread them with his fingers, seeing John open her thighs again and thrust himself into her, and he, Bob, worked his tongue inside, causing her to groan and to leave off pleasuring him so she could concentrate on her own pleasure.

Bob and Jen Face Another Crisis

It was a relief to be doing physical work. He had thought it would be difficult to work beside John again, but he found a kind of comfort in his company. They shared knowledge of two women that no one else in the plant shared; they were a fraternity of two. At lunch John asked him how Jen was doing. Shannon was worried about her.

Bob assured him that Jen was all right. She just needed some time to think, was all.

"How about you? How are you doing?" John asked.

It took Bob a moment to reply. Finally he said, "I've been feeling a lot of different things. And I've been constantly horny since Saturday."

John laughed. "I know what you mean, about the horniness anyway."

"What about you and Shannon? Emotionally, I mean."

He shrugged. "It's not a problem for us. We're not deep people."

Bob laughed, although he could see John meant it.

"Do you think you'd like to do it again? Maybe we'll invite Don and Leslie over too. Or we don't have to."

"Maybe. Give us some time."

"Sure. We're not going anywhere. I see those sores on your arms are clearing up. Have you been putting vinegar on them?"

"Yes. It works."

On Friday, as Bob was punching out, Ace asked him to come to his office. He told Bob he was letting him go at the end of his probation period, next Friday. Ace said he had been watching Bob and he just wasn't strong enough to keep up with the other men.

Bob objected. He admitted the first week had been hard, but since then he had been pulling his weight.

Ace shook his head. He wanted to tell Bob in advance so he could start looking for another job. The best time to apply for a job is when you already have one, Ace said.

Bob didn't tell Jen until the next day. They decided not to say anything to her parents when they saw them at supper later. There was always the chance that Ace would change his mind.

Eating lunch Monday, Bob told John that Ace had fired him.

John was surprised. "I know some of the guys didn't think you would make it the first week you were here, but now you're as strong as any of us. Just a minute."

He got up and went into the warehouse and came back with a man Bob had seen a number of times driving a forklift but had never talked with.

"Ron's our shop steward," John said. "Tell him what Ace said."

After Bob told him, Ron said, "You're still on probation?"

"This is my fourth week."

"So you're not in the union yet. Next week, if you stayed, you would join the union and then there would be something I could do."

"That's what I thought," Bob said.

"I don't know what else I can tell you."

"That's shitty," John said.

"I know, but that's the way it is," Ron said.

During the afternoon when there was a free moment, one or another of the men Bob worked with came over to commiserate.

They said they could not understand why Ace was letting him go after he had proved himself. Some said what John had said, that they'd had some doubts about him during his first week, but by the second week he had gained strength and had been able to hold his own.

At the mid-afternoon break, John disappeared. When he returned, he told Bob that Ace had admitted he hadn't observed him after his first week and that Bob may have improved since then, but he had to make his decision based on what he had seen, and what he had seen showed him that Bob didn't have the physical strength to do the job. John asked him to take another look before making his final decision and Ace said he would.

Bob was doubtful, but the other men seemed to feel a kind of relief on his behalf. Through the week, one or another of them would come over and say something to try to reassure him that everything would work out.

Ace didn't come by. Friday, after Bob had punched out, Ace came out of his office to ask him if he wanted to drop by next week to pick up his last check, or did he want Payroll to mail it to him?

John was waiting for him in the parking lot.

"I'm gone," Bob said. "They're going to mail me my check."

"Shit. I don't know what to say. I'm sorry."

"I'm pretty used to the idea now. I didn't think he would change his mind."

"You're more cynical than I am. I thought he would."

"I'd say I was being realistic."

"Yeah. Realistic is a better word. Well," John said. He extended his hand and Bob took it. "Give me a call if you want to get together. We shouldn't let a job tell us if we can be friends or not."

"That's a nice way of putting it. Thanks, John. I'll call you."

Oink

Years later, at an exhibit of part of the Peggy Guggenheim Collection at the Palazzo Strozzi in Florence, he would be struck by the title of a painting, Leonora Carrington's Oink. It would bring back to him a dream he'd had when he was eighteen and Jen and he were together in the apartment two blocks off of Harbor, the main thoroughfare of Fullerton, California. The dream was of a single image, a pink-skinned infant swathed in the protective fat that adorns healthy children of that age.

He had awakened from the dream upset, as though wanting to deny something about it, but unable to, and over the years, every time he recalled the image, it upset him again, although not as strongly as the first time he saw it. It wasn't a still image, as in a photograph. The child was fat and round and pink and it reminded him of the suckling pigs he had seen once at a county fair. Perhaps that was why the title, Oink, brought the vision of the infant back to him. It would smile a little and then the smile would leave its face and it would drool, the fingers of its right hand in its mouth, and the few blond hairs on its head moved as though under the influence of a breeze.

The first time he saw it, when he and Jen were living in the apartment near Harbor, he didn't know what to make of it or of his upset. Only decades later, when he saw the Oink at the Strozzi, would words occur to him that expressed the insight, if that's what it was, it provoked the first time he saw the vision of the infant and every time since.

The words were "Is that all we are? Only need?"

I'm Trying Not To Get Cynical

David was concerned. He asked, "What are you going to do?"

"Apply for unemployment. Then look around for another job. That tree-spraying outfit I worked for last year should be hiring again in a couple of months. I'll call them and let them know I'm still around."

"Do you think you'd like to cook chicken?"

"What?" Jen said.

"I asked your hubby if he wanted to cook chicken. Do I mumble when I talk?" He was teasing her. Bob always enjoyed listening to the banter between David and his children.

"Sometimes you do mumble, David," Carol said.

"Never," he said.

Peter laughed.

"What's this about chicken?" Jen said.

"I read in the paper about a new company that broasts and serves up chicken. The customer calls in his order or drives up and orders what chicken parts he wants and how many and the restaurant broasts them right there and gives them to him. After he gives them his money, of course. So I called them. They're selling franchises. I've always wanted to own my own business, and I thought this might be my chance."

"What's 'broasting'?" Bob asked. "A combination of roasting and broiling?"

"You got it, Buckwheat." David had never called him Buckwheat before. Had he become David's child? Bob felt comforted but uneasy at the same time.

"What about your job?" Peter asked.

"I'd keep my job. I figured I'd put up the money for the franchise and this guy here could run it. They'd train you," David said. "Teach you how to operate the machines, all that good stuff."

That was something else Bob had heard Jen say—"all that good stuff"—but she was talking about his semen.

"I don't know," he said. "My parents owned a couple of restaurants. It's hard work."

"You're strong. You've proved that."

"I mean it's long hours. And at the end of the day you smell like fried meat. But it can pay. My folks were turning a profit only a year after buying the first restaurant, and it was a new place. New building, new shopping center. Everyone said it would take two years before it began to make money, but my folks did it in one. My father lost forty pounds in the first six months they owned it, and my mother had a physical breakdown, but they made a go of that place."

Bob hesitated, reluctant to say any more, but the immediacy of the memory pushed it out of him. "One evening—it was around nine o'clock and we had closed early to clean up. It was a Thursday, I think, the night each week when I buffed the floor. My father had been going over some receipts or doing some other kind of paperwork. My mother had worked the kitchen that day—she often did that when a cook was sick or just didn't show up—and one of the waitresses had stayed late to help with the cleanup. There was another man there, someone from the kitchen, but I don't remember what he was doing. Something regarding to the kitchen, I suppose. And we were all sitting at one of the tables in the front, taking a break together and just talking. I must have been ten or eleven. I don't remember where my sister was, but she wasn't in the restaurant with us. She may have been spending the night with one of her girlfriends. She did that sometimes.

And then it was time to get back to work, if we wanted to get out of there before midnight, and we all stood up at the same time. But my mother didn't stand up. She just sat there on her chair. My father said, 'What's wrong?' and she said, 'I can't get up,' and she began to cry. She was so tired, her body wouldn't obey her. It wouldn't do what she wanted it to do. And then the waitress shoo-ed my father and me and the other man toward the back of the restaurant and she went and sat down with my mother and talked quietly with her, quietly enough that I couldn't hear what they were saying, and after a while my mother stood up and we all went back to work."

Even as he was speaking, Bob realized how proud he was of his parents. He was surprised. He did not remember ever thinking of them before as they were when they were younger, when…what? When they had confidence that they could make something for themselves that hadn't existed before, something other than their children?

David was watching him. So was Jen. So were Peter and Carol. Jen put her hand on his arm. Bob wondered what showed on his face.

"Have you talked to your parents lately?" David asked.

"No."

"Well, I'll talk with this company next week. I have an appointment Thursday night. You don't have to go. You can come over here and buff our floors if you want to. And even after I talk with them, you don't have to commit yourself to anything. I'll let you know what they say."

"I didn't know you had all those feelings about your parents," Jen said on the way home.

"I didn't know I had them."

"Do you miss them?"

"I didn't think so. But now I don't know."

"My father really loves you."

"I know. He's been very good to me."

"That's because you married his only daughter and he really loves her."

"I know. I love her too."

John called Monday evening.

"I thought you would be interested—the guy who took your place is Ace's nephew."

"Wow," Bob said.

"Yeah. There's no way you could have kept your job. You could have been Superman and Ace still would have found a way to let you go."

"Yeah."

"Well, I thought you'd want to know. Any chance of you guys coming by this weekend?"

"Not this weekend. We're having dinner with Jen's parents on Saturday and a friend of ours is having a party on Sunday. We said we'd be there. I'll call you next week."

"Tom's party is next Saturday," Jen said after he hung up.

"I know, but John's been after me, after us, to come over again, and I don't know what to tell him."

"You could just tell him no."

"Is that what you want me to do?"

"I don't know what I want. Sometimes I feel that if we did it again with them, it would help me get past it. Other times, I feel like they raped me and I don't want to even think about doing it again. Also, I don't want to have to watch you with Shannon. I don't want to watch you with anybody. I want to believe that I own your body. Are you sure you didn't come in her?"

"Yes, I'm sure."

"Okay. I don't want to think about it anymore. What else did John say?"

"The guy who replaced me at work is the foreman's nephew."

"You're kidding."

"That's what John said."

"Can they do that?"

"They did it."

"Can you talk to the foreman's boss?"

"The owner? Ace has been there for twenty years. He would say I wasn't up to the job and his nephew is. The owner would side with Ace even if he didn't believe him."

"I'm trying not to get cynical."

Carol had prepared fried chicken, corn on the cob—"sweet corn," she called it—black-eyed peas and mashed potatoes with white gravy, an all-American meal, if you lived in the South or were raised there.

"I fixed chicken because I thought you and David were going to go into the chicken business," she said. "I wanted to celebrate."

"You knew yesterday that we probably weren't going to," David said.

"Well, but I had my mind set on chicken."

"It's really delicious," Jen said.

"Me too," Peter said. "I love fried chicken."

"'Me too'? You're really delicious too?" Jen said.

"What? What are you talking about?" Peter said.

"You said—"

"I'm not delicious. I don't think I am. But I've never tasted me," Peter said.

David cut in, "So I went down to their office Thursday and they showed us the broaster ovens they use and they explained how they worked, how they made their chicken different from other people's, and they said they would maintain the ovens for us. And they talked about the system they used to keep track of the call-in orders, and how the restaurant—they don't call it a restaurant, but I don't remember what they call it; they have their own word for it—how the restaurant's floor plan has to be a certain way so you don't confuse call-in orders with walk-ins. And they talked about how the company supports their franchises, and the things the franchisee, if that's a real word, has to do to keep the franchise, and actually it all sounded pretty good. They warned us that the business would require long hours, especially at first when we're getting established, but I figured, hell, they're not my long hours, they're your long hours, and then they handed out the contracts. They said we didn't have to sign immediately, although they would like us to, but we could think it over and then come back when we were ready to sign. But they wouldn't let us take the contract out of the building. They said we should understand that the contract was not negotiable. We either agreed to everything as it was written or we didn't. And they counted the copies of the contract that they collected at the end of the night. So, what do you think? I haven't signed anything."

"I don't know. I haven't read the contract," Bob said.

"Exactly. That's a problem, isn't it? Because I couldn't take a copy of it to show you. Another problem, or part of the same problem, is that I don't remember the details of what the contract said. For instance, I don't remember what we would be charged for maintenance on the ovens. I don't think there was an exact figure, but I don't remember for sure. And that's the kind of detail that can kill you if you're not careful. You've heard that old saw, 'The devil's in the details'? Well, I think that may be true in this case. I mean, what kind of company doesn't allow you to look at a contract at your leisure, or consult a lawyer?"

"You could call them," Carol said. "Maybe they would tell you what maintenance costs."

"I was just using that as an example. I would want a lawyer to look over the contract before I signed it, if I signed it. I think this company has a good idea, but they make their money by selling franchises, not by cooking chickens. So, I'm sorry to have gotten your hopes up, if I did get them up, but I just don't trust a company that won't let me show their contract to a lawyer. Are you disappointed?"

"To tell you the truth, I wasn't looking forward to working eighteen-hour days," Bob said.

"I don't blame you. I'm disappointed though. I may not get another chance to own a business."

At the door, as Bob and Jen were leaving, Carol put a fifty-dollar bill in Jen's hand.

She put her hands over his eyes. It had been months since she had done this and she caught him by surprise. He pushed her away. "Goddamnit! What are you doing!"

She came back at him, trying again to blind him. He could see ferocity on her face, which he had not seen there before. He grabbed her shirt and pulled her away and then he shoved her so that she fell back against the passenger door. She came at him yet again and he punched her in the chest with his fist. When he hit her, he felt that he had stepped through a gateway and the gate had closed behind him. He had the sense that he had made a mistake a long time ago and he was paying for it now, or that someone else had erred, maybe even before he was born, but the debt was still his to pay. And Jen's.

"That hurt! Goddamnit, you hurt me, you shithead!"

There was a supermarket ahead and he pulled into the parking lot and stopped the car.

"Get out," he said. "You can walk the rest of the way."

She glared at him. "I'm not getting out."

"If you try that again, I'll hurt you a lot worse than I just did."

She turned her face so that the windshield was in front of her. "Drive," she said. "Bastard."

He started the car and pulled cautiously out of the lot. He was afraid. He wished he hadn't hit her.

The Party

The occasion for Tom's party was the end of finals week. Everybody was there: Gerry and Janice and Kevin and Barbara; Harold and a woman Bob assumed was his fiancée; Phil, down from UCLA; Justin with an elegant, long-haired girl nobody knew, wearing a sleek dress and an emerald choker; others Bob hadn't seen before. Jazz was coming from the stereo Tom had set up on the table beside the wine bottles. Cal Tjader. Bob used to have that record.

"Fred said he might drop by later," Justin said. "He and Toni were going to spend the afternoon in bed and he didn't know how much energy they would have to go out afterward."

"That sounds like something Fred would say." He poured Justin a glass of white wine. His girl was talking to Harold. "Who's Toni?"

"Fred's fiancé. You met her. They're getting married at the end of the month. I thought I told you."

"Maybe you did."

"They're going to move up to Berkeley. Fred was accepted for graduate school there."

"I didn't know that. 'That old gang of mine.'"

"What's that?"

"A lyric from an old song. My father used to sing it."

"Have you seen your dad lately?"

"No. Nobody. Not even my sister."

Jen wobbled over on elevated shoes she had bought with money her mother had given her. Bob caught her by her elbow. "You should take those shoes off. You're going to hurt yourself."

"She should take everything off," Phil said, appearing out of nowhere. Bob ignored him.

"I'm doing all right," Jen said. She was already buzzed.

"Have some more wine, my dear," Phil said in the faux accent of a European movie seducer.

"Don't hit him," Jen said.

Phil looked at her. "I wasn't going to hit anybody."

Justin laughed.

"She was talking to me," Bob said.

Phil's eyes widened and he walked away.

Justin's date came over. "This is Sara," he said. "And this is Bob, who I've known for many years." Justin was also a little drunk. Sara didn't say anything.

"I used to know another girl named Sara," Bob said. "Do you spell it with or without an aitch?"

Jen punched him in the stomach.

"Ow," he said. "Not fair. You know I won't hit you back."

"Better not."

"It's a common name nowadays," Sara said. She didn't answer the question about the spelling.

"A common name. Present company excluded, of course," Jen said. "Oops. I meant to say 'Common name for common girls, present company excluded.'" She had trouble saying "excluded" the second time.

Sara glanced at Justin.

"Are you in a sorority?" Bob asked.

Justin laughed again. "She's a Communist."

"I'm not a member of the Party yet, but I've been asked to join. But I used to be in a sorority."

"Congratulations," Bob said, not quite sure what he was congratulating her for. He was feeling the wine too.

Her forehead furrowed.

"Seriously," he said, although he was not being serious.

"Why did you think I was in a sorority?"

"You look like you would be in a sorority. They way you're dressed, the way you carry yourself, your hair. Everything is just right."

"I don't know how to take that."

"I'm sorry. I don't know how I meant it." He said to Justin, "There's something I've been saving to tell you, but now I've forgotten what it is."

"Was it important?"

"I doubt it."

"Nietzsche's my man," Phil said. He was standing off to the right, talking to Tom.

"*Thus Spake Zarathustra*," said Tom.

"*Geneology of Morals*. But yeah, *Thus Spake Zarathustra* too."

"Actually, I don't know what to think of *Zarathustra*."

"'You go to women? Remember to take your whip!' Or something like that." Phil laughed.

"That's kind of crude," Sara said.

Phil turned to her. "What is?"

"You are. Talking about whipping women."

"Not me! Nietzsche! I was quoting him."

"And laughing about it. Do you have other friends like him?" she asked Justin.

"Most of my friends are very nice," Justin said.

"Hey!" Phil said.

"Actually, I like Rousseau," Kevin said, having come over from another conversation.

"Jean-Jacques!" Phil cried. "He's my man, too!"

"You seem to be drawn to men," Sara said.

"What!"

"Freedom. That's what it's all about. Natural man," Kevin said.

"Even if you have to kill your children," Phil said.

"What?"

"Didn't you know? Jean-Jacques and his mistress gave all of their children to an orphanage as soon as they were born."

"So? That's not the same as killing them. That's just giving them up. It's bad, of course, or at least not good for the children, or may not be, but—"

"So back then most children in French orphanages died before they reached adulthood. Rousseau knew this, but pretended not to. All the French knew it, but pretended not to."

"Like today every Frenchman says he fought in the Resistance, but it's more likely he was a collaborator," Tom said. "Everybody knows it, but they go along."

"Don't you just love hypocrisy?" Phil said.

"I do. Hypocrisy makes the world go 'round."

"I'm part French," Sara said.

"Of course you are," said Phil.

"What's that supposed to mean?"

"Never mind. You can't help it."

"You're really taking a beating tonight, aren't you?" Bob said to Sara. "Sorry, that was an accident. I wasn't referring to the whip."

He didn't see Jen.

"She's in the bathroom," Phil said. "Want me to check on her?"

Bob ignored him. He saw Harold talking with Gerry and went over to say hello. Harold introduced him to Kathy, his fiancée. She was a self-assured woman of middle height who seemed to be at ease with everybody.

"Tom told me you got married," Harold said. "Congratulations."

"Thanks. When's your wedding?"

"Next month," Kathy said, a wide smile on her face. She was clearly in love.

"Well, congratulations to both of you," Bob said.

"This idiot just lost his job. How the hell do you expect to keep a woman if you can't hold a job?" Gerry said to Bob. He was very drunk.

"What happened?" Harold asked.

"The foreman fired me so he could hire his nephew. I wasn't in the union yet, so it was easy."

"That's terrible," Kathy said.

"That's shitty," said Harold.

"I didn't know it was like that," Gerry said. "I'm—"

Bob walked outside and stood on the porch for a minute. Then he walked downstairs. He heard laughter in the parking lot and walked back there and found Jen and Phil sitting cross-legged, facing each other beneath a street lamp, a jug of gasoline between them. They were trying to talk but their laughter kept getting in the way. One of them would get a syllable out and then throw his or her head back or double over and then the other would do the same thing.

Bob sat down beside Jen in the shadow of a car and waited for the effect of the fumes to pass. "Oh God, oh God," Jen gasped, and fell over on her side, laughing convulsively. "Don't hit me," Phil said, and he leaned to his side and then rolled onto his back, choking with laughter. In a moment his laughter ceased and he began to breathe heavily. Jen's laughter had also ended and she asked him, "Are you all right?"

"I'm fine. Fine." He sat up and coughed and then was still. He seemed to be staring at something directly in front of him.

"Say something," Jen said. She placed her hand on his.

"I want to fuck you," he said.

"No, Phil." She withdrew her hand.

"I'll be better to you than Bob is. I'm smarter than he is."

"I can't. You're my friend—"

He got to his feet and, standing, looked at Bob as if he hadn't realized he was there. "Sorry," he said, and then, facing Jen again, said, "What good is being your friend if I can't get into your pants?" He turned and walked back to the party.

"How long have you been sitting there?" Jen asked.

"A few minutes," Bob said.

"Well, I didn't fuck him, and I won't."

"Why are you angry with me?"

"I don't know. I didn't know I was, but I am." She managed to get to her feet. The effects of the gas were gone, but the alcohol was still there. She started back to the apartment, stopped and asked, "Are you coming?" and then continued on.

Sara was sitting on the sofa, Justin's arm around her shoulders. Phil was sitting on a chair opposite her, looking up her dress, ostensibly interested in what she was saying.

"My sister told me that she woke up one morning—this was when she was in prison—and looked up and saw the blade of the guillotine coming down on her. It wasn't really, of course. There was no guillotine and she was safe and secure in her cell. But that's what she saw. She was a fraction of a second away from being beheaded. So, yeah, she believes in reincarnation. She thinks what she saw actually happened to her in a previous life."

"Don't you think she was having a dream?" Justin said.

"It's not for me to try to explain it. She said she was completely awake. She had just woken up and she saw this blade coming down on her."

"It's Zen," Justin said.

"It's not Zen. Not everything that's inexplicable is Zen," Phil said. He leaned forward and put his hand on Sara's knee.

"Hey!" Justin said.

"It's all right," Sara said. "He's just being needy."

Phil pulled his hand back and stood up. He walked away.

"That was harsh," Justin said, laughing.

"I know, but I couldn't resist." Sara tilted her face toward Justin and he kissed her.

"...and Kevin put the knife in him," Gerry Crowe was saying.

"Don't talk about that," Kevin said. Barbara was staring at him.

"It didn't really happen," Gerry said. "It was all a dream. I made it up."

"Was it really just a dream?" Barbara asked Kevin.

"Yeah. It wasn't even my dream. It was Gerry's."

"I just realized," someone said, "Mickey's not here. Where is he?"

"He went back to Florida. Him and his girlfriend slash fiancée. They're gonna get married there," Harold said.

"I'll never leave you. Even if you left me, I could never leave you." Was that Jen? Who was she talking to? Bob searched, but didn't see anybody he thought might have said it. He wondered if he had made it up, but he had clearly heard a girl's voice, although maybe not Jen's. Had someone come inside for a moment and then left?

"So I'm drillin' her from behind and she starts to moan, and I'm sayin' to myself, "Mmm mm. Man, you doin' good." Who was that? He sounded like a guy Bob used to work with at the warehouse. What was his name? Bob couldn't remember.

"But that's what it sounds like—fucking. That's how it sounds when you're doing it. It makes that sound like sucking, but with an F." That was Jen, he was sure. But he couldn't find her. Looking around, he realized that he knew only half of those who were crammed into the apartment, maybe fewer.

"We had this girl in our class—we all sat in a circle on the floor, don't ask me why. The teacher probably thought we would get to know each other better than if we sat at our desks. It would be more intimate. And I guess it was, because every time this girl got up she would hike up her skirt and she was never wearing panties. My husband was the first one to notice, of course. He thought she was wearing red panties, but she was a redhead and it was her pubic hair."

That was Jen! She was laughing and the people around her were laughing.

"Every morning I get up and I think, 'What lie shall I begin with today?'" Bob heard someone say from inside the jumble of voices.

"...the moral autonomy conferred by one's first sexual relationship...," someone was saying. Was that Fred? Fred could have said it, but he wasn't here, was he? Bob was drunk. He realized that now. He set his glass on the table beside the empty and half-empty bottles and went over and sat down on the couch next to Sara. She and Justin were still kissing. Was this the same kiss he had seen, what? a half-hour ago? Or had they come up for air and then gone back down? Justin was massaging her breast and her hand was on his thigh.

"I didn't want to get married. I kept running away, taking these little trips to test myself, to see how I would feel living away from her. But after a while, I felt as though she was with me, even when she wasn't. It was as if she was tucked away somewhere inside me, no matter where I went." Is that me? Bob thought. That could be me. Almost. That could almost be me.

"That's love," Kevin said.

"It's a good thing she's so small. She wouldn't take up much room," someone else said.

"My life tells me that I have to do everything twice. I have to repeat myself at least once before I learn what I should have learned the first time I did it. What a waste of time!"

"He was one of the first American soldiers who went into Dachau. After that, he said, whenever they captured an SS officer, they gave the interrogators carte blanche to do what they wanted to him." That was Tom.

"Who's that?"

"One of my professors. He was in military intelligence during the war."

"That's kind of an oxymoron, isn't it—military intelligence?"

"You think that once you're married, you'll be able to reveal all the secrets you've carried inside you, and maybe you will, but immediately after the ceremony or even before it, you start growing new ones, and you can't reveal them, at least not to your husband." That was Janice, Bob was pretty sure.

"Give me, give me, give me," Someone said. Bob thought of the pink infant of his dream.

"Every revolution is made by the middle class. The followers may be the poor, but the leadership is always made up of people from the middle class."

"That's bullshit. Where'd you get that?"

"Crane Brinton. A great American historian."

Tom: "So I said, 'But we're not a democracy, we're a republic.' And, holy shit, you would have thought I'd dropped the bomb. I didn't know that's a catch-phrase of the John Birch Society."

Gerry: "I'll have to remember to say that when I take that class, just to piss people off."

"One of my professors knew John Birch in China. He said Birch was a fool who got himself killed by his foolery."

"Is 'foolery' the right word? Wouldn't 'foolishness' be better?"

"He said Birch was with a Nationalist unit that was being overrun by Communist troops and everybody was leaving. But Birch stopped and started swearing at the Commies. He wanted to let them know what he thought of them. So they shot him. What a fucking idiot. And the people who named their cult after him are fucking idiots too."

"What's a Parthenon shot? Did I say that correctly?"

"Parthian shot."

"Oh. I guess I didn't say it right."

"Nietzsche can beat up Jean Jacques any day of the week."

Was that Phil? Had he come back? Where was Jen? And Janice, where was she now?

Gray light was beginning to seep into the room. Bob sat up. He was on the sofa. He wanted to stand up, but waited to see if he was sick enough to vomit. His stomach seemed okay but his mouth and brain felt as though all the moisture had been wrung out of them. He went into the kitchen and got a glass of water and drank part of it. It made him a little dizzy, but he was able to keep it down. He seemed to be alone in the apartment. The mingled smells of cigarette smoke and stale beer and old wine clung to everything. He remembered sitting down next to Sara on the couch and leaning his head against her shoulder. Then nothing.

He had to pee.

When he came out of the bathroom he saw that the door to Tom's bedroom was ajar and he peered in. In the drab light Tom appeared to be asleep, his arm draped over someone next to him. Bob knew who it was even without looking. He turned to leave, but he wanted to be certain, or perhaps he wanted the pain of certainty, and he moved closer to the bed. Jen was asleep beside Tom, her back to him. Both were clothed. Okay, Bob thought, I can live with that. He stepped back from the bed and saw her panties on the floor. They were hers, he knew, because they couldn't be anybody else's. He thought of leaving them there but then, in a flash of malice, he picked them up and brought them to his face and smelled them and then stuffed them into his pants pocket. Let her look for them. Let her wonder.

Outside, the sun hadn't come up yet. He heard a single pigeon in the neighbor's dovecote. He went out to the parking lot and then remembered that Jen and he had walked to the party. He pictured her in their flat when they were deciding whether or not to take the car, and then opting not to because they might be too drunk to drive home. Such a mundane activity preceding the end of the world. He forced the beginning of a sob back into his chest. He walked home, his fingers rubbing the soft fabric of Jen's panties in his pocket.

He was masturbating when Jen came in. He watched her as she undressed. Her flat stomach, her breasts, her rib cage, the black pubic hair.

"Don't stop," she said. She was completely naked now. She sat down beside him on the bed and moved his hand away from his penis. "Let me."

After a while she said, "Are you going to be able to come?"

"Let me look at your vagina," he said.

She hesitated. "I haven't washed." Then she positioned herself so she was sitting cross-legged as she stroked him and she raised her knees. The hair on her labia glistened—with Tom's come, he knew. He thrust violently into her hand.

"Give me," she said, mounting him.

Two men in just a few hours, Bob thought. He came almost immediately but was hard again even before his penis began to shrink. She was smiling, her eyes closed, her face tilted toward the ceiling, as though she were watching something joyous behind her eyelids. He visualized Tom in her and he grasped her buttocks and spread them and pretended Tom's cock was between them. He remembered how John's penis had looked as he withdrew it from her vagina, coated with his semen and Bob's, and Bob imagined his penis coming out of her with his semen and Tom's on it. She smelled of dried sweat, and he wondered how much of it was hers and how much Tom's. He drove into her, harder, expecting her to ask him to stop, to tell him he was hurting her, but she only made that "unh, unh" sound she made when she was surrendering to pleasure, and then he came again, crying out, and she was kissing him, his eyelids, his mouth, his eyelids again and the corners of his eyes, and it was then that he realized he was weeping. "I had to," she whispered.

"Did you sleep with Karen?"

Before he could answer, she said, "Please don't lie to me. I know you want to."

He tried to remember what Tom had seen that night. He thought that what Tom knew, he had only surmised, but he said, "Yes."

She had been lying against him, her head on his shoulder, but now she moved away and lay on her back. She put her hand on her chest, as though she were having trouble breathing.

"Are you all right?"

She shook her head. "How can I be all right? Look what you've done to me. And you didn't even have the courage to tell me. Did you sleep with her more than once?"

"No."

"Can I believe you?"

"It was only that one time."

She looked at him. "I think you're being honest. Apparently you won't lie if I ask you a direct question. Why did you sleep with her? Aren't I enough for you?"

He put his hand over his eyes. She was in such agony—he

couldn't bear it. She moved his hand away. "Look at me. Tell me."

"I don't know why I slept with her. It wasn't because I was missing something with you. I don't know why I did it. Why did you sleep with Tom?"

She lay back again.

"Because he asked me to. And I was drunk. No. I was drunk, but I would have gone to bed with him anyway. Because he asked me to."

"Would you have gone to bed with anyone who asked you to? What about Phil? He asked you to."

"How do you know about that? Oh, I forgot you were there. I would never go to bed with Phil." She made a dismissive motion with her hand.

"Did you go to bed with Tom because of Karen?"

She made that motion again. "He only told me afterward. I was crying and he was trying to make me feel better. I felt so guilty." She laughed. "What a klutz."

"Who?"

"Tom. He was trying to help me, so he told me the worst thing he possibly could have. Well, he didn't know."

"He knew," Bob said.

After a moment she said, "What are we going to do, Bobby? I don't know who you are. I don't know who I am."

He didn't know how to respond.

"My heart is breaking," she said.

Is This the World?

Everything had gotten distorted. Was this the world? He had looked for clarity but had found only distortion and illusion. Was this the world? Did the world operate as though it did not see itself as through one of those funhouse mirrors that balloon you into something grotesque, or thin you into something straight as a screwdriver, narrow as a toothpick? Or did it see itself as it was, but was indifferent to what it saw? Was this the world—deceit and self-deceit and indifference?

Night after night they lay beside each other, staring into the darkness until first one and then the other turned on his or her side and went to sleep.

During the day he stayed away from the apartment as much as he could. He would leave at midmorning, go to a Denny's, buy a newspaper and look at the want ads. It was summer now and he was competing for jobs against students on their break, and they had more education than he had. That is, he would have been competing against them if he applied for any jobs, but he didn't apply. Soon enough he would need work, but there would be tree spraying before too long. He thought about enrolling in summer school at the junior college, but didn't.

He began to write a story, or at least fragments that might turn into a story. Then he began another one. He had not written in almost a year and the writing came new to him, almost as if he had never written, although he could tell that some of the things he had learned before were carrying through. He paid more attention to the rhythm of sentences than he had, and in his mind he likened writing to the composition of music.

When he thought about what he was doing, or how he was doing it, he realized that he was still under the influence of Kerouac. But he had no control. He was surprised again and again by how something could turn out so different from what he had imagined it would be when he began it. He didn't remember writing being like this before. But he was glad he had it and that it gave him pleasure. It was a kind of consolation for the losses in his life.

When he returned to their apartment, Jen was often there, but sometimes she wasn't. They didn't ask each other how they spent their days. One afternoon he went home and she was wearing her terry-cloth robe. She wasn't wearing underwear.

"Waiting for Tom? Or has he already been here?"

She began to cry. He wanted to help, but he was afraid to touch her. He was afraid to lose his anger, his hurt. Finally he went over and sat down next to her on the sofa and put his arm around her. He smelled her hair. She had just showered.

"Won't you make love to me?" she asked.

He did his best to give her pleasure, to keep her from thinking, to stop her pain, at least for a while. He did not ejaculate; he didn't know why. Staring at the wall in the dimming light, he said, "Maybe we can go on like this."

"Do you think we can?" She was lying on her side, watching his face.

"I'm willing to try."

"I don't want to lose you."

He put his hand on her hip, then sat up and bent and kissed her thigh. "I don't want to lose you either." He said, "I want you from the rear."

She rolled onto her belly and raised her hips. With his finger, he followed the crease between her buttocks down to her anus and pushed. It resisted. Her flower. Her rosebud. He was certain Tom hadn't been there. He got to his knees and pressed his penis against it. "I won't go inside," he said.

He masturbated until he came and then he smeared his semen on her anus with his fingers.

"That was strange," she said after he lay down next to her again.

"Did you like it?"

"I think so. I didn't dislike it. Did you really want to have me in the ass, but decide to do that instead?"

"I just wanted to see my jizz on your anus."

"Why?"

He didn't answer. Instead, he said, "I thought our days of experimenting were over, but I guess not."

She placed her hand on his belly and turned so that she was lying on her side beside him again, the length of her body in contact with his.

"Your body is changing," she said. "Your chest has more hair on it than it used to."

But sometimes when she wasn't home when he returned, he wanted to scream loudly enough to destroy the world. He imagined himself yelling at her, throwing things against the wall—a lamp, dishes, an ashtray—and he would pace the living room, unable to keep himself from looking out the window each time he came to it, hoping to see her in the distance, walking back to their apartment from Tom's.

Masturbation helped. It tired him; rage required such energy. While he stroked himself, he visualized Tom on top of her, his cock moving in and out of her, or his head between her legs. He saw her swollen labia part to welcome Tom's tongue. He saw her with her mouth enclosing Tom's cock, her eyes looking upward to meet his, to see if she was pleasing him. Sometimes he saw her with John again, John's cock coated with her vaginal fluid, Bob's semen and his own.

He could not guess what she and Tom talked about, so everything he saw was accompanied by silence, though he wondered if the sounds of her pleasure were the same with Tom as with him. If he could have heard them, her cries or the words they spoke, it would have been worse, he thought. But the worst was knowing that she had a life apart from the one she had with him, one in which she had found someone in whom she could confide as she used to do with him, someone with whom intimacy was unqualified. Bob knew that his life with her would end as soon as one of them found the courage to walk away.

He would masturbate to orgasm and then he would doze, as he did after coitus with Jen. But soon enough he would wake and he would be energized again, his anger having returned. He hoped she was suffering too. Yet when he saw her, saw how unhappy she was, he felt he would do anything to make her unhappiness go away.

He wondered if she was sad only when she was with him or when she was with Tom too, until one day, driving home, he saw them strolling on Harbor, window-shopping and holding hands. She looked...what? She looked happy, yes, but she also looked... carefree. Yes, carefree. It was something, this absence of woe, he hadn't seen on her face in a long time, since before they married.

And Tom? He, too, seemed happy, his face red with sun. They were talking as they walked, oblivious to everything around them, oblivious to Bob's observing them.

When she came home that evening, he said, "Maybe we should split up."

She was shocked. "Why?"

"You don't love me. I make you unhappy. And I'm unhappy

too."

"I didn't know you were unhappy. Why are you? And I do love you."

He stared at her. How could she not know? How could she not see what he was going through?

"Why am I unhappy? Why do you think?"

She didn't answer and for the rest of the evening he concentrated on not phrasing anything else as a question.

He thought often of leaving her. He thought it would be better, for him, at least, to leave her than it was waiting for her to announce she was going to live with Tom. He thought he could simply leave one day when she was away. He owned very little. He still had the duffel bag he had used when he moved out of his parents' house. He could buy another one at a surplus store if he needed one. And the car was his. But he told himself he needed to stay so Vern would know where to find him when the spray season began, and he stayed.

One night he said to her, "You haven't put your hands over my eyes since...the last time." He didn't want to say "since I punched you," and wished suddenly that he hadn't said anything at all.

"You said you didn't want me to. I will if you want me to. If you won't hit me. That hurt." She laughed. "Jesus, that was dumb, putting my hands over your eyes. Why did I do that?" She laughed again. "It was fun though. I liked making you mad."

Karen had moved away from home and gotten her own apartment. Her mother gave Bob her phone number. She was working part time as a nanny and taking a class in summer school at Long Beach State. Bob asked if she was free on Tuesday. She wasn't, but she invited him for dinner on Thursday.

She had gotten hold of a Burgundy and they drank it with dinner. Bob felt light, almost free. He laughed at something she said and realized that he couldn't remember the last time he had laughed. He kissed her and she returned his kiss. This was a different life from the one he had been living.

She excused herself and went into her bedroom. When she came back she was wearing a sheer chemise and she sat down on the couch. He sat down next to her and kissed her again. He had forgotten how heavy her breasts were, and how they tasted of vanilla. He thought to ask her someday if she put something on them to make them taste that way. He lifted her chemise over her head and kissed her again. She asked, "Aren't you going to take your clothes off?"

"If I do, I'll have to take my hands off you."

She smiled. "I don't want you to take your hands off me. I'll undress you."

He stood up and she stood up too and began unbuttoning his shirt. He kissed her again. She unfastened his belt and opened his fly and he kissed her hair and ran his hands over and between her buttocks. They, too, were heavier, fuller, than Jen's. Only a year older than Jen, Karen's body was already an adult's.

"Let's go to bed," she said. She grasped his penis as though it were a handle and led him, both of them laughing, into the bedroom.

She had just broken up with her boyfriend, she said. Then she said no, he had broken up with her. Her father had gone to his apartment and said something to him, she didn't know what, and the next day Marcus broke up with her. He wouldn't tell her what her father had said. He said only that her father was insane. "That man is crazy," he said. She hadn't thought that her father would do that.

She thought that what her father said had something to do with Marcus' race. If it wasn't about race, it could have had to do with what her father had done to her. He had done something to her when she was small and he had continued doing it until finally she moved out. She asked Bob if he knew what she was talking about; she didn't want to say it. Bob said he thought he knew. She had hinted at it before. She must have forgotten; they had been drinking then too.

He put his arms around her and she huddled against him. She began to sob, her tears hot on his chest. Finally she said, "I shouldn't have told you. Now you'll hate me."

"I don't hate you. Why would you think that?" Bob said.

"I don't know. I just thought you would. I don't know why I told you."

"Oh, Karen," he said. He kissed her hair.

He sat up. Karen was awake; he could feel her eyes on him. It was almost four.

"I have to go," he said.

"I know. I have to get up soon too."

He walked out to the living room and found his clothes and put them on. Karen was still in bed when he went in to kiss her goodbye.

"Thank you for last night. For listening to me," she said. "I hope you don't hate me."

"I don't understand why you think I would hate you. Your father is the one I hate." He put his hand on her cheek. "Thank you for last night. I'll call you in a few days, okay?"

"You don't have to worry about me."

I do have to worry about you, he thought. I won't be able not to worry.

Driving home, he thought: Other people have their own lives, their own sorrow. He would have liked to tell this to Jen, but he knew he wouldn't, out of loyalty to Karen.

He hoped Jen wouldn't be home when he arrived. Rather than having to talk to her now, he would have preferred her to have spent the night with Tom. Or, if she was home, that she would be asleep and, at least for a while, he wouldn't have to confront their unhappiness again. It's like a wound that refuses to close, he thought. The sky was only beginning to lighten when he pulled up in front of their building. The apartment was dark.

When he let himself in, the bedside light came on.

"You scared me," Jen said. She was wearing one of his tee shirts. The globes of her eyes were pronounced and all around them was dark and hollow; she had been crying.

"Sorry," he said.

"I didn't know what to think. You haven't done this before."

"I should have called. I'm sorry."

"I thought you had left me. What are you doing?"

"I'll sleep on the couch."

"Why?"

He didn't have an answer.

"Come to bed with me. Please."

When he was beside her, she said, "Would you like me to suck you off?"

"You don't have to."

"I want to."

She stopped. "You smell like her." She took his penis in her mouth again. She was more accomplished than she was the last time they did this.

"I'm going to come," he said. She nodded. She gagged only a

little.

"It tastes sweet," she said. She moved up and kissed him, her tongue going into his mouth. She asked, "Do I taste different?"

"No." He kissed her back. "Thank you."

She turned off the lamp and then turned back and moved under his arm. "Did you come in her?"

"No."

"Liar."

"Does Tom come in you?" It hurt to think of them together, her offering herself to him. Bob visualized her naked, lying on her back, parting her legs. He saw Tom, naked also, looking at the glistening hair on her pudendum, then opening her legs even more with his hands and slipping between them and tasting her salt, smelling the sea inside her.

"You're hard again. My superman. My super Bobby. I have homosexual dreams. Fantasies, not dreams. I think of Shannon kissing me and then I think about a girl I knew when I was thirteen. We used to touch each other. Then I fantasize about your old girlfriend—Sherry, isn't that her name?—and make up in my mind what she looks like. She has red hair, doesn't she? I imagine discovering her red pubic hair and wondering what it must taste like down there. And then I think about Karen because that's who you're fucking now. You don't have to deny it. It hurts to think about it, you with her, but I get excited when I do, as if I'm you and I'm taking her through you. Is that how it is for you when you imagine me with Tom, that it's actually you fucking me when he's fucking me? In my fantasies I do it with Karen. I think it's because I want to tame her, or domesticate her—maybe I mean own her—so I can own you too. But all that's too cerebral, trying to figure out what something means when the important thing is what my pussy wants. Is that how it is for you? Once your penis gets hard, you just want to put it in any girl who's available?

I'm not just prattling now. I need to know what to expect from you. When you get hard, does it matter to you who you put it in?"

"Of course it does."

"So you're in love with Karen."

"No. I care about her. We've only done it twice."

"Liar. But that's all right. I can live with your lies because I know you're only trying not to hurt me. Tell me again. Are you in love with Karen?"

"No."

"All right. I'll believe you. So it's just sex."

"Are you in love with Tom?"

"Shit. I knew once I asked you about Karen, you'd ask about Tom. I don't want to answer."

"You don't have to. I already know."

"You've lost your hard-on. I don't know if I can live like this, Bobby. I have a question: would you want to make this permanent, if you could? I mean, me with both you and Tom? I think I could overlook Karen. I think we've talked about this before."

"You're asking me if I could accept you having Tom and me too?"

"I don't want to lose you, Bobby. And I don't want to give Tom up. I wish we had done it again with John and Shannon. Maybe I could have learned just to pay attention to the sex and not all the stuff that goes with it. Oh, Bobby, what are we going to do?"

"I love you," he said, "but this is killing me."

"It's killing me, too."

"Does Tom love you?"

"He says he does."

"Do you believe him?"

"Yes."

"Lucky girl. Two men in love with you and you get to fuck them both."

"Fuck me. Fuck me in the ass. Come on my tits. Are Karen's tits as big as they look when she's wearing a sweater?"

"Yes."

"What do they taste like? Do they taste like mine?"

"They taste like vanilla."

"Vanilla! And she has such dark skin. How are her legs? Does she have cellulite?"

"No."

"No? I would have thought she did. Do you care if I touch myself? I'm getting excited again, talking about your lover. Do you eat her? Do you kiss her pussy? Do you put your finger in her? Of course you do. Everybody does that. Do you lick her juice off your fingers? It gets me so hot when you finger fuck me and then lick my juice off your fingers. Are you hard? Oh yes. Is it for me or for her? Who are you thinking about? Who am I, Bobby? What's my name?"

He hadn't seen Jen's parents in almost a month, though Jen had dutifully gone for supper every Saturday.

As in the past, conversation began once they were seated around the table. David asked, "How goes the job hunting?"

Before he could answer, Jen said, "Tom is working for his friend Gerry and he said he could probably get Bobby a job there too."

She hadn't mentioned this to him, that Tom was working with Gerry or that he had offered to get him on.

"Who is Tom?" Carol asked.

"He's our friend. I've told you about him. Bobby used to live with him."

"Oh?" Carol appeared not to remember.

"What do Tom and his friend do?" David asked. "Is he really

named Jerry?"

"Tom and Jerry?" Peter said.

"They paint houses. And he is," Jen said.

David's eyebrows rose. "New houses? The economy must be picking up."

"Actually," Bob said, "that tree-spraying company called. I'll be going back to work for them in two or three weeks. Part time."

"You didn't tell me that," Jen said.

"I thought the season began in August," David said.

"Early season. They're bringing on some us who worked for them last year before they hire for the regular season."

"Will the season end again in…November, was it?"

"I assume it will."

"You must have done a good job for them last year if they want you to start early. You might consider this house-painting job though. It might last longer. I'm talking about the rainy weather putting a halt to painting this winter, not any trouble you might have."

"I know."

"Of course, you might be able to paint indoors when the weather changes. Or do they have another crew that paints the insides of the houses? I assume your friend is working outdoors in sunny weather. Getting a good tan and all that." He directed this to Jen.

"I don't know."

"Still"—this to Bob—"you might think about the painting job. If the economy is picking up, it might turn into something long-term, even with the winter layoffs."

"I'll think about it," Bob said.

At the door, Carol pressed some money into Jen's hand. David put his hand on Bob's shoulder. "Don't worry," he said. "It'll pass."

Bob wondered what David knew. Did he know about Jen and

Tom, or did he see something in the way he and Jen were acting toward each other? Maybe he was showing his unhappiness in spite of trying to conceal it.

"If nothing else works out, there's always the paper route," Peter said.

"When did they call about the tree-spraying?" Jen asked.

"Yesterday. The day before. No, yesterday."

"Why didn't you tell me?"

"I don't know. I didn't think you'd be interested. No, that's not true. I don't know why I didn't tell you."

"That was embarrassing, your telling my parents without telling me first."

"So, what's this about Tom offering to get me a job? When did that come up?"

"All right, so I'm guilty of not telling you stuff too."

"I didn't even know he was working with Gerry. When did he start?"

"Last week. He said they were looking for more people and he thought you might be interested." She turned to face him. "Are you interested in what Tom is doing?"

"We were friends once," Bob said. "But I don't see him inviting me to work alongside him. Not now."

"It was my idea." She said it as though she was giving up something she didn't want to give up. "He didn't think it would work either, but he said he would ask if I wanted him to. I knew you needed a job and I was just trying to do something right for a change, okay?"

He pulled onto their street, drove slowly between two sedate rows of houses, old trees, maples, overhanging the street, and rolled to a stop almost directly in front of the door to their building. Jen was weeping again, soundlessly.

"Do you ever feel that your life is being wasted? That you could be doing something else that would make you happy, or go somewhere else where you could find something that would be important to you?"

"All the time. Every day."

"Really?"

"Yes."

"I thought so." Large tears were crawling down her cheeks. She had cried so much lately that he was becoming numb to it. He made no effort to comfort her.

"Why did you ask?"

"I wanted to be sure."

He met Karen at a coffee shop neither of them had been to before.

"Say something that will make me feel happy," he said as he sat down.

She burst out crying.

"I'm sorry. It's just that my own life is so unhappy now," she said.

He put his hand on hers and she turned her wrist so that she could grasp his fingers.

"I should be wearing my smiley face now. I'm sorry," she said.

"Your smiley face?"

"That's what our teacher used to tell us when I was in the third grade—we should always wear our smiley face when we're with other people, or they won't like us."

"You don't have to wear your smiley face with me."

"I know. But I still think I should. Isn't that stupid?"

He squeezed her hand.

"I'm parked in front. Do you want to follow me back to my apartment?" she asked.

He Didn't Know How She Got There.
He Didn't Know How He Got There.

"You lost weight. Didn't you used to be heavier?" Alberto said. He had turned the nurse truck off and was sitting beside Bob on the soft dirt between two grapefruit trees.

"I don't know," Bob said. "I don't know what I weigh now."

"Maybe you got taller. How old are you?"

"Eighteen."

"Eighteen. Weren't you eighteen the last time I saw you?"

Bob thought. "Yeah," he said.

"Well, you still got time to grow. Maybe you haven't lost any pounds. I thought you looked different when I saw you back at the barn. Maybe you're taller. How tall are you?"

"I don't know. I haven't measured in a while."

"You don't know how tall you are? You don't know how many pounds you weigh? Are you sure you just eighteen? You sound like, I don't know, eighty-four, eighty-five to me. You sound like my grampa."

Carl laughed.

"And you look like my grampa," Alberto said to him.

"Fuck you," Carl said. "For all you know, I might be your grampa."

Dick Miles was not on any of the crews. No one had seen him since last season. Carl and Bob alternated driving with spraying. They drove slowly, sometimes stopping altogether to allow the sprayer time to wet the trees on both sides of the lane. Sometimes Alberto, bored with waiting for them to empty the tank on the rig so he could refill it, took the second spray gun and doused the trees on one side. He was very fast but very thorough. After he passed through, the leaves of the trees on his side dripped water and compound for half an hour.

They knew this because Marion came by some time after they had wet a lane and told them that whoever was spraying the right side needed to adjust the nozzle of his gun to a finer spray. Almost a mist, he said. He looked at Bob, but Alberto stepped up and admitted that he was doing it that way because he was bored and he wanted to use up the water fast so he could bring more.

Marion put his hand on Alberto's shoulder. "Bored, huh? Well, if you don't get your boredom under control, you're gonna kill these trees. They can't tolerate all the poison you're putting on 'em."

"Okay," Alberto said. "I won't let myself be so bored."

"Good man," Marion said. He looked at the trees. "Good thing these are young ones. We don't have to man the tower. You're not putting anyone up there, are you, Carl?"

"No sir. Don't need to."

"All right. See you tomorrow, probably."

Marion walked back to his pickup. He was heavier than he was last year. Fatter. And he seemed a little distant, but maybe that would change as the season progressed.

They worked only eight hours that day, including traveling to and from the grove and refueling the rig and the nurse truck back at the barn. Bob was home before Jen returned from visiting her mother. With both the men in her life working, she had time on her hands.

"I'm thinking about catching the second half of summer school," she said as they ate. Bob was about to bring up the expense of buying books—the spraying job had come just in time, but he wouldn't get a paycheck for a couple of weeks—but she said, "My mom gave me a hundred dollars."

"That much? Does your dad know she gives you so much money?"

"I don't think so. Sometimes he gives me some too. I don't think he would if he knew mom does."

Bob nodded.

"What if I asked you to give Tom up? Would you do it?" He hadn't known he was going to say this. He hadn't even thought about saying it.

She stopped eating. She stared at him as though she were assessing him as a threat. She seemed to be on the edge of panic.

"You said you wouldn't ask me to do that. I remember you saying that."

"I know I said it, but it's really hard for me, Jen. Some days…"

"What?"

"Some days I think I'm going crazy. Today has been good because I'm tired—I don't have the energy to feel everything I feel about you sometimes. But even today on the way home, I was thinking about how it would be if you weren't here when I got home. I started thinking about you and Tom together and—"

She said, "I've never heard you whine before."

When he didn't respond, she said, "Tom was at work and I was with my mother. I told you last night that I was going to see her today."

"I know, but it doesn't matter. I don't trust you anymore."

"You don't trust me? I find out months afterward that you fucked Karen, and you don't trust me? You didn't even have the guts to tell me!"

He had been holding his fork in his hand from the time he brought up Tom. Now he placed it carefully on his plate. He didn't want to hear its small, singular chime when he set it down.

"Besides," Jen continued, "you have Karen now. Do you think

that doesn't hurt me? Do you think you have to tell me how you feel when you think about me with Tom? I feel the same way when I imagine you with her. I'm hurting too, and I don't see you doing anything to help me. Just the opposite, it seems to me."

"Tom helps you?"

"Yes, he does. Doesn't Karen help you?"

Bob got up from the table and went over to the bed and lay down. After a moment he sat up and took off his shoes and then lay back again.

"Are you going over to Tom's tonight?"

"I won't if you don't want me to." She was looking at her plate, or at the table.

"I don't want to interfere with your life, Jen. If you need him—"

"Shush. Don't do this to yourself."

She came over to the bed and stood beside him.

"Can I lie down with you?"

He moved to make room for her.

She lay down and placed her hand on his chest. "Do you want to make love?"

"No. I'm too tired. Sorry."

"It's all right, baby. I'm tired too. It's nice just lying here with you."

They found a shaded area of loose dirt and stopped the trucks and turned off the hoses and sat down to eat lunch. After eating a sandwich, Bob ate the apple he had packed. Then he lay back, the black soil absorbing the tiredness in his body. He was at the edge of sleep when Alberto said, "Your woman, man."

He opened his eyes and turned his head toward Alberto.

"What about her?"

"A little girl with black hair, right? She got a sweet ass, am I right?"

Bob didn't say anything.

"I saw you maybe three, four months ago in Fullerton. You were walking by the stores and you were holding hands. Maybe five months ago. Very sweet, man. I got to say, she don't got much in the titty department, but she got a very fine ass. Here, you want a Oreo?"

"I'm not hungry. Thanks, anyway."

"That's why you're losing weight. You're not eating any Oreos when someone offers them to you."

He extended his hand again with an Oreo in it and Bob took it.

"Thanks," he said.

"So, you married to her?"

"Yeah."

"Yeah? You got married, man?"

"Holy shit!" Carl said. "What'd you wanna do that for?"

Bob sat up. "I don't think I'll be married much longer."

"Uh oh," Alberto said.

"Well, if you're gonna do it, it's best to do it quick. Like pulling a bandage off a wound. Hurts like hell, but it's less painful in the long run," Carl said.

"Ask Carl," Alberto said. "He knows the best ways to get divorced. You married to her for real or just shacked up?"

"For real."

Carl shook his head. "That's why I like to shack up. It's easier when you want to leave."

"Or when she leaves you. Right, Carl?" Alberto said.

"Well, it happens that way, too."

"So what is it, man? You leaving her or she leaving you?"

Bob shrugged. "I think we're leaving each other."

"That sounds serious. I bet she found somebody else, huh? Or you did. Yeah, I bet it was you. I remember you were a real stud last year. I bet you didn't give up your stud ways when you should have, did you?"

"A man should never give up his stud ways. He should take his stud ways with him to the grave," Carl said.

Alberto and Bob laughed.

"Old Carl," Alberto said. "So, hey, man, how about introducing me to her, your woman?"

"She's got somebody else," Bob said.

"All the better reason to introduce me. I'll get her back for you. Well, maybe not. But I can get her away from this other guy. What's his name?"

"Tom."

"Tom? Like Tom Turkey? Tom Cat? No wonder he got her away from you. What kind of name is that? That some kind of American name? Carl, you ever know a guy named Tom Cat?"

"I don't think I ever heard of anybody with that name. Tomcat? No."

"So, Bob. Is that an American name?"

"I don't know. Probably."

"What is 'Bob' in Spanish?"

"Roberto, I think."

"Yeah? Roberto? That's a very good name. So, Roberto, if I can get your woman away from this Tom Cat, can I have her?"

"You won't be able to."

"You don't think I can? I can give her something this Tom Cat doesn't have. I bet you don't have it either, or you wouldn't have lost her to this guy."

"What's that?"

"I ain't tellin' you, man. If I tell you, you can use it too."

"It's drugs," Carl said.

"No, man, it ain't drugs. You think I need drugs to get a woman to beg for it? You think I need drugs to make a woman want to have a baby with me?"

"I'm just jerkin' your chain. I didn't mean nothin'," Carl said.

"So, Roberto, what do you say? If I can get her to beg me for it, can I have her? What's her name?"

"I don't think I should tell you," Bob said.

Alberto laughed. "See? That's 'cause you know I can do it."

"Maybe you can. I don't know. But I'm not going to help you. Why are you even asking me? It's up to her. I don't own her."

"You don't own her? Aren't you married to her?"

"Yeah. For now."

Alberto looked at him. "That's your problem, man! You got to be in command of her! I bet this other guy, this Tom Cat, is. Women want that, man!"

He wasn't joking. He was truly angry. Bob could feel contempt radiating from him. Bob stared back. Alberto got up and went over to the nurse and started it up. Carl and Bob got to their feet and walked over to the rig.

Jen wasn't there when he got home. He tried to bring himself off in the shower, but didn't succeed. He dried off and put on clean clothes and heated a can of soup.

When Jen came in, he could see a kind of cheeriness in her face, but only for a moment. When she saw him, the cheeriness vanished and she turned away, but then she turned back and said, "Hey."

"Are you wearing underwear?" he asked.

"What?"

"Show me."

"I'm not going to show you."

"Take off your jeans."

"No! What are you talking about!"

"Goddamnit!" He stood up. "Goddamnit! I don't know! I don't know!"

He could hardly see for the blur of water in his eyes, but he knew she was frightened. Then she was on the floor. For a moment he didn't understand how she got there. Disbelief was on her face. Then he remembered feeling something move in his shoulder and his arm and he understood that he had hit her. He was afraid. His scalp and the skin on his arms tingled and his face was tight and he felt himself start to separate from himself and he took a step toward her. She scooted away, terror on her face, watching him. His heart was breaking. This was not what he had wanted. He didn't know what he had wanted, but it was not this. He stepped back. He wiped his forearm across his eyes.

"You can't stay here," he said. It's too dangerous for both of us, he thought, but didn't say it, or maybe he did. "Grab some clothes. Grab what you need. I'll take you wherever you want to go. You can come back for the rest of your stuff later."

Neither of them spoke as she pulled her clothes off hangers, underwear out of drawers. He got some grocery bags from the kitchen and handed them to her, but she wouldn't reach for them. He put them on the floor and backed away and she picked one up and stuffed clothes into it and then she did the same with another bag.

"Where do you want to go?" He thought she might say her parents'.

"Tom's."

He took the bags of clothes down to the car and put them on the back seat. After he closed the door, she opened the door on the other side and got in behind the passenger seat.

He slid in behind the wheel and turned on the engine. He

looked in the rearview mirror. She was watching him. Neither spoke.

He pulled into the lot behind Tom's apartment. He got out and took the bags out of the car. Jen got out by the opposite door. He carried the bags to the foot of the stairs leading to the apartment and set them down. He turned, almost bumping into her. "Goodbye," he said.

"I don't know if he's home," she said. He heard her running up the stairs as he walked away.

That night it occurred to him that she hadn't come home from being with Tom because Tom would have been working. He didn't know where she had been.

Lying in bed, he thought, Who am I? Who am I? I am someone who must watch himself. I must take care.

His Heart Was Almost Okay

The next morning Alberto and Carl didn't say anything to him. They must have been able to read something in his face or in the way he moved. At lunch, Alberto gave him a Benzedrine. Bob had never had one. Alberto said it would make him feel good.

It kicked in shortly after they resumed spraying. Bob imagined himself playing a trumpet, sounding a lot like Miles Davis, but hotter, faster. The sounds coming from his horn took up his entire head so that he wasn't thinking about Jen at all. He decided to take up the trumpet. Somehow he would find a way to pay for lessons. He heard his future self as the hottest trumpet player ever, wrapping the notes around trees, utility poles, flagstaffs, anything that stood upright. He saw the notes as you see the stripes on a barber's pole, spiraling their way toward the top, flowing to infinity. The world felt structured, orderly, as though everything made sense. All he had to do was adhere to the structure.

He was spraying full bore, running between the trees to make certain he didn't miss anything, drenching the undersides of the leaves as well as their sun sides.

"Hey! Hey!" Carl yelled, stopping the rig. "Ease up! You're using too much of that stuff!"

He corrected the nozzle of his gun—he didn't remember adjusting it to full-on—and continued spraying. He had so much energy! He wondered if this was how Phil felt when he was high on gas vapors and went on those long sprints. He wondered if Phil had taken speed before sucking in the fumes those times.

He had an erection. He didn't remember that happening, but

there it was. He thought about Karen, her thighs opening, drops of moisture on her pubic hair like the condensation of dew on grass. He thought about her breasts flattening against her chest as she lay back. He thought of her legs parting and her arms rising to receive him. Jesus Christ! Was he going to come? That would be embarrassing. He was certain Carl was watching him in the sideview mirror. Maybe Alberto was watching him too. He turned quickly but Alberto wasn't behind him. He didn't see the nurse truck.

His heart was hammering his rib cage. It hurt. He didn't care. It was just this curious observation he made. Then he did care: it really hurt. He thought he could work past the pain and after finishing the trees behind the tank truck he moved up along one side of the rig and then the other, spraying those trees even before the rig could catch up, lumbering as it did over every bump in the shallow ditch, in and out of every depression.

Carl turned off the engine. He was laughing. "We're almost out of poison. We'll have to wait for Alberto to find us. What was that pill he gave you?"

"Fuck if I know," Bob said. He lay down between two trees. "Benzedrine, he said. I didn't know Benzedrine was an upper." He was very tired now. His heart was still beating against his ribs, but not as violently as before.

He heard the nurse truck lurch up, and then Alberto's and Carl's laughter.

"They don't call it speed for nothin'," Carl said.

"It took me twenty minutes to find you," Alberto said. "Is he all right?"

"Just a little hung over," Carl said.

"I'm gonna give you only half a tank, maybe less. It's already two. They want us back at the barn by three. Hell, let's go back now. I'll load you up in the morning. Can he get up? Hey, Roberto!

On your feet!"

Bob sat up. His heart was almost okay.

"That's the last time I give you a Bennie. It took me almost half an hour to find you. I hope you did a good job on those trees. If you didn't, Marion will let us know. And you don't want Marion on your ass."

He woke up earlier Friday than he needed to, but he couldn't get back to sleep. An image of Jen in shorts and a buttoned top came into his mind, and he placed her naked beside him in bed. He was hard and he grasped his cock. Jen was talking to him, but he couldn't hear what she was saying. He turned his head and kissed the air where her breast would have been, and soon enough he came in his hand. He felt something in his chest and then it came out too—a sob, which surprised him.

They weren't working weekends yet, and he called Karen on Saturday after he did his laundry. She didn't pick up.

Jen called on Sunday. She wanted to come over to get the sheets and dishes and everything her parents had given them when they got married. He told her he would collect it all so all she would have to do was pick it up and go.

He had hoped she would come over early and leave early because late afternoons and evenings were hard for him and he didn't want her to see him when he was having a bad time, but it was almost five when she arrived. She still had her key and she let herself in. She was wearing the shorts she had worn in his fantasy a couple of nights before, but her top was a pullover. When she saw him, she stopped short.

"I thought you would be gone."

"No. I don't know why you would have thought that."

"Tom's outside."

He shrugged. "Okay. Do you want me to help you, or are you going to make a couple of trips?"

"I've got it."

She gathered up the linens and left.

Tom came up for the dishes and the flatware. Bob hadn't seen him in a long time and couldn't help but feel again some of the affection he used to feel for him. Tom's face was very ruddy. At first Bob thought the climb up the stairs had winded him, but then he remembered that Tom was working outdoors now.

"Sorry, man," Tom said. Bob thought he meant it.

"That's okay. You shouldn't feel guilty."

"I can't help it." His face scrunched up and Bob turned away, thinking Tom was going to cry.

"Do you need help with this stuff?" Bob asked, although there was only one box.

"I think I can get it."

"Take care," Bob said.

"You, too."

He went to a supermarket and bought some plastic dishes and cups and bowls and two settings of silverware.

He called Karen again, but again she didn't pick up.

He masturbated every night, unable to get to sleep without it. And after waking up at three or four in the morning, as he had started doing, he couldn't get back to sleep until he had brought himself off again.

He couldn't always retain the narrative line of his fantasies and sometimes they devolved into a series of images brought up from memory, each displacing the one preceding it, seemingly on its own. He tried pushing away images of Jen with some of Karen or Sherry or Sara, but these lingered for only a moment before they vanished and Jen reappeared. Some of the most painful were those he imagined with Tom on top of her or taking her from behind, her small breasts swinging with his movement, the flesh of her buttocks rippling. The most powerful images were of her and John as he grabbed her ankles and spread her legs before inserting his penis in her, and then the semen, his and Bob's, on his penis as he pulled out of her.

He missed Jen's father. He wondered what he made of their break-up. He wondered what Jen had told him.

He stopped calling Karen, though he knew she could bring him solace, as he could her, if only they could get together, if only for a moment.

He Showed the Lawyer the Certificate of Marriage

The storefront was no longer a lawyer's office but a shop that sold serapes and souvenir trinkets. On the next block he found another lawyer's office and went inside. He explained that he had gotten married in Tijuana a few months ago and now he wanted to get divorced. He showed the lawyer the certificate of marriage the first lawyer had given them.

This lawyer said he had never seen one of these before. Bob told him what the other lawyer had said about a proxy wedding in Mexico City. The lawyer looked puzzled. He picked up the phone and dialed a number and spoke into the mouthpiece. He waited, then spoke again and waited again. Then he spoke again and said "Gracias" and replaced the phone in its cradle.

"Your marriage is not registered," he said. "You were not married in Mexico."

"What about the proxy ceremony in Mexico City?"

"Mexico does not have weddings by proxy. If you were married, your marriage would be registered. It is not."

"Okay," Bob said.

"I won't charge you."

"But I still want to get divorced."

"You weren't married. You don't have to get divorced."

"I want to. There must be a form to fill out. I'll fill it out and I'll pay you and then I'll be divorced."

The lawyer pulled two forms out of a drawer in his desk and put a sheet of carbon paper between them and rolled them all into the typewriter that sat on top of the desk. He typed, then rolled the papers through, withdrew the carbon paper, and handed Bob the forms.

"Sign there."

Bob signed.

"Sign the other one too."

Bob signed the second one.

The lawyer signed both and gave the original to Bob.

"Now you're divorced. That will be fifty dollars."

Bob gave him fifty dollars and then offered his hand. The lawyer shook it and walked Bob to the door.

"Good luck," the lawyer said.

It was early afternoon and Bob wandered through the city, away from the tourist areas, for a while. He discovered himself walking behind a small, black-haired woman without realizing that he was following her. She approached a policeman and Bob saw her head tilt in a gesture of a kind and the policeman gave a slight nod and looked past her at him. When she turned to her left, Bob turned right. In a moment he was back among the tourists. He asked a cab driver where he could find a whorehouse.

"Cherry Hill," he said. "I can take you."

"No, I don't want to go to Cherry Hill." He had heard a lot about Cherry Hill. "Somewhere here in town."

The cab driver gave him directions. Bob offered him ten dollars, but he refused it. "We all have our needs."

He followed the alley the cab driver had indicated to a three-story, adobe-colored building. Stopped in front of the door, he was trying to figure out if this was the house he wanted when a fit-looking man, twenty-five or twenty-six, came out. Bob asked him if this was a brothel. "Yes, my friend. Just go in." He turned and opened the door for him and Bob walked inside.

The ground floor was spacious but empty of both people and furniture and Bob walked up the stairs to an alcove where he saw another young man, this one with three or four days' growth of beard, talking with a woman Bob guessed to be in her thirties. He had come up behind the man, startling him so that he spun around and stared at Bob as though he thought Bob was going to accost him. The woman laughed. Bob seemed to be the only customer in the house.

"Señor," the young man said.

"I'd like a girl. She should be small and her hair should be short and dark, not dyed. And she should be young." Bob told him how much money he could spend.

The man nodded and asked Bob to wait, and he and the woman went to the rear of the house. In a moment he came back with a short, plump woman with dark hair. She was also in her mid-twenties and she was wearing a merry widow and panties. Jen was not plump, but Bob said okay and gave the woman the money.

The young man said something to her and pointed to a room. She led Bob inside where he asked her if she sixty-nined and she said she did. He watched her strip her panties off and he undressed and lay back on the bed and she straddled his face and bent forward and took his penis in her mouth. She emitted a vinegar-y smell, but he pressed his tongue into her and after a minute or two he felt his cock hardening as though it had an expanding steel shaft inside it. He rolled her off him and told her he wanted to fuck her and she parted her legs and he went inside her.

Soon she began to groan and thrust her pelvis toward him each time he pushed into her. Her eyes were closed and her expression could have been that of pleasure. He was surprised because he had thought prostitutes did not allow themselves to feel pleasure with a customer. After he came he kissed her forehead and said, "Jen." He couldn't help himself.

He lay down next to her. "I'll rest for a minute and then I'll leave," he said.

But she jumped up and said, "Wait." She slipped her panties on and, turning to him, said, "Do you want to be in a film?"

He didn't say anything and she said "Wait" again and left the room.

He got dressed and stepped out of the room. No one was around. He heard movement—footsteps, the creak of a weak spot in the floor—but it seemed to come from the floor above. He walked to the alcove leading to the stairs. He heard someone behind him and ran down the steps. Outside, he did not run, but walked rapidly away from the house into the alley. He turned and saw the young man who had brought the woman to him staring at him from the doorway. Bob waved to him and shook his head no and the young man went back inside.

Walking through the alley, it occurred to Bob that this might be the one where Kevin stabbed the guy who tried to rob him all those months ago.

Part Three
(1980, 2014)

Remember? Remember?

He had spent a good part of his sabbatical doing research on a small island in the western Pacific and now, having returned to Seattle, he could not settle in. Little things, by American standards, upset him: an associate professor in the sociology department—Bob recognized him even if he did not recognize Bob—cutting into the line ahead of him at the post office; a bicyclist spitting on his windshield when he was stopped at a light; a young mother slapping her squalling toddler, then handing him to his father who slapped him again. Bob knew what was wrong. He always got this way after coming back from Polynesia. He even knew how long the depression would last—four months, six months, perhaps a little longer—and then it would go away, the worst parts of it anyway.

He still had a few weeks before he had to resume teaching and he decided to drive down to San Francisco and get a motel room and stay there for a while. His favorite short run was from the marina to the Coast Guard station at the base of the Golden Gate Bridge on the San Francisco side of the bay. He liked running into the cold wind coming off the open ocean into the bay, the sun on his head and back, the spray wetting him when he left the trail to run along the water. The combination of cold and heat and water and sweat made it the happiest run he thought he would likely ever experience, and it was on one of these runs that it occurred to him to try to find Justin. He knew Justin had moved up here after he got out of prison and had found a job teaching at a private school, and he looked him up in the telephone directory.

His wife answered the phone and gave him Justin's work number. He was living there now, she said.

"I was thinking about you just the other day," Justin said. "Maybe Phil can come down. He lives in Santa Rosa."

The school was in a converted two-story house on a residential street just south of the Presidio. The lower floor was comprised of two large rooms and a kitchen with a small storage area for canned and boxed goods behind it. The lights were on in the nearer room, which Bob surmised was the classroom for the younger children, given the diminutive sizes of the chairs and tables and a couple of jackets that had apparently been forgotten at the end of the day. Butcher-paper posters of crayon scrawls—"Call it Expressionism," Justin said. "Or Dada," said Phil—and rudimentary human and animal figures were taped to the walls and the chalkboards.

Justin was thinner than Bob remembered him, and tireder. His face was already lined. Phil had become rotund and his face was more sanguine than when he was a kid. He looked like a caricature of a bourgeois of the last century as a Marxist might have drawn him then. Justin and his wife—ex-wife—had only recently divorced and he had furnished the storage area with a cot and some of his personal belongings, "until I can save enough to get an apartment. Lindsey pretty much got everything."

Phil and his wife had also split up and he was out of work as well—"Bad things come in bunches," he said—but he had decided to take out a loan and go back to school; he had never completed his undergraduate degree. He had spent the last seventeen years on marijuana, he said, and had quit only after his wife announced that she was leaving and taking the children. He had had the idea of persuading her that he had changed, that she wouldn't regret moving back into the house with him. He had not intended to quit forever, only until he got her back. But she had found someone else, probably before she moved out, and she wasn't willing to try again with Phil. But, all things considered, he didn't regret the break-up because it had led him to stop smoking and he was seeing the world as though he were a child again, as though everything was new and shiny or moved in ways that he did not expect. And he had begun painting again. And of course he was going to return to school. He did miss his kids, although, truth be told, not that much.

In the course of conversation—"Whatever happened to...?" "Do you remember...?" "What's Fred doing now?"—Phil said something about Jen's brother dying and Bob fixed his attention on him.

"You didn't know? It was seven or eight years ago. I assumed you knew."

"I haven't seen Jen in years," Bob said. "Peter was twelve the last time I saw him."

"You heard that Tom and Jen got divorced," Justin said.

"No."

"What have you been doing for the last twenty years?" Phil said.

"I left eighteen years ago," Bob said.

"Yeah. I lost seventeen myself."

A few days later the man Bob's sister was in love with was killed skydiving, and Bob went down to Orange County to stay with her. She was crying a lot in those first days after Michael's death and when she wasn't crying she was sleeping, or trying to, and Bob had time on his hands. Until Phil told him about Peter, Bob hadn't thought about either him or Jen in years, but now he found himself recalling images of her and of Peter and their parents.

He remembered Jen telling Phil the joke about her being a Martian with her sex organ in her thumb, and Phil's screeching laugh as he jerked his hand away when she said the punch line.

He remembered Peter offering to get him on as a paperboy when he was out of work. He didn't remember their mother well, except that she was blonde and overweight whereas her children were athletic and dark-haired like their father. He remembered Jen as she looked without clothes.

Finally, one evening after his sister had gone to bed, he got Jen's number from the phone book and called her. Later he would not remember all they said. She must have been surprised to hear from him, but he wouldn't remember her saying so. He told her he had just heard about Peter and felt compelled to call, and she said she had thought of him after Peter's death. She knew how fond of him Bob had been and thought he would want to know, but she had not known how to get hold of him. She hadn't thought to call his sister.

He asked if she had time to get together, maybe for dinner or a drink. "For a drink," she said, and gave him the name of a bar near the airport where they could also get something to eat if they were hungry. "Friday," she said. Her children would be with their father.

He arrived first and took a table and ordered a glass of wine. At the next table were a flight officer and four flight attendants, a steward and three stewardesses. They were drinking heavily and the steward's hand was on the thigh of the attendant nearest him. He seemed to be trying to goad her to respond, but she ignored him and continued talking with the flight officer seated across from her. The steward was becoming irritated. After several minutes the attendant rose and left the bar, taking her handbag. When she returned, her legs looked different, paler. Bob realized she had taken off her pantyhose. She sat down and resumed her conversation with the flight officer as the steward slid his hand under her skirt.

Jen came in just as the attendant and the flight officer stood up to leave. Bob didn't have time to search for the expression on the steward's face. He was amazed that Jen looked as she had when she was seventeen. She seemed not to have gained any weight, her hair was cut more or less the same, but she walked differently: her hips did not sway as they did when he first met her. He did not remember if they still swayed at the time they separated.

"Hi," she said, seating herself opposite him. She smiled tentatively. The smile, slightly off center, her lips a little more open at the right side of her mouth than the left, was the same. She ordered a glass of Cabernet and a grilled sandwich. "I didn't have time to eat. I had to get the kids ready to go to their father's. Tom picks them up on Friday night and brings them back on Sunday."

It was the same arrangement Bob had with his ex-wife when he was in Seattle.

"Do you see Karen much since you got divorced?"

"Karen?"

"Didn't you marry Karen, that girl you knew in high school?"

"No, I married someone I met in Colorado when I lived there. I don't know what became of Karen."

"I wonder who told me you married Karen. Maybe I just assumed you married her after we split up."

The barmaid came over and Bob put his hand over his glass. Jen ordered another Cabernet. She stood up and came around and sat down in the chair at his right. "I can't hear you with all this noise. It gets pretty loud on Friday nights."

She asked how many children he had, then said she also had three, a boy and two girls. The boy was the oldest.

He asked what happened to Peter.

He went crazy, she said. And then he killed himself. Schizophrenia. "We could see it happening, his descent, but we couldn't do anything about it. He went to a gun store and bought a gun, but my father found it and took it back and asked the owner or manager, whatever he was, not to sell Peter a gun again because Peter was crazy. Everybody could see he was crazy just by the way he talked, the way he looked at you. Then he bought another gun there and my father went back and begged the store owner not to sell Peter any more guns and the owner said as long as there was no law against it and Peter had the money to pay for it, he would sell Peter whatever he wanted. The third time, Peter bought the gun and shot himself before my father found out he had it. Nobody was home, but the neighbors heard it, the shot. It broke my father's heart. There was a little smile on Peter's face when we saw him, as though he had finally found a place where he could be without pain, but it broke my father's heart. A year later, on the anniversary of Peter's death, my father had a heart attack. He died the next day."

Jen's hand went to her left cheek and she brushed it lightly with the tips of her fingers.

"I know you liked Peter," she said. "And my dad. I wish I had called you."

Bob caught the barmaid's eye and she came over and he ordered a sandwich and asked for a glass of water. Jen ordered another glass of wine.

"In one year I lost my father and my brother. That was the year after I lost my husband."

Tom had become a contractor, putting up drywall, but he remained close to Gerry Crowe who had also gone out on his own as a contractor, so when Gerry got a job he tried to get the developer to hire Tom too, and when Tom got a job, he did the same for Gerry. "You knew Gerry and Kevin, didn't you? They and Tom have been friends since they were children."

But there was a recession and no one was building anymore, so there wasn't any work. "Gerry and Janice had put some money away, but Tom and I hadn't—it never occurred to us that anything like this could happen—and Tom started drinking more. I don't know if you remember, but he always liked to drink. But now he was drinking every day and I was getting more and more scared. We had three children and two cars and a house we were paying on. I kept asking myself what would happen if we lost the house, and I kept asking Tom too. Tom said I was like a puppy, the way I followed him around. He told me I'd better not pee on his slippers. He thought he was being funny, but I was scared and I couldn't stop myself from nagging him because I needed him to tell me everything was going to be all right.

"He was drinking a lot. A lot. He had closed the office and he had nowhere to go, so he stayed home and drank and I nagged him. Then he started hitting me. Just slaps, but… It wasn't like him. I knew he loved me, but… And he started talking about Jews. That wasn't like him either, I thought, but after we separated and I began to think more clearly, I realized he had always demeaned the Jews, but I had ignored it. He knew my father was Jewish and he loved my father, but he started putting Jews down, although not where my father could hear. And then he started blaming the Jews for everything that was wrong with his life. With our life. Our life together. And he started listening to Wagner again. I had made him give up Wagner when we got married—it was the only condition I imposed on him. Not because Wagner was anti-Semitic, but because he was too loud. Tom played him too loud. It hurt my ears.

"Of course, the Wagner and the anti-Semitism—even then, when I was being eaten up by anxiety over money and watching my marriage fall apart, I knew the anti-Semitism was aimed at me. I had never thought of myself as Jewish. My mother had had Peter and me baptized when we were small. But I knew Tom wanted to hurt me, and he did.

"Once, when he was drunk, he beat me up badly enough to… When I went to the hospital and got x-rayed, I found out he had cracked my pelvis, my cheekbone, some of my teeth—that's enough for a short list. Even before I went to the doctor, before I knew how badly off I was, I took the children and went to my parents' house. My father and my brother were still alive then.

"A couple of days later, Tom came over. He wanted me to move back with him. He was sober and denied having hit me. He said he had no memory of that night, but he was sure he hadn't beaten me up. 'I wouldn't,' he said, as if the way he thought of himself was the way I should think of him too. He couldn't explain what had happened to me if he hadn't beaten me up, but he insisted that he hadn't done it."

"I hit you too. I'm sorry," burst from Bob. He had intended to apologize to her but he hadn't known he was going to blurt it out like he did. It had weighed on him all evening. "I want you to know I haven't hit a woman since." Why did he say that? Would she care whether or not he had ever hit another woman? He had put in too much time in the academy, he thought.

For a minute or so, she was silent and he began to worry that she wouldn't forgive him, but finally she said, "You never hit me. You may have wanted to, and I wouldn't have blamed you if you had—I know I was cruel to you—but you didn't. I would remember it if you did. I have a very good memory. And, believe me, I know what it's like to be hit."

He didn't know what to say. She seemed so certain, but he could still see the events of that evening vividly—her fear, her crawling away from him even as her eyes remained fixed on his face, trying to anticipate what he was going to do next—and he couldn't believe he had invented something so terrible and lived with it for so many years. If he had, why would he have? He still felt the weight of his shame.

He said, "You don't have to protect my feelings."

"I wouldn't. Not about something like that. You were very angry with me the last couple of weeks we were together, and you had reason to be. But you didn't hit me. Maybe you're confusing me with someone else."

"No, I'm not. I don't know what to think. I could have killed you."

"If you could have, you would have. Listen, I want to continue with what I was saying. It's important to me. So, listen. I was living at my parents' house and Tom came over and he wanted me to move back with him. And I thought about going back. I even went to the house one day when the kids were in school. There was a hole in the wall that neither of us could explain. Finally I realized from the height it was from the floor that it must have happened when he broke my pelvis. He had hit me hard enough to knock me through the wall.

"I couldn't go back to him. Do you remember telling me, the last day we were together, that I had to leave because it wasn't safe for us to be together anymore? Well, I knew it wasn't safe for me to be with Tom anymore. By the way, why was I the one who had to leave? Why didn't you leave?"

"You could go to Tom's or back to your parents'. I had nowhere to go."

"Okay, that's a good reason. So, when I was ready, medically I mean, I got an apartment for me and the kids. Tom paid for it and my parents helped out. But it was too hard, financially and emotionally, and I went back to him."

After her father died, she went crazy. She had seen Peter when he was crazy and locked up and she had come to fear the lithium shuffle: you know, shoulders slumped as if collapsed on a hanger; chin dropped on the chest as though in sleep; hands dangling, incapable; feet sliding forward in a slow, measured pace, as if you'd fall over if you raised your foot from the floor. Well, now she was crazy and she had herself institutionalized in the same institution Peter had been in. It was while she was in Camarillo that Tom filed for divorce.

The woman he left Jen for was his brother's ex-wife with whom he had been in love since before she married his brother. She moved in with Tom as soon as her own divorce was final.

"In less than two years," Jen said, "I lost all the men in my life." When Tom dumped her, all of their friends went over to Tom's side. Even Kevin, with whom she had become close after Barbara died. "Oh, you don't know. Barbara died from an asthma attack when Kevin was out on a job. He was working for Gerry. He came home after work and found her."

What enraged her now, she said, was thinking about how wealthy Tom was, the comfort in which he lived, the big house, the cars, the fucking poodles, for Christ's sake, for with his new wife he had grown rich. It wasn't fair that he and Lisa should have everything and she nothing. All she had was a shit job she hated that paid only a little more than minimum wage. Tom hadn't touched her during the last two years of their marriage and—was this a nonsequitor or did it follow from her talking about Tom's new wealth?—she lost the confidence in her sexuality she had always had. Maybe Bob remembered how she had been.

Now, except when she had her children for the weekend, she used Friday and Saturday nights to pick up men. So far she hadn't gotten sick and she hadn't gotten hurt, although she had been frightened once by a man who told her when she started to get out of the car at the motel, "You touch that door handle and I'll break your fucking arm." He was really angry with his ex-wife.

"I can't have friends. What I have on Friday or Saturday is all I can have." With her fingertips, she brushed her left cheek. It was fourteen years more before Bob understood that she was tracing the memory of a river tears had cut.

When Bob said he wanted to make love with her, she said, "I was beginning to think you weren't going to ask," and said there was a motel nearby. "I don't like to bring men home, even if the kids aren't there."

When she came out of the bathroom, she looked as he had remembered her but for the Caesarian scar. "I thought about saying something, but I figured, What the hell, he can take it or leave it."

At love, she was uncannily as he remembered. Her flesh rose to meet his hand, his hand moved to place itself just so. Bodies have their own memories. But he couldn't finish. Giving up, he lay down beside her. Her hair smelled the same as he remembered it. "Well, I got mine," she said. "Do you want me from behind? Some men..." She turned over and raised her hips. After placing himself inside her, he brought his fingers to his nose and inhaled the scent from her vagina. When he came, it happened so quickly that there was not even a thought of holding back.

"Hey, do you remember our first date? You took me to a jazz club. I mean, what seventeen-year-old knows about jazz clubs?"

"I was trying to impress you."

"You succeeded. I knew then that I was going to give myself to you."

"You should have told me. I wouldn't have worked so hard to get you into bed. But I don't think it was our first date. I think we had been seeing each other for a while and may even have gone to bed by then."

"No, if it wasn't our first date, it was very early in our relationship. And we hadn't made love yet. At least we hadn't had intercourse yet. I remember thinking that I wanted to give you something for being so thoughtful. And I decided that night to give you my body."

"Do you remember who was with us?"

"Justin. And a girl. I don't remember who she was. Do you remember—we went to a motel for our birthdays? Our birthdays were close together and I asked you if we could get a motel room instead of doing it in the car like we usually did. Not that doing it in the car wasn't always good, but we had never gone to a motel. We must have done it five times that night. I remember being amazed that you could keep it up."

"I remember seven or eight times, but that may be vanity."

"We did it so much, your penis was raw. Poor little Bobby." Jen laughed.

"And the lips of your vagina. Little Jen."

"But we wouldn't stop. We weren't going to let a little pain keep us from fucking." She was still laughing.

"I don't think that was the first time we went to a motel. What I remember is that we had gone to motels a number of times, but I hadn't had any money for a while. Then when I got that job spraying orange trees I did have some money, and we decided to rent a motel room as our birthday gift to each other."

"I don't remember you spraying orange trees."

"It was the first job I got after we began seeing each other, not counting working in Justin's father's wood yard."

"I vaguely remember you working with Justin."

"Do you remember that time someone was yelling and banging on the door of our room in this cheap motel we were in, and you went and hid in the bathroom while I waited for him to come through the door? I had an ashtray in my hand and I was going to brain him with it."

"I don't remember that, but I believe you would have tried to protect me. Do you remember getting stuck in the sand on the shoulder of the road when we were trying to make love, and that nice man who came along and pulled us out? Out of the sand, I mean, not you out of me. We hadn't gotten that far in our lovemaking yet."

"I do remember. He liked you. You reminded him of his daughter."

"How do you know that?"

"I had gone looking for help. I left you with the car and I told you to lock yourself inside. And I found the man who owned the land we were on, actually, and he and I drove back in his pickup to rescue you and the car, and on the way he told me he had a daughter our age."

"I don't remember that. I remember him just showing up."

"Are you sure I didn't hit you?"

"I'm sure. Maybe my memory isn't as good as I thought it was, but I would remember that."

"Okay. How did we... I don't remember how we finally accomplished...what? Your deflowering? One of my students a couple of years ago called it 'devirginizing.' Did we finally do it in a motel?"

"We did it on my parents' couch. It was white and we put a towel under me and the blood soaked through and I was rushing to clean the couch before my parents got home. I told them the couch was wet because we had spilled coffee and I'd had to bleach out the stain. They just took it in stride. I'd just given up my virginity and they were talking about prices at the Thriftway."

"I remember now. I remember wanting to just lie down with

you afterward, but there was no time because we, or you, had to clean up the bloodstain."

"Yeah, that's how it was. Thank you for remembering now, and telling me."

"Do you remember putting your hands over my eyes while I was driving? You did it several times. I've never been able to figure out why you did it. I don't think you realized how dangerous it was."

"I liked to make you angry."

"Why?"

"I liked sex with you when you were angry."

"What!"

"After we made it with that other couple—I don't remember their names—I was really angry with you and I wanted to scare you because I was scared, but all I did was make you angry. But after one of those times, we made love and it was so good that I wanted to do it again, just that way. So I looked for a way to make you angry so you'd do me the same way you did it the first time. The first time you fucked me when you were mad at me, I mean."

"You were doing it before we made it with John and Shannon—"

"Yes, those were their names."

"—so you must have had some other reason for doing it."

"If I did, I don't remember it."

"You could have killed us."

He was intensely, disproportionately angry. He felt as though he had been betrayed yet again. But his thoughts were scrambled. What did it mean, her wanting to anger him? He didn't believe it was for sex, despite her explanation. And now she was trying to distract him—her sudden focus on John's and Shannon's names. What did their names matter? He didn't know where his rage had come from—the depth of it! It was something very old, older than the war he had fought in, older than his and Jen's…what? Love affair? Marriage? What was he to call the relationship they'd had? Had? If it was something that had passed, why was he in bed with her now? He knew this feeling, but from when? He did not remember when he had last been this angry. Was this the way he felt when he hit her, if he hit her? Was this how he felt during the last weeks they were together? But it didn't matter when it had begun, with Jen or earlier. It was there; it wasn't going to go away. It was inside him.

He felt as though he were being smothered, as if someone were pressing a pillow against his face. He had spent the major part of his life trying to convince himself that he was free of the constraints of the past, of a life determined by obligation. Sex with Jen, for a while, had been his route to freedom. And, he thought, hers. Yet here she was, telling him not only that she had deceived him in a way he had not known until now, but that nothing was as he had thought it was; he had deceived himself from the very beginning. The evidence was there; it had been there all along. He had seen it, but he had ignored it. Why had he pretended to himself that things were other than what they were? Was making love with her so important that he had overlooked everything else? No, he hadn't overlooked everything. After all, they weren't together now.

She was saying: "You were always so remorseful after you hit me, if you want to call it hitting. That was why I kept doing it, so you would feel bad. After the first time I knew that for a while, at least, I could get you to do anything I wanted. Don't you remember?"

She stopped. She had detected something. Was she afraid? She slipped out of bed and started putting her clothes on. Bending to step into her slacks, half-naked, exposing the swell of her hip to him, the sway of her breasts—he knew he would never see her like this again.

"I shouldn't have said that," she said. "It was inappropriate."
Inappropriate. She must have picked that word up in therapy.
Would that have been when she was institutionalized, or
afterward? What did she see that she felt she had to say it? What
was she feeling? Fear? Resignation? He couldn't tell. He thought
to ask her not to go, but he did not speak.

The Woman on the Train

They had gone to the Anne Frank House. Afterward, Jessica was withdrawn and Bob went for a walk in the park by their hotel in order to leave her alone to try to regain control of her emotions. Over dinner she told him how sad she felt for Anne, and how bitter about what had happened to her.

The next morning they were on a train to Antwerp when Jessica leaned back and closed her eyes. Instantly, she saw a woman's face, grim, elderly, a grandmother's face but a grandmother who had known hardship, rushing toward her. Jessica thought the woman was going to collide with her and she opened her eyes. No one was there. The train was speeding ahead, Bob was sitting beside her, and other people were dozing or chatting.

It had not been a dream. It had felt nothing like a dream, and Jessica hadn't been asleep. Her inclination was to see the vision as relating somehow to Anne Frank, but she didn't know how it would. She had never seen the face before, although the bonnet of gray hair on the old woman's head seemed to recall something in her memory. What, she didn't know. She thought the old woman may have been an emissary from her mother who had died a few months earlier, but then thought that whoever she was, she had nothing to do with her mother. Then she settled on the thought that the old woman was one of the six million, of which Anne Frank was another one.

Three weeks later Bob was sitting on the floor of their living room with their dachshund, debating whether to look for something on TV or pick up one of the books he had started reading but had set down unfinished. Gus was settled beside him, tearing at a stuffed giraffe he held between his paws. Jessica had moved out. Or maybe she hadn't. She had taken only a single suitcase. Most of what she owned was still in the house. She needed some time, she said. She didn't say for what.

The phone rang but he didn't get up to answer it. It rang four times and then stopped. Since she had moved out, Jessica had called him every night, but tonight he didn't want to talk with her. He was content to sit with the dog and think about turning on the TV or reading a book. The last time he and Jessica talked, she said she was unhappy with him because he had been unfeeling when they were at the Anne Frank House. How would she know what he was or wasn't feeling? he had thought to say, but hadn't.

After a while he got up and checked the voice mail. There was a single message, from Jessica, of course, and it asked him to call her at a number he didn't know but which he recognized as having an Orange County area code. (What was she doing in Orange County? He wondered if she had really left, if she was with someone else now.) Her voice sounded thicker than it usually did, as though she had a cold or had been drinking.

He listened to the message again and wrote the number down, and while he was writing it, he realized that the woman on the phone had said "Jennifer," not "Jessica," and he set his pen down. He thought at first that it was a solicitation and he crumpled the bit of paper he had written on and was about to toss it in the recyclables when something else occurred to him and he stopped. He returned to the living room. The giraffe was on the floor, but Gus had gone to another part of the house, probably to Bob and Jessica's bed.

He had thought of her only infrequently. When he did think of her, he remembered the different aromas her body emitted, particularly that damp, child smell that her skin sometimes gave off when she was sixteen. And he remembered, too, the desperation he had felt about their lack of money and his struggle to find work; he remembered that at one point they gave up coffee as too expensive and drank tea instead. But over the last thirty years or so an increment of melancholy had infiltrated his heart, and when he thought of her, he could not help feeling sad. He remembered how she had brushed invisible tears from her cheek as she listed the things she had lost from her life.

But only this morning, on the verge of waking, he had been visited by a memory of the last evening he had spent with her in the apartment they'd lived in in Fullerton. At least he thought it was a memory; the sense of immediacy that accompanied it, the detail, the tactility, was nothing like the feeling of a dream. He was angry, he remembered. He was certain of that. Sometimes he had played at anger, but this time he was not playing. He was sitting on the couch and she was lying across his knees, her buttocks bare. He remembered that they felt cool in the palm of his hand before he began spanking her. This was not one of their games; she was squirming, trying to free herself. He slapped her, hard. He did it again and her buttocks began to redden. He remembered the odor of her arousal and that he had become aroused too, and he had been embarrassed by his own excitement. He let her go and she eased herself onto the floor. She watched as he unfastened his belt and unzipped his fly and kicked his pants and his underwear away, and she turned onto her elbows and knees and he penetrated her without consideration of her and in only a moment he came and then she came. It was afterward that he had told her she had to leave, that her staying would be unsafe for both of them.

When he dropped her at Tom's apartment she did not know if he was going to come back for her or if it was the end of their marriage. How did he know this? How did he know what she thought? She must have told him, but when? He had not seen her in more than thirty years. Was it the evening they spent together in that motel by the airport? He couldn't remember.

Fully awake, he began to think that, in fact, he had not spanked her that evening, that his memory had invented this episode in order to shield him from the worse shame of having beaten her, assuming he had, in fact, beaten her. He was certain he had, even if she had denied it. But now he felt equally certain that he had not beaten her, but had spanked her in what had started as one of their games, but became an assault and ended in sexual arousal for both of them, and then coitus. Both could not have happened, not on the same day.

He did like to torment himself.

He sometimes thought of a man he had met when he was in his late twenties. He was an organizer then, in the last years of the War on Poverty, and he had gone to the man's home to try to get his support in persuading the legislature to pass a particular bill that would benefit the poor, at least some of them. He had hated going there, hated the idea of it. Even though he had not met the man, he resented having to beg for money or favors, for that was what it was—begging, asking for charity from people who have what others don't. It—his commitment to the have-nots of the world—would eventually cost him his marriage. Certainly there were other factors, but without the stress that went with organizing and lobbying, his marriage may have weathered them. Although who ever would have thought Maggie would barter him to his enemies in return for a tenure-track position? Who would have thought she kept book on the things he told her?

The man he had gone to win over lived in a cozy redbrick house with a cheerful wife. A log was burning in the fireplace in the study when Bob went inside. Bob and Maggie and the kids had a house with an unreliable furnace. The man who sat behind the wide desk near the fireplace had enough wealth to donate to causes that appealed to his sentiments. He was arrogant, as so many people of his class are, as if they merited the money they inherited, though he probably didn't know he was arrogant, and he had opinions on everything, from people whose secrets he was privy to to the morality of the current war.

Then he said that his son, who would have been about Bob's age, had he lived, had killed himself some years earlier, and he began to weep. When he pushed back from his desk to get a tissue out of a drawer, Bob saw that he was in a wheelchair.

Everybody suffers. Some suffering we visit on ourselves and some is handed to us. If your life is long, you suffer more.

Bob was distracting himself with memories not of Jen.

How would she look now? He pictured her as he had last seen her, her carriage mature, but her body still that of an adolescent.

What would she say?

She would say, I was thinking about you and I looked you up on the Internet and discovered your book about the war. Do you know, as I was reading it I began to feel something and it took me a while, but I finally figured out that what I was feeling was pride—pride in your work. I don't know why, but I did. I do. Weird, isn't it?

But before that he would ask, How did you ever find me? I've moved half a dozen times since we last saw each other. What is it, thirty, thirty-five years?

And she would say, I remembered that you lived in Seattle and I just called everybody who had your name or initials on the chance that I would eventually find you. It didn't require a lot of ingenuity. She would say she wanted to apologize for having treated him so badly when they were together. Would she really say this? She might. She would.

And he would ask what she was apologizing for, how was she

cruel? And she would say, I was so childish.

And he would laugh and say, But we were children. You don't owe me an apology.

She did, she would say, but again she would not say specifically why, only that she had been childish; she had made a mistake.

She would say she had called to apologize, but also to thank him for being so kind to her. She had been thinking about the men she had known and she remembered him for his kindness and his patience with her: he hadn't insisted that she do anything she wasn't ready to do.

And he would think, Jesus, because again he would remember hitting her despite her denial thirty-five years ago that he had. He would think, What must the others have been like?

And she would tell him that she had called also because she wanted to be able to talk to someone who knew her, who shared some memories with her. She couldn't talk to Tom. She had nothing in common with him anymore except their children, and also she didn't like him. Anyway, he had Alzheimer's now. Saying this, she would give a short giggle. She would say she had this fantasy in which they, she and Bob, would get together somewhere for a glass of wine—she was allowed only a glass a day now, but she would make sure it was filled to the top for the occasion—and they would share memories of their life together. She would especially like to talk with him about their sex life. Sex was such a big part of our lives, she would say, and Bob would agree. Sex was really important to us, wasn't it? she would insist, and Bob would say yes.

She would ask if he ever thought about her, and he would say of course he did, and she would ask what he thought about when he thought about her, and he would remember again how her head felt in the cup of his hand, the scents from the different parts of her body, the black vee of her pubic hair lush against her skin, how she looked as she climbed into bed, the things she used to say to him when they made love, but he would not say any of this because he would be afraid of revealing too much, and he would say instead that he remembered what she had told him about her life when they had drinks that time three decades ago, about Peter's death, her father's, her going into an institution, her telling him that in the space of two years she had lost all the men in her life, and later, in the motel, her telling him that when they were younger she had liked angering him because when he was angry was when she most enjoyed sex with him.

She would say she didn't remember telling him all this, although it was all true. She would remember meeting him in a bar near the airport and getting smashed, but she wouldn't remember going to a motel with him. There's a lot I don't remember about those days, she would say. I was drinking a lot then.

He would say, We talked about your job and how some supervisors give out incomplete information so that the people who work under them have to be wrong if their supervisor wants them to be wrong. And you said you worked for someone like that.

And she would say, I did work for someone then who made my life miserable.

But she would remember having sex with him on the floor of the kitchen in her house. And she would apologize for this too, saying she should have respected him more, they should have made love in her bed, but she didn't like to have men in her bed in those days, although that was no excuse.

And he would say he didn't remember having sex on her kitchen floor. He remembered going to a motel with her. He remembered her coming out of the bathroom, naked, and his surprise at how little her body had changed, except of course for the Caesarian scar, and here, perhaps for a minute, perhaps for half a minute, she would not respond until finally she would say, I don't have a Caesarian scar. All of my children were born through normal channels, and she would give that short giggle again. And he would not know what to say. He would want to say, Are you sure? but wouldn't say it, recognizing how silly it would sound.

Maybe you're thinking of somebody else, she would offer, and he would have a hazy memory of her having said that to him once before, though he would not remember when or the conversation it was embedded in. He would say, I remember so clearly how you looked, standing in the bathroom doorway, and what you said. You said, I thought about telling you, but I figured, What the hell, he can take me as I am.

And she would say, That wasn't me. Sorry. And again he would not know what to say. And later, a day or two after this conversation, this first conversation, he would remember that two years after he last went with her to a motel, he made love with an American woman he met in the Philippines and noticed her Caesarian scar. And he would recall that this was the first time he had ever seen one. So he had transposed Peggy's scar onto Jen's belly in his memory of that evening with her. Why had he done this? What purpose had it served? He didn't know.

And she would ask, Do you remember, when we were kids, going to a motel and making love and then falling into a sound sleep—you falling into a sound sleep, not me—because you had worked all day and were exhausted? I was irritated—we didn't get to go to a motel all that often–and I was not tired because I had not worked all day and I got up and walked over to the dresser where you had put your cigarettes and helped myself to one of your Lucky Strikes and sat down on a chair next to the bed, wearing only my underpants, and I watched you sleep while I smoked the cigarette. I felt so sophisticated, sort of Lauren Bacallish.

And he would say, I remember. I even remember one or two

of the details of our lovemaking that night. I don't remember you smoking a cigarette, Lauren Bacallish, but I remember your being annoyed with me because after we made love I just couldn't stay awake. I must have been working as a tree sprayer then, to have been that tired.

And she would say, How out of it I was. I didn't have a clue. I was so naïve about work and earning a living. I certainly learned about it later, but that was no help to you. One more thing to apologize for.

And he would say, Why do you keep apologizing for things that don't matter anymore? Are you in some sort of twelve-step program where you have to make amends to everybody you've wronged or think you've wronged?

And she would not answer, but instead would say, I loved your body. I missed your smells, even the way you sometimes smelled in the morning. Sometimes you'd sweat in your sleep and in the morning you'd smell bitter and old, and I loved that smell too. I loved your hands. That's what I remember most. How did you know how to touch me?

And he would say, I never knew what I was doing. I just did what I thought your body wanted me to do. I was just making it up as I went.

And she would say, We both were.

And then she would say, I took this art class a couple of years ago, just to kill some time. They'd alternate between models. A woman and then a man. And I figured out that what interested me were the imperfections in the women. I'd gloss over the imperfections in the men. They looked like cartoon figures in my drawings, but the women were all sagging breasts and dimpled thighs and balding pussies, even if they were young and beautiful in real life. I was always afraid of losing you. Did I tell you that when we were together? I always thought you'd leave me for someone prettier or someone who had bigger boobs. Maybe I left you so I wouldn't have to worry about it anymore.

She would say, Life's a crapshoot, isn't it? You roll the dice and they careen and bounce and whatever comes up is what you have to live with. All you know, maybe all you should know, is that sooner or later you're going to be confronted with what you're most afraid of. That sounds a lot wiser than I am.

And he would think but not say, Love endures, whether or not we will it, despite the world and despite ourselves.

And then she would say she had had cancer and had had fifteen feet of her colon removed and then had chemotherapy and that had killed the cancer or put it in remission. She would say she tried not to think of the possibility of its recurring and concentrated each day on what had to be done—her exercises, her medication for her depression, and so on. She would say the chemotherapy had left her with a loss of feeling in her hands and feet as well as a loss of balance. Her balance was returning, although slowly—she was able now to put on a pair of pants without holding onto a chair—but her hands and feet remained numb. Her oncologist looked at her as a success story, but she didn't feel successful. Her oncologist looked at anybody who survived five years after a bout with cancer as a success story. It had been eighteen months since her cancer went away, or at least since it became undetectable.

And she would say, And I wanted to talk with someone who knew me when I was full of myself and could imagine myself as Lauren Bacall, and naïve enough to think I wouldn't have to earn a living for myself and the children I would have, but would be provided for forever.

And he would say… he would say…

"Jen?"

"Bobby? Bob?"

Jerome Gold is the author of seventeen books and chapbooks of fiction, nonfiction and poetry. He has published in such journals as *Boston Review, Fiction Review, Hawaii Review, Left Bank, Chiron Review* and others. He lives on Fidalgo Island in Washington State.